Praise for Vivian Arend's
Rocky Mountain Rebel

"Arend sure knows how to corral readers' attention and lasso them in without a hitch. Book five of the Six Pack Ranch series is raunchy and dirty like a super-sexy, sweaty cowboy."
~ *RT Book Reviews*

"It is one read that you do not want to miss, and I happily recommend it to all contemporary romance readers."
~ *Long and Short Reviews*

"This spicy story was a fun read and I am delighted to have found a new author to follow and will be looking for the earlier tales centering around the Six Pack Ranch."
~ *Night Owl Reviews*

"Another superb winner from Ms. Arend that left me sighing from happiness and anxious for more!"
~ *Under the Covers Book Blog*

"...I definitely recommend to fans of contemporaries with hot cowboys and strong family ties."
~ *Smexy Books*

"...I can assure readers that this is a series that doesn't disappoint."
~ *Romance Junkies*

"All in all I continue to fall more and more in love with this series as it progresses."
~ *The Book Pushers*

Look for these titles by
Vivian Arend

Now Available:

Granite Lake Wolves
Wolf Signs
Wolf Flight
Wolf Games
Wolf Tracks
Wolf Line
Wolf Nip

Forces of Nature
Tidal Wave
Whirlpool

Turner Twins
Turn It On
Turn It Up

Pacific Passion
Stormchild
Stormy Seduction
Silent Storm

Takhini Wolves
Black Gold
Silver Mine
Diamond Dust

Six Pack Ranch
Rocky Mountain Heat
Rocky Mountain Haven
Rocky Mountain Desire
Rocky Mountain Angel
Rocky Mountain Rebel
Rocky Mountain Freedom

Xtreme Adventures
Falling, Freestyle
Rising, Freestyle

Bandicoot Cove
Paradise Found
Exotic Indulgence

Print Collections
Under the Northern Lights
Under the Midnight Sun
Under an Endless Sky
Breaking Waves
Storm Swept
Freestyle
Tropical Desires

Rocky Mountain
Rebel

Vivian Arend

Welcome to the Ranch Susan,

[signature] 2014

SAMHAIN
PUBLISHING

Samhain Publishing, Ltd.
11821 Mason Montgomery Road, 4B
Cincinnati, OH 45249
www.samhainpublishing.com

Rocky Mountain Rebel
Copyright © 2014 by Vivian Arend
Print ISBN: 978-1-61921-901-4
Digital ISBN: 978-1-61921-540-5

Editing by Anne Scott
Cover by Angela Waters

First Samhain Publishing, Ltd. electronic publication: May 2013
First Samhain Publishing, Ltd. print publication: February 2014

Dedication

There's nothing like the writing community for shared support and wisdom. Cheers to Laurie London who helped me with the horses, Denise Tompkins who smacked me over the head with true ranch spirit, and Elle Kennedy who kept me writing. Thank you, ladies!

Chapter One

Playing *connect the dots* was his newest obsession.

Joel Coleman took another drink, the tepid coffee left in the bottom of his cup barely registering. He was too fascinated with the smooth, exposed line of Victoria Hansol's neck as she stood one table over taking down an order. With her shining brown hair pulled into a ponytail, his contemplation lingered on the freckle he wanted to nibble. Leading up to the one on her jawline. Right before he tasted the one hovering to the side of her luscious-looking mouth.

He could play this game all day if his estimate of how far her freckles extended was accurate.

"You're drooling."

Joel dragged his gaze off the woman he'd been ogling, and focused across the table. His brother's grin was familiar enough. Joel saw pretty much the same face every time he glanced in a mirror. Dark hair, square jaw. As identical twins, he and Jesse had their share of mistaken-for-each-other stories.

Jesse peeked over his shoulder, turning back with a laugh.

"Vicki *Hansol?* You're not serious." Jesse leaned forward and lowered his voice. "I mean, yeah, she's hot. But—"

"Whoa, hold it." Joel shook his head in denial. "Just because she's built doesn't mean I want to get involved with her. I'm admiring the view, that's all."

"View is rather tasty." Jesse's brow rose, and he hummed for a moment. "How come we've never gone out with her?"

Damn it. Joel's stomach clenched. "We? Jesse, will you fucking stop that? There is no 'we' when it comes to dating, okay? There are girls you date, and girls I date."

"Fine. No need to bite my head off." Jesse flopped back in

his seat, hands raised in mock surrender.

Joel fixed his twin with a firm glare until Jesse laughed and returned to his plate. This was not a matter Joel was willing to bend on. Not anymore. They'd gotten a reputation over the years, him and Jesse. Not as wild as the Hansol family, but that was probably because the oldest of their immediate Coleman kin were squeaky clean and respectable. As the youngest of the Six Pack clan—literally the youngest by all of thirty minutes after Jesse's arrival—Joel was ready to move on.

He stared at Vicki's legs as she stood at the far end of the café, topping up a customer's coffee. He'd seen the woman around town for years. Gone to school with her, in fact, although he and Jesse had been a couple grades above her. He knew about the Hansol girls, or what the community gossiped about them. The rotating door on her oldest sister's bedroom had been discussed during many a late-night drunken boast-session among the less-than-courteous males who'd taken Sarah up on her willingness to share.

The short skirt that was part of the waitress uniform swirled around Vicki's limbs as she moved, and Joel fought to find something else to concentrate on. Because there was no way, no matter how attracted he was, *no way* was he going to get involved with one of the town's bad girls.

This was the year he made some changes. He was done with college, back on the ranch, and ready to move forward. Didn't mean he wasn't going to have any fun, but he planned to watch his step a little more.

Which put Vicki Hansol on the *drool over at a distance, but avoid* list.

Suddenly, there she was, a polite smile that didn't quite reach her eyes pasted on her lips. "Either of you boys want dessert?"

Jesse shook his head. "Not for me, thanks."

He pulled out his cellphone to answer it, talking quietly toward the window.

Joel gazed up at Vicki, working hard to focus on her face and not the amazing rack pushing the front of her uniform.

"You bake today? Because, frankly, no one else here can beat your pies."

Her smile came alive, brightening her entire face and making her brown eyes sparkle. "Made a dozen this morning. You want cherry or lemon meringue?"

Something inside twisted. Her obvious pleasure at the simple bit of praise struck him as odd. As if she didn't receive many compliments. "A piece of each, please."

Vicki nodded, reaching for the empty plates in front of them before retreating without a word, her skirt swaying over the rounds of her ass as she vanished into the back of the café.

Jesse hung up and pushed his phone into a pocket. "When you're done lunch, Dad says to meet him at the seed store. He's going to order for next year. Wants your opinion on some new strains."

"No problem. Are you finishing the south fields this afternoon?"

Jesse wrinkled his nose. "Probably take all day tomorrow as well to get done. Blake took a break to hit some prenatal thing with Jaxi. Can't fault our big bro for taking time off to do his family duty, but there's more to finish than possible in one run."

Joel nodded. "He should have said something earlier. I can give you and Blake a hand in the morning if the third tractor is running."

"That would be great. Hey—did I tell you? We got an invite to a party in Red Deer this weekend. You want to head out Friday night or Saturday?"

Neither. But not for any reason Joel wanted to explain. "Whose place?"

"Some friends of friends of Travis. Boats, barbecues and bikinis."

"Bikinis?" Joel laughed out loud. "It's the first week of October. Are they crazy?"

Jesse shrugged. "Forecast is for clear skies. If Indian summer hangs on for another couple days, it'll be fun. I already

11

said we'd be there, so if you pick up the beer I'll swing the food."

Typical. "Of course, I get the booze, and you'll sweet-talk someone into making grub for you. Jaxi? Ma?"

Jesse looked offended at the suggestion. "I am capable of pulling together a couple dishes for a potluck."

"You're going to bring cheese buns and pepperoni sticks, and call them cowboy pizzas." Joel thought back over all the weird things his brother had done to avoid cooking. "Or maybe hit the bulk aisle and nab premade chicken wings and frozen ranch fries."

Jesse grinned. "In the cooler in the back of my truck already. Why switch out a winning combination?"

"You're such an ass."

His twin rose to his feet and checked his watch. "I'll see you in a bit, right?"

"I'll be there after I finish up with Dad." Joel tried his own subtle prodding. "Of course if you completed the repairs to the corral fence before I got back, I wouldn't be upset."

"Ha. I think I might get distracted before hitting that part of the work list." Jesse winked and waved, heading out the door with nods to the locals.

Joel leaned against the rough fabric of the seat cover, easing his legs under the table as his twin drove off. While he liked his growing independence, there was something a touch weird about it. He and Jesse had been into every sort of trouble over the years, but always together. At school, in the fields. Where one was, the other was never far behind. Getting themselves into situations, or talking themselves out of it.

Joel swirled the liquid in his cup, trying to ignore the internal grumble reminding him it was usually Jesse who got them into mischief, leaving it his responsibility to get them out.

Even something simple like the party this weekend. Last place on earth he wanted to be. Friends of friends...

Screw it. Nope.

He wasn't interested, and he'd make that clear when he saw Jesse later. Maybe it had been a long summer or something, but he was tired of the nearly forced good times they'd been having weekend after weekend. Joel didn't want another wild party. He wasn't ready to sit at home and do nothing, but a little time with local friends and family would be a nice change of pace.

Even the smallest of scenery changes was enough for a while. Like stopping at the café for a bite to eat. Bachelor-pad cooking got old real fast, although he was better than Jesse. The café was a soothing place to fill his belly and take a quiet break from rattling his bones on the ranch equipment. He glanced around contentedly, the familiar setting part of his life over the years. Plates of fries at noon during school, the occasional date he'd brought there.

Comfortable.

The place wasn't packed, and the diners were spaced far enough apart that low-spoken words weren't usually overheard. Not like the ruckus three tables over was making, with loud laughter ringing out from the four men in suits. Business lunch or something.

Vicki stepped from the kitchen area, nudging open the swinging door with her hip, and Joel dragged his gaze up to her face as rapidly as possible to avoid being caught staring at her more-than-ample chest. Because, yeah, getting fixated on her tits would just prove once and for all he was stepping up his A-game.

She lowered a plate in front of him. "Cherry and lemon, as requested. I added a scoop of ice cream."

His mouth watered, but it had little to do with the pies, more to do with her leaning past him to lower the serving. Her scent filled his head and barreled down to his nuts. "You're too good to me."

Her brow rose the longer he stared into her face, but he couldn't seem to look away. A couple of long curls had escaped from her ponytail, the dark brown strands framing her delicate features. Blonde highlights shone in her hair as the fall sun reflected in through the windows.

"Do I have something on my face?"

"No, of course not." He looked down at the table.

She ripped off his bill and slid it under the edge of his plate. "Will I see you tomorrow, then? I'll be making peach pies."

Laughter roared out, and Joel glanced down the room. Considering they were businessmen, he'd expect different behavior, but it seemed some rednecks wore ties.

Vicki frowned—then she was gone. Back behind the protective barrier of the countertop, fidgeting with a dishcloth and topping up pitchers.

Her sudden departure was odd enough to catch Joel's attention. They weren't friends that he'd expect her to make tons of small talk, and yeah, there was something a touch awkward between them as he tried to hide his attraction, but up and leaving was borderline rude. Her chin was lowered, eyes fixed on her task, as if attempting to block out everything else.

The first bite of pie turned sour on his tongue as he struggled for what to do next. Not to mention, he was pissed at himself for being drawn to the one girl in town he should avoid.

Joel stared out the window and fought his frustrations.

"Bad case of blue balls, that's for sure."

Joel whipped his head around to see who needed their face rearranged, but the comment wasn't directed at him. The guys in suits had increased in volume. Joel recognized one of them as Eric Tell from the bank. The man had been in the same grade as Travis, so a few years higher than himself.

"You should have stopped in to see Sarah Hansol," Eric advised his seatmate. "She opens her legs so often there's a landing strip between them to make the approach easier. Whole family's the same. Easy sluts, the lot of them."

Idiots. Joel ignored them. Even considered abandoning his pies. It was one thing to know about Sarah's reputation, and another to shout rude comments in a public—

Fuck it. The rest of Eric's words fully registered.

He glanced to the right as Vicki's petite form flashed past. She skidded to a halt directly in front of the loudmouth's table. Joel rose and stepped forward, but not in time to stop her from dumping the contents of an entire pitcher of cola over Eric's head.

While the man was still blinking in surprise, she threw her first punch.

The roaring in her ears drowned out the shouts of anger, dimming everything to a low buzz as she got in a satisfying second hit to the asshole's jaw before she was captured from behind and dragged off.

Vicki squirmed, fighting for release, but the arms around her could have been made of iron for how much give they allowed.

"What the hell was that for?" Eric was on his feet, towering over her, his companions at the table all rising as well as chairs screeched over the floor. He grabbed his napkin and dabbed at the rivulets of liquid running down his face, blood flowing from his nose where she'd got in a blow before being pulled away.

"Calm down, everyone." Joel's voice carried over her shoulder, and she debated digging her elbow into his ribs for stepping in when she hadn't asked him to interfere.

"Should we call the police?" One of the jerks accompanying Eric had his cell phone out. Vicki glared daggers at Eric, daring him to make one wrong move.

"No police." Eric waved his friends off. "Sit, it's okay. It was an accident. The waitress tripped."

Goddamn bastard. Vicki opened her mouth to lambast him, but all the air in her lungs emptied as Joel snuck a hand around her waist and squeezed in warning.

"Everything fine, then?" Joel asked.

"So sorry." The café manager stepped in, passing over an extra towel before wiping up the mess on the table. Sherry spoke soothingly. "Accidents happen. The meal is on the house. Let me replace anything you gentlemen need."

Eric settled back in his chair, still eyeing Vicki as if she might burst from Joel's clasp and resume swinging. She wiggled in an attempt to get free, because that was exactly what she wanted to do, but Joel only tucked her against his body.

A distant part of her brain noted this was about the closest she'd ever been to a guy, with Joel's thigh shoved between her legs to give him something to brace her against. His bulky biceps pressed the side of her breast. All of that registered in a flash before being ignored for the more important craving to knock Eric's head off. Yet, even the dim awareness of Joel was another reason to hate Eric's guts. She wasn't able to appreciate the intimacy of her contained position, as twisted as that enjoyment might be.

Vicki focused on the asshole who'd started this mess.

He'd stopped the bleeding and had the audacity to smirk. A benevolent type of smile, forgiving and oh-so-condescending. "Don't fuss, Sherry. Your waitress had a bit of a balance problem. Everything is forgotten. In fact…"

He took out a dollar coin and flipped it at Vicki. Almost as if he were giving her a tip. Only at the last second he pulled his toss and allowed the coin to fall at her feet.

It was a good thing Joel still had her in a tight grip because at that moment she really might have killed Eric without thinking. Her heart raced, adrenaline and fury whipping through her icy cold like a winter's storm.

He'd as good as called her a hooker.

The others at the table found new places to look. At the floor, out the window, anywhere but at Eric and Vicki.

Air brushed her cheek as Joel whispered, "He's a fuckwad. Prove you're better than him and let it go."

The iron grip on her arms eased, as if he expected her to listen and not leap across the space between her and Eric to throttle him with her bare fingers. Vicki took a deep breath and released it slowly. For a moment she allowed herself to lean against the firm bulk of Joel's torso as a reward for behaving.

Then the rush of anger turned, now directed inward, and she fled to the back of the café. She worked to calm her breathing as she stood in the middle of the staff room and stared into space.

She wasn't supposed to let him get to her. Every time it happened and she lost her temper, she thought she'd learned her lesson. He'd say and do anything to get her goat. This time she'd even spotted him ahead of time and hauled herself aside, vowing to not take whatever bait he offered. Yet once again, she'd simply walked into his trap and allowed him to be the one in charge of her behavior, instead of herself.

It was going to cost her. It *always* cost her, and not him, and that's why a change had to happen. She knew it, but damn if controlling her temper was getting any easier.

The door opened. Sherry entered and sat, waiting in silence.

Vicki turned toward her supervisor. "I'm sorry. I should have pretended I didn't hear him."

Sherry shook her head. "Honey, you had a good reason. Only, you always have a good reason for losing your temper. I can't afford to have you taking it out on the customers."

Oh shit. "I'll keep it under control. It's just..."

Sad regret filled her supervisor's expression. "I can't keep someone on staff I can't trust. And I can't keep covering your butt, no matter how justified you feel you are in hating Eric's guts. He lives in Rocky. He comes into the café a couple times a week. You seeing him around town is inevitable, so you've got to give up this vendetta."

Far easier said than done. "I'm trying."

Sherry paused. "I know you are. But you'll have to try while working somewhere other than at the café."

Vicki waited for yet another flash of anger to hit, but this time there was nothing but resignation. "I understand. It's not a great idea to be anywhere near knives until I get this under control, right?"

Sherry chuckled. "Probably not. But when you're not taking potshots at the customers, you're a good worker. I'll give you a letter of reference, if you want one."

"Thanks." She was going to need every bit of help she could get. "You want me to finish my shift?"

Sherry rose to her feet. "It's slow enough Carrie and I can deal with the customers until Tina comes in."

Sherry patted her on the shoulder and headed into the main lobby. Vicki grabbed her backpack and cleaned the few things out of her locker. Not much there. In a few minutes only empty space mocked her.

Behind her the door clicked shut with a hollow echo. Another door shutting on her future. Another possibility turned from positive to negative.

Vicki paused as she examined the alley. Graffiti marred the brickwork in a few places, but mostly there were orderly dumpsters and a few cars parked outside shop rear-exits. The alley wasn't a dirty mess, but it wasn't a place of beauty either, and Vicki's breath caught in her throat.

This was her. Trapped between two things. She wasn't a foul mess, but she wasn't doing what she needed to get the hell out of the hole she'd fallen in.

Fallen, or been shoved?

No, she wouldn't play the blame game. No matter how she'd been treated while growing up, no matter what her family's reputation, she was an adult and responsible for her own actions.

Right now? There was no one to blame for being unemployed but herself. She'd love to say it was Eric's fault, but he wasn't the one who'd moved his fat head into her fists.

She shouldered her backpack and headed down the alley, thankful he hadn't pressed assault charges. He could have, and it would have been nothing more than another round of he said, she said... The town bad girl acting out against the star valedictorian.

Another round with another loss for her.

The end of the alley was mere steps away, the sunshine on the sidewalk her goal, when someone stepped around the corner and she jerked to a stop.

Images of vindictive mob-crews sent by Eric vanished as Joel Coleman blocked her path. She paused, making sure she was in position to run if needed. Not that Joel had ever done anything to threaten her, but being cautious was only smart.

"What?" If the word came out sharp and defensive, so be it.

Joel examined her carefully. "You okay?"

"Just peachy," she lied, the sarcasm in her voice tinny and bright.

"Don't fuck around," he growled.

The words rumbled over her, dark and rough, and for once she allowed herself to look him over. To take in the broad width of his shoulders stretching his T-shirt. Massive biceps pushing the sleeves. Narrow waist and well-worn jeans, with a lighter patch right *there* where her gaze shouldn't dwell. He shifted his weight, and the impulse to stare a little longer was hard to fight when his thighs and his...

Vicki dragged her gaze up to the relative safety of his face. Only it wasn't safe, not by a long shot. Bright blue eyes twinkled at her, a lazy love-em-and-leave-em smirk on his firm lips. His hair long enough she wished she could step in closer and thread her fingers through it to see if it was as soft as it looked.

Yeah, if it wasn't the stupidest idea ever, she would love to get a taste of Joel Coleman. Always had wanted one, never would take herself up on the craving.

She took a deep breath and stared over his shoulder. "Sorry. I'm still riled up."

"I figured." Joel stepped to the side, his body swaying back into her line of vision, and the concern on his face nearly killed her. "I really did want to make sure you were okay."

"I'm fine." Vicki paused. The words stuck in her throat, but he had helped. "And...thanks. I mean, earlier, at the restaurant."

"No problem." He glanced at his watch. "You finish your shift already?"

No use in lying. He'd find out soon enough she'd been canned. "I'm going to look for a different job. One more suited to my personality. Sorry, no peach pies tomorrow."

He nodded. "Sorry to see you go."

Vicki needed to get home. Needed to hide, and not have to think for a few minutes. "See you around."

She shouldered past him, ignoring his hand that brushed her arm as she walked by. She was at the edge of the alley, stepping into the sunlight, when he spoke again.

"I heard Orson's Hardware is hiring stockers."

Vicki paused. Glanced over her shoulder. "Thanks. That might be a better place for me. I'll look into it."

"Vicki, if..." His words trickled to a stop, and the strangeness in that alone was enough to pin her feet to the ground.

She turned to face him, waiting for him to finish. "What?"

Joel was looking at her. Really looking, as if seeing beyond the tough-girl façade she wore like armor. She tugged her backpack a little closer, hiding behind it.

"If you ever need, well, someone to talk to. Or a hand. Let me know, okay?"

She should have responded. Should have blurted out a noncommittal *thanks,* but his offer knocked all logic from her brain and left her with nothing but emotional turmoil.

They stood for a moment, nothing said, just a growing sense of disaster looming as Vicki fought the urge to give in. Because giving in would be a bad idea—she was sure of it.

It seemed like an earnest offer. Maybe. Or maybe more of the same of what she'd been handed over the years. People who appeared to be one way, while only wanting to take advantage of the trusting and the naïve.

A bad girl desperate to change her spots couldn't allow the lure of attraction to lead her astray. She lifted her chin and turned without a backward glance, walking away from temptation in the form of one Joel Coleman.

Because the last thing this rebel needed was to get involved with another rebel.

Chapter Two

Vicki spent all Friday dropping off resumes around town, managing—barely—to ignore the snarky comments at a few places. She collapsed onto the couch and stared at the ceiling, flipping through the nasty comebacks she hadn't voiced.

Fuck them for being small-minded, small-town bigots.

From flat on her back, not only the ceiling but the kitchen and the door to the bathroom were visible. Her couch was a daybed she turned into her real bed for the night. The tiny bachelor suite had everything she needed to be independent, but at times, man, did the walls close in.

It was the best she'd been able to manage when she escaped the family home. Hadn't been easy. None of it. Which made her current lack of job situation even more annoying. She knew better. She knew she needed to keep her cool.

The wind rustled the curtains, bringing fall air to swirl around her. The moment's refreshment helped her refocus, and her breathing calmed.

Okay. She'd blown it. But it wasn't the end of the world—not yet. She'd planned and saved and scrimped. She had a couple months' rent squirreled away, and hopefully Joel's job lead would play out in her favour.

Joel.

She shouldn't think about him. Shouldn't imagine his gorgeous eyes focused on her for real. In a time and place she could give in and take a little pleasure.

Vicki scrambled to her feet. Nope. The option was totally out of the question. Even if the Coleman twins weren't known as sexual whirlwinds, Joel was in a whole different camp. The kind of kids who back in school wandered the hallways taking up more than their share of space and attention. It wasn't as if the better-off folks in Rocky wore a lot of designer jeans or fancy duds, but the Colemans and the Hansols were not in the same pecking order, and she knew it.

Joel might have worn hand-me-downs from his big brothers, but they were always clean and well mended. Vicki had made sure her and her sister Lynn's stuff was always washed, although it meant learning how to do their own laundry at ten years old, but there were no hand-me-downs she wanted to wear.

The phone rang, and she grabbed it. "Hello?"

"Vicki Hansol?"

"Yes."

"Mark Orson at Orson's Hardware. You put in an application for the position in the stockroom."

Vicki straightened, even though the instinctive move was invisible. "Yes, sir. I'm looking for full-time hours. I have a recommendation from my—"

"Skip it. My manager was in the café yesterday right before you got your walking papers."

Shit. Bubbles burst even before the job offer was on the table. "I see. Well, thank you for calling."

The man's laugh broke over the line. "Slow down, girl. I'm not brushing you off. In fact, from what Davis told me about the situation, I like your spunk. If you're a hard worker, I can use you. It's minimum wage to start, salary increases quarterly if things work out. Two-week trial, though, to make sure you fit in with the boys."

Vicki clutched the phone in shock. "Really? I mean, that would be fabulous. When do you want me to start?"

"Come in Monday at seven a.m. I'll get you to fill in the paperwork, and you can pull a shift." Mark paused for a minute. "You'll be working with a full crew of guys. Can you handle that?"

Since Eric didn't work there, she figured she'd be okay. "No problem."

She crossed her fingers she wasn't lying through her teeth.

"I'll find a spare coverall for you to wear. My daughter used to work in the shop before she moved away, and I think she left a couple around."

"Thank you."

Vicki hung up somewhat in shock. Only one-day unemployed and back into the swing of things. Stocking shelves was far safer as well. Sherry had been right. Eric was at the café all the time. He'd never pop his head into a hardware and seed shop. Probably had fancy mechanics and other flunkies to do his manual labour.

The world looked a tiny bit brighter. She slipped to the wall calendar and added a couple notes. October stretched before her, and the happy little image of a cartoon turkey decorating Thanksgiving Day mocked her.

Should she try to get together with her family, or was that asking for more heartache?

The thumbtack holding the calendar to the wall nudged loose and everything fell to the floor, the pages flipping like some fancy art shot in a movie, and Vicki stilled. Months spinning past. Her life whirling away, minimum wage and dead-end jobs. Tossing her fists every time someone made a comment about her family.

Was that all she had to look forward to?

God, she was an emotional mess today. She hauled open the fridge and grabbed a Coke, plopping down on the edge of the mattress harder than she should. When the creaking settled, she glanced around, shaking her head in frustration.

Tiny apartment. A small pile of clothing. Her motorbike—so little to show for her life so far. Not even a high school diploma.

Nothing but her pride, and lately even that kept taking a bruising.

And yet...

She'd made a difference when it counted the most. She nabbed the picture frame from beside the bed, the one showcasing her middle sister. Lynn's innocent smile shone out with unmarred joy.

You were strong enough to do what's right. The words whispered through her head.

She just had to believe it.

The phone rang, and she snatched it up, panicked for a moment that Mark had changed his mind. "Hello?"

"Hi, Vicki, it's Karen Coleman. You got a minute?"

Well now, this was unexpected. Karen belonged to another of the local Coleman clans—the Whiskey Creek side. The woman had gone to school with Vicki's oldest sister. Vicki swung to vertical so she was seated comfortably and listened carefully. "No problem. What's up?"

"I've got a far-out idea, and I want to run it past you. Remember when you helped at that kids' camp a couple years ago? You were the chef's assistant, right?"

A shiver shook Vicki as memories swept in, but somehow she kept her voice steady. "Yeah?"

"I'm trying to organize something for next summer, and I thought of you. It's not set in stone yet, but if things work out the way I hope, I'll be running weeklong camps in the Willmore Wilderness Park. I'm coordinating the horses and wranglers, all that side. My partner has already got a head cook lined up, but he'll need help. I thought of you."

Two job offers in one day? Maybe life was taking a turn for the better.

"When would it start?"

"First trips with customers begin the May long weekend. We'd get together early in the month to make sure things are in place, then you'd work in shifts through the summer. I've got a friend who has an on-site camp you could move to on your days off. It's a pretty transient job, but I figured you might enjoy the change of pace. Plus, you get to ride horses to the job site and out—fun stuff."

Elation at the idea of getting the hell out of Rocky mixed with instant terror as Vicki heard she would have to ride.

God, how was it possible to simultaneously feel two

conflicting emotions like this? She'd love to move away. She'd love the cooking. The rest of it? Not so much.

Her mouth had gone dry with fear. "When will you know details?"

"I hope to have all the contracts in place by early January. I figure that would give you enough warning. And Vicki? The dude ranch I'm coordinating with always seems to need a new full-time assistant-chef come the fall. If they like what they see over the summer, there's a chance they'd hire you full time for the winter season."

The trap caging her in edged open a crack.

Vicki ignored the potential trouble screaming at her and focused on the good points, allowing herself to hope. "It sounds wonderful. Thank you for thinking of me."

"You're a good kid. Got lots of compliments when you did the camp. I remember hearing that."

Karen obviously didn't hear any of the other details Vicki had fought to keep under wraps, which was a good thing. "Let me know what you need. If I can help out at all beforehand."

Karen agreed to stay in touch and left Vicki with her head buzzing with possibilities.

The future had just changed. A way out of Rocky, and away from harsh memories. Only...*trail rides*?

A shiver shook her entire body. Horses. Damn it.

Why'd she have to be the only girl on the planet who was afraid of the silly beasts?

Something hard hit his shoulder, dragging Joel's attention from the saddle he was fixing. "What the hell?"

Jesse stalked toward him. He kicked aside the dustpan he'd thrown before putting the stiff bristles of a push broom to the floor and raising dust. "You're in dreamland. Get your act together. I want to leave in the next couple of hours."

Ah, damn. He'd forgotten about Jesse's grand plans. "I'm not going."

His twin pulled to a halt in mid-sweep. "You got a better idea?"

Joel shrugged. "I figured I'd head to Traders."

Jesse damn near rolled his eyes. "We can see the family every fucking week if we want. Traders Pub is old and boring. This is new people, new faces...new women."

God, he was so not interested. Plus, he wasn't going to let Jesse get away with that kind of bullshit. "Family is not a problem to hang with, and you know it."

"They're falling like flies, man. I'm not ready to settle down."

Joel laughed out loud at the panic in his twin's voice even as he wondered at the huge leap in logic Jesse had taken.

"Settle down? Good grief, what are you talking about?" Joel hung up the saddle and turned to his brother. "No one expects you to get hitched."

"But look at them all." Jesse lifted his finger and pointed in a general circle around them. "The three oldest in the family are done for. Daniel's got the three boys now, and Blake and Jaxi are expecting their third. Matt and Hope are planning a winter wedding. You know Ma's gonna start plotting things for Travis and us soon. She wants all her boys hooked up and happy."

"Doesn't mean anything." Joel smacked Jesse on the shoulder. "You seriously think she wants us to get married? Hell, no. The way she carried on when we moved across the road into the trailer was bad enough."

Jesse snorted. "Still miss the three square meals a day we got when we lived at home."

"Bullshit on that as well," Joel called over his shoulder as he headed toward the other end of the barn to finish his chores. "You're mooching at least two meals a day from her, so don't go trying to sound as if you're hard done by and starving."

Joel measured out oats for each of the horses, taking his time and enjoying their easy movements as they crowded toward the front of their stalls and waited. Comfortable with him, with his step and body language. The newer animals were stabled separately, but these were the family's usual rides—steady and consistent. Happy to be brought out to check fence lines or wander through the cattle, although with the distances involved on the ranch, often the horses rested while the boys used quads or trucks.

There was something special about having the horses available, though. Joel bumped his gelding's head aside with his torso. "Move your fat head out of the way."

He'd barely tipped the bucket upright when Trigger retaliated, nose against Joel's side to push him off his feet.

Joel laughed as he caught his balance. "Mischief maker."

If a horse could grin?

Trigger snorted before lowering his head and concentrating on more important things like demolishing his dinner.

Jesse stuck his head around the doorframe. "You serious about not joining us?"

"Serious as shit." Joel moved steadily. He was nearly done his to-do list and eager to get to the end of it. "Go on. I bought beer. You can grab the case from my truck. You and Travis have a blast, and tell me about it later."

"Your loss." Jesse paused. "Hey, but thanks for the brewskies. I'll be back sometime on Sunday if things go well."

Joel strolled through his remaining chores, a strange peace hovering over him at having no frantic plans for the weekend. He wandered outside in time to catch his oldest brother Blake parking one of the tractors in the common equipment yard between the two main Six Pack ranch houses.

Blake nodded as he swung down, closing the door behind him. "You have a good day of it?"

"As always."

Blake took off his cowboy hat and wiped his brow with his sleeve. "Yeah, you pretty much always have a good time, don't you? You and Jesse coming to Traders tonight?"

"I'll be there. Jesse's got other plans, Travis as well."

His oldest brother grinned. "Trouble as usual—that much is also consistent. Make sure those two remember they're expected to stick around for Thanksgiving next weekend, okay? No wild getaways, just a nice quiet day with the family."

"Quiet?" Joel laughed. "Hell, what rock are you living under? The last family get-together the kids were loud enough to raise the dead."

"My sweet angels? *Nahh.*" Blake dropped an arm around Joel's shoulder as they walked to his truck. "It's all Daniel's boys. Bunch of hoodlums, just like their uncles."

Blake left him with a hearty pat on the back, his big brother whistling as he headed into the trees and the short path that led to his house on the other side of the coulee. Joel paused in the middle of starting the engine, suddenly struck by something. Blake was marching home to his wife and two little girls.

His brother's wife Jaxi had been one of Joel's playmates growing up, and while having her in the family felt right, there were still times he had to flip his brain back into gear. It was proper to have her around, but she wasn't *just* someone who'd always been there, she and Blake were married. Lovers. Now parents. They had a family of their own, and everything that went with it.

Maybe that was part of where this weird sensation was coming from. Jesse could protest until the cows came home he didn't want to settle down yet. Joel was online with that sentiment as well.

Only having someone special to spend time with? It wasn't an unwelcome idea. After years of casual dating and lots of fun, what was wrong with wanting to move to the next stage and have a steady girlfriend for a while?

It was damn crazy, though, how the first image in his brain was of Vicki Hansol. Not the wild child he'd heard gossiped about all over town for so long, but as he'd seen her the previous day after she'd been sacked.

Kind of lost and alone looking. Fragile, even. None of the tough girl left, just someone who needed a helping hand. And if his daddy had taught them anything in the Coleman clan? Taking care of women and helping them was important.

Joel parked outside the trailer he shared with Jesse, his brother's truck already gone. He headed inside and laughed. Jesse had pulled a couple bottles from the case of beer and left them on the table along with a bag of potato chips and a note.

Here you go, you party animal.

He popped a cap and took a long drink on the way to his bedroom. Yeah, Jesse was still a great guy, even if they had a few moments of frustration between them at times. Typical family stuff—brothers being brothers.

Hell, he had an awesome family and tons to look forward to.

Life couldn't get much better.

He was standing under the shower when the image of Vicki's big sad eyes hit him again.

Come to think of it, he'd never heard much negative about Vicki other than her fighting. Chatter about her had usually been mushed in with the easy sexual habits of her older family members, but specific dirt-talk about Vicki?

He couldn't think of anything past high school.

If he thought he had a task ahead of him to break free of the weird reputation he and Jesse had been labeled with, how much more of an issue would it be for someone like her to change people's minds? With her sister and mom still adding to the rumour mill.

What would it take for a town bad girl to find redemption from a bunch of small-town attitudes?

The thought clung to him throughout the rest of his evening.

Chapter Three

Vicki pulled her motorbike to the side of the road and cursed her foolishness. She'd debated with herself until she was dizzy, always coming back to the same conclusion.

Fate was giving her a chance, but she still had to work for it.

She needed to get over her fear of horses without letting Karen discover her anxiety, because wouldn't having a horse phobia go over like a ton of bricks? After wracking her brain, her possibilities had proven to be limited. The best person she could think of to help her was Joel Coleman, if his offer the other day had been sincere.

Oh God, let it have been sincere.

But having made that decision she was still lost. The worst part wasn't wondering if she was making some huge mistake, it was logistics. How to get in touch with the man? With her new job, she'd be buried in the back room of the hardware shop. It wasn't as if he'd stop by, and she could casually bring up the idea.

Calling him was out. Nope—this had to be done in person.

But her brilliant idea of taking a casual Saturday morning drive past his place and if she spotted him, stopping, had just fallen apart.

How was she supposed to know at a distance if it was him or Jesse?

She was such a twit.

She was still considering her options when the gods of karma must have decided she'd suffered enough. Joel's truck appeared before her, coming to a stop beside the driveway leading to the trailer Jesse and Joel shared. The door opened and Joel stepped out.

"You need a hand?"

She shut down the engine and loosened off her helmet.

His eyes widened as he discovered who she was. "Well, now. Hi, Vicki. What brings you out my way?"

"I'd like to talk."

He nodded, pointing toward his trailer. "Sure, come on in."

"No." The word jerked out far too quickly to be polite, and Vicki swore under her breath. "I mean, could we go somewhere else to chat? I don't want..."

Even explaining she didn't want her bike seen outside the twins' place was a horrible way to start to ask for a favour.

Joel frowned. "Coffee shop?"

"The Tree?"

He snorted. "You want to talk down at the high school kids' make-out field?"

Yeah, it wasn't much better. Frustration tore at her. "Never mind. It was a stupid idea to begin with."

He stopped her from putting on her helmet and racing off. "Slow down. If you want to talk without being interrupted, we can go to the river. Follow me."

He didn't give her an opportunity to protest, just got in his truck and pulled a U-turn, back toward the main highway. She did up her helmet and followed at a safe distance as he turned down a narrow gravel road leading into Coleman land.

Once they'd crested the hill and disappeared on the other side, she relaxed. Out of sight of curious onlookers was good. She backed off to allow the dust to settle and stop choking her vision. Instead, she admired the rolling fields around them, clear signs of fall displayed everywhere. Hay cut to short stubble, bales neatly stacked along the sides of the field. As far as she could see was Coleman land, and something inside twisted as she considered her tiny rented apartment.

He was so out of her league.

A pounding rang through her brain. *Didn't matter.* It *didn't* matter. The differences in their status had to be ignored. He had something she desperately needed, and she would damn well put her pride on hold and ask for help.

She parked on the inside of his truck, an instinct for secrecy still riding her even this far into the backcountry. Vicki slipped her leg over the bike seat and pulled off her helmet, hanging it from the handlebars.

Joel had found a spot on the fading grass beside a sturdy bench, his position allowing both of them to overlook a section of a slow-moving waterway.

She ignored the long line of his body as he stretched out his legs, instead dropping onto the bench and breathing deeply. "Pretty. I didn't know this was here. Is that Whiskey Creek down below?"

"Yeah." He plucked a stalk of tall grass and nibbled on the end as he pointed. "The Whiskey Creek Colemans' land is straight to the west of here, Angel land beyond that. Moonshine clan owns the spread to the south."

"And this section is Six Pack." She twisted to look back at the road they'd traveled, amazed at the extent of it all. "Seems so big. Kind of endless."

He laughed. "Especially when you're on a tractor and have to cover another section before dark. Endless is right."

They sat in silence for a minute, no words, just the rush of the water below them bubbling over the rocks and past branches that leaned into the water. Vicki pulled her gaze away from the pretty place and focused on Joel. He'd lain back on the ground and tipped his hat over his face to block the sun. The rest of him relaxed and delicious looking.

All her tightly wound secrets and desires were going to kill her, bundled up and hidden from everyone. The moment to share most of them was not here, and definitely not with Joel.

Focus. She had to focus.

If he'd asked her right away what was up, it would have made it easier, but the silence stretched between them until it was in her face, tension rising. The peacefulness of the spot vanished under her hopelessness.

If she wasn't brave enough to ask a simple favour, how on earth was she going to face the damn horses?

She loosened off her white-knuckled grip from the edge of the seat and forced herself to lean forward. "How good are you at keeping secrets?"

He leaned up on an elbow, adjusted his hat back into position and seemed to really consider his answer. "Depends what the secret is and why it's a secret. My mama got that foolishness of keeping secrets just to keep secrets out of me when Jesse and me were in grade school. Secrets that hurt someone, don't tell me, because I'll be bound to try to fix it. Secrets that can make a person happy, like surprise parties and such? I'm good at."

Fair enough. "I have a secret, and it's not hurting anyone but me."

"You want to tell me?" He glanced around them. "Is that why the hush-hush meeting and all?"

Vicki opened her mouth to answer then paused. Shit. Should she tell him? Did she hope he'd understand and give her a break, even if he didn't want to help?

She was stuck between a rock and a hard place. If she didn't get his help, Karen would eventually find out about her issue. If he didn't prove trustworthy, Karen would find out sooner and the job offer would be pulled. Simple enough.

Something tugged on her wrist, and Vicki blinked in surprise to discover Joel was no longer sprawled a few feet away on the ground, but beside her on the bench, lowering her hand to her thigh.

"You were biting your nails," he pointed out.

She looked up at him, their difference in size more obvious than ever at close range. "Shit, you're big."

A huge grin burst out for a second before being wrangled into a more controlled expression. He cleared his throat as he leaned on the seat back, opening space between them. "What's got you chomping on your fingers?"

Resignation set in. Either sharing worked, or it didn't. "I got a job offer for next summer I'd like to take, only there's a problem."

"And your secret is involved in this job offer?"

Vicki nodded. "Your cousin Karen is setting up trail rides, and I can go along as cook, only..."

He waited, and she debated getting up and pacing because the longer she sat there, the bigger he seemed to get. The size of his arms, the mass of his body. The fresh clean scent of him— and wasn't that fucked up? She was trying to get her life set on a new path, and all she could think about was how good he smelt.

Stupid mucked-up hormones.

Anger at herself rose. Bullshit on this farting around. "I'm afraid of horses. The last time I worked at a camp I had limited interaction with the brutes, and I still was too sick to work a couple times. Just from having to walk past their corral."

Concern and confusion showed in his eyes. No pity at least, that was good. "Did you have a bad experience with a horse?"

Blurred images flashed in her brain. "I remember only bits and pieces, but yeah. It was before we came to Rocky, so I might have been about six. I think we were at a fair. My sister and I wanted to pet them, but while we were in the yard one of them acted up. Someone got kicked—not us, we got hauled out right away—but now even the idea of getting close makes me nauseous."

Joel nodded slowly. "Which is why they say to get back up on the horse right away. Your fears make sense—it's not uncommon."

That made her feel a little better, but still. "They're just so bloody big, and unpredictable. And they smell."

His lips twitched.

"What?" she demanded.

"I'm sorry you got scared when you were little, but they smell?" The words squeezed out through tight lips.

Dammit, he was trying not to laugh. "They do," she

insisted.

"Chickens smell. Are you afraid of chickens?"

Her frustration would have been higher if he hadn't said it so deadpan. As it was, her sense of humour snuck in to point out that part of her complaint was a little on the stupid side. She bounced to her feet and planted her fists on her hips, staring him down as straight-faced as she could. "Only when I have to ride them."

Joel let his grin escape. "Sorry. I shouldn't tease, and I am taking this seriously. So what are you going to do about it?"

"The job?"

"The horses. I take it you'd like the position."

"God, yes." She jiggled in place. "If I wasn't worried about puking my guts out while on the trail with Mister Ed, I'd be pleased as punch."

Vicki absently noted their eyes were at nearly the same level with him seated on the bench. Talk about big beasts.

"That's the answer then. You need to get over your fear of horses. How long you got?" Joel stretched one leg to the side, still sprawled on the bench, his arm along the seatback.

"Until May." She eyed him cautiously. "You're not going to tell Karen, are you?"

"Don't see anything to tell. If you were offered a job that required you learn to rope between now and May, I think you could do it. I don't know all the mental stuff involved in dealing with your fear, but—"

"I need you to help me get over it."

He stopped. "I'm a rancher, Vicki, not a shrink."

"But you have horses."

Laughter broke out before he calmed himself. "Sorry, not laughing at you but, darling, what are you thinking? That I can help you get over your fears? I don't have a clue where to start."

Shit. Options were fading fast. "But...you're not afraid of them, right?"

"Of course not."

"That's all we need." It had to be enough. She faced him square on, arms crossed, daring him to turn her away. "Teach me what you know."

The earnest hope on her face was hard to resist, as was the rest of the package bouncing on her heels in front of him. High strung, high energy—hell, maybe he'd lied when he'd said he didn't know the first place to start. If this was how she acted around horses, no wonder they freaked her out. The animals would pick up on all her tension and react. Nothing more temperamental than an edgy horse.

The desire to scoop Vicki into his arms and teach her how to relax grew by the minute, but Joel needed to keep this under control. No matter how much her bossy attitude turned him on. "Fine. Let's teach you to like horses."

Her eyes widened. "Seriously?"

He caught hold of her wrists to stop her from rebounding away from him. "First off, you need to slow down. If you want, we can go over to the barns—"

She froze, face going white. "Shit."

Panic setting in already? He rocked forward to reassure her. "Don't worry. I'm not planning on throwing you up on one right off the bat."

She shook her head. "It's just..." She twisted away and stomped along the top of the lookout, curses rising the entire time she paced. Joel hid his smile at a few of the racier terms. Not often he heard that kind of language from the ladies— although he'd been impressed with how raunchy his sister-in-law Jaxi could get.

Vicki had a far more extensive vocabulary.

She pivoted on the spot and glared. "Here's the issue. If I start showing up at the ranch, people are going to notice. Either we tell them what we're doing, which doesn't work to keep Karen in the dark, or we tell them something else."

He shrugged. "Not like we have to tell them anything, really."

"They're going to assume we're seeing each other."

Oh hell. She was right.

The initial dismay that struck faded far too quickly. Only two days earlier Jesse's suggestion he had the hots for the woman had made him squirm.

Why wasn't he nearly so upset with the idea anymore?

He kept their gazes locked together, refusing to look her over, no matter how much he wanted to. "So what?"

"So...it's not true. We're not dating. I'm not going out with you, because if I did, people will then assume I'm also fooling around with Jesse. I'm not a slut."

He could have sworn his jaw hit his chest. He'd never expected to hear those words pop out of her mouth. "I never said you were."

Her chin rose a fraction of an inch. "Plenty of others have said it."

She was right about that.

His brain whirled with ideas. He wasn't sure why this woman had gotten under his skin, but damn if he didn't suddenly want to toss everything to the side and help Vicki make a change. He had a feeling an even break wasn't something that came her way very often.

No matter how much trouble it was, he made a decision. He was in. One hundred percent. If the town rebel wanted to clean up her act, he was game.

"You're planning on moving out of town, if all this works out?" Joel asked.

Vicki nodded.

"If I promise there will be no games with Jesse involved, will you go out with me?"

Her righteous anger blurred into confusion. "Go out—? Joel, I want to learn to ride."

He tried, he really tried, but he couldn't stop his lips from twitching, even though he buried the full-out grin.

She swung a fist into her thigh hard enough it had to hurt.

"A horse, you ass. Yes, I know the goddamn song, but I want to ride a *horse* without freaking out."

"And I promise we'll work at that as well. But maybe diving in at the deep end would help deal with the idiots. I'm not saying I won't try to help if you don't date me. But if you and I are hanging out together for a long, steady time, that could go a long way to killing some of the..."

Shit. How much did he want to admit about the talk of the town?

"The rumours how the Hansol girls are loose and easy? You don't have to try to protect me, Joel." She glared up into the tree where the leaves were slowly changing colour. "I've heard pretty much everything you could repeat. Hell, Eric Tell doesn't even feel the need to temper his talk during full daylight in public places."

"Yeah, but he's an asshole."

She snorted. "No arguments there."

Joel reached for her hand. "We could do this. We can make sure it's crystal clear it's just you and me involved, and frankly..."

He trickled to a stop. Vicki's body language was all tied up tight, and she wasn't giving an inch yet. She'd been honest with him about her fears. Maybe she needed a little reciprocated honesty.

"In a way, you'd be doing me a favour. You know that reputation you're worried about? Jesse's and mine?"

Lord, the faces this woman could pull.

"If you two were women you'd have been painted as harlots ages ago. Instead you're held up as sexual heroes."

"I know, it's damn unfair, but honestly I'm getting tired of it. It's time to get this town to see me and Jesse in a different light, and you and I dating would help a lot."

Vicki stepped back a pace, freeing her hand, her alert gaze looking him over. "And Jesse's going to simply agree with you? Because if he fucks around, it won't help either of our situations."

"I'll take care of Jesse." Confidence was rising. "Not a problem."

"And you'll help me get over being afraid of horses?"

"I'll give it a shot."

Vicki stared out over the water for a minute. "We're both crazy, but it might work. You're right. I shouldn't give a damn what the town thinks, especially if I'm leaving, but I still do. I want what I shouldn't bother wanting."

"You're not your family. You've got every right to change the things you don't like about your life."

God, listen to him. He was still finding his own way and now he was giving out advice?

When she turned, some of the bounce was back, a touch of the anger, but now, something else as well. He waited for her to share whatever was going on in that intriguing mind.

Vicki stepped in close.

"You're right. It's time to get moving forward with my life. So what do I want?" She took a deep breath as if gathering her courage. Then she held up one finger. "I want you to teach me to deal with the bloody horses."

Joel grinned as he dipped his head in acknowledgement.

A second finger rose. "I want people to stop talking about me like everything my family does is etched on my back simply because we share a name. If you're brave enough to try and help me fight that bullshit, I'd be damn grateful."

"Deal." A trickle of pride in doing something honourable—doing something that could make a difference in a person's life—struck again. Even though he'd get some benefit down the road, it was going to take some energy to accomplish this.

He was ready for the challenge.

Then she caught hold of his shirt and leaned in. "And just so you know, that girlfriend thing? I've never been anyone's girlfriend before."

Both her actions and her words made something inside tighten as he fought to understand. "You've never had a steady boyfriend?"

She moved in close enough their lips were nearly touching as she whispered the words. "I've never had a boyfriend, period. I want to learn all there is about being a girlfriend, Joel. Everything. And I want you to teach me."

Chapter Four

Joel's brain wasn't working properly. Even skimming through what he knew, her words didn't make sense. "Vicki..."

She released him and backed up. "Great, I did that well, didn't I?"

He grabbed her wrist before she could run away. "Would you slow the hell down? And explain a little better? I'm just...what do you mean no boyfriends?"

Vicki heaved out a huge body-shaking sigh. "Okay, I did have one boyfriend. Back in fifth grade, Danny Webster gave me a Valentine's card that said 'Will you be mine?' For three days straight we sat on the swings during lunch and talked. I figured he was working his way up to stealing a kiss by Friday or something. Only my older sister Sarah got in trouble, and Danny's parents said I wasn't a nice girl to spend time with, so he dumped me the following day."

Grade five? She was going back to grade *five* to find a guy she'd been interested in? He was sure there'd been another huge blow-up just a couple years ago.

"But you went out with Eric Tell in high school."

Her lips pressed together into a tight line. "Now we're back to secrets, and I'm not ready to share that one. I know from watching people what a girlfriend does, yet I've never done it, okay? And before I get the hell out of this godforsaken town I want to experience them at least once. The little things. And the big things."

She caught his gaze, the dark honey gold in her brown eyes seeming brighter than ever. "I'm trusting you with a lot, Joel Coleman. Please don't let me down by talking out of turn."

Then as if she couldn't maintain eye contact, she stared at

his fingers. He wasn't sure when he'd begun to rub his thumb over the inside of her wrist. It had started without thinking, her soft skin drawing him. He'd love to take that stroking touch and slip up to the inside of her elbow, teasing her along the way with delicate kisses.

"I can keep a secret," he reassured her. Being her boyfriend wasn't going to be a sacrifice at all, but *holy shit*— "Little things like...?"

"I've never held hands with a guy," Vicki whispered, trying to tug her hand free. "I've never been kissed."

Sweet mercy. Joel's pulse picked up. "And the big things?"

He had a good idea by now, no matter how impossible it seemed.

Vicki lowered her chin and looked him in the eye as she spoke. "I'm a virgin. In everything. So if you're up for the challenge, go ahead, teach me to ride."

The response of "you're fucking kidding me" wasn't the right one, but damn, he'd never been so tongue-tied in his life. Her wrist slipped from his fingers, and she moved away, staring down the ravine at the creek.

Silence stretched between them, different this time than before. It wasn't him patiently waiting for her to gather her courage. This time there was anticipation along with the discomfort.

The discussion had totally not gone where he'd expected, and all his images of being a knight in shining armor and helping her redeem her name were buried under a sea of *holy fuck, holy fuck, holy fuck...*

Her being a virgin was impossible, and yet why would she lie? And she wasn't lying, not that he could tell.

"I'm trying to absorb this, okay?" Joel spoke softly, like he would around skittish horses—ironic, that. He didn't want to scare her off, but he needed time to process the information. "I'm totally going to work with you on the horse thing, and dealing with your fears will require us to at least pretend to date each other. All of that, I'm good with. I'll do it."

He stood and walked to her side. Vicki had crossed her arms over her chest and she wasn't bouncing anymore. Just standing, motionless.

It was awkward, towering over her. He shifted uneasily on his feet before pulling her back toward the bench. "Sit, I want to ask you something."

She went willingly enough, curling up on one side of the sturdy bench and drawing her legs to her chest. She wrapped her arms around them and rested her chin on her knees. "I kind of blew your mind, didn't I?"

He nodded. "I won't push for the secrets right now, but...holy shit, yeah. I want to ask you something."

She lifted her head and waited.

"Why me?"

A crease folded between her eyes. "Why you, what?"

Joel shrugged. "I promise to help you no matter what, so it's not like we have to fool around to make this work. If you've gone this long without having sex, why do you think you have to change things up now?"

"Because you don't want to have sex with me?"

Oh God. He beat down the images flashing into his brain. "Because most women I know want sex to be something special. Especially their first time."

Her mouth twisted into this teasing grin. "You saying you suck in the sack, Joel? That's not what I'd heard."

"You're not making this any easier," he complained.

"Look, if it's too freaky to consider then, whatever. But sex is sex. I have my own reasons for not having had it until now, but..."

She turned those bright eyes his direction, and something inside just about melted. Whether it was from how hot she made him or her total lack of self-consciousness, he understood a little better what a deer felt like when the headlights hit them.

Vicki squirmed closer. "You've always been on my radar, although I never did anything about it, both because of my family and the *you and Jesse* thing. But honestly, if there's

43

anyone in this town I want to get intimate with, it's you. So why don't you think about it for a while and get back to me."

The absurdity of her statement struck like a bat. "Call and let you know I'm okay with fucking you?"

"Don't think being crude is going to scare me off." She knelt on the bench. "And don't be stupid. I feel like some hick-town kid as it is. What happens when I get the hell out of here, and I meet some guy I like? I'll be all messed up and stereotypical, and I'm so goddamn over being left out. I want what I want for once in my life. And yes, that means I want to fuck you."

There was just enough of the ridiculous in the situation Joel found his lips curling into a smile. His amusement increased instead of fading, especially when Vicki arched one perfect brow.

Her eyes widened. "You think this is funny?"

"Well, it sure as shit isn't sad."

Her lips twitched this time as well, and she bloomed. Sunshine in her eyes, delight dancing across her face. "You gonna help me, Joel Coleman?"

"Seems like we need to get this straight. We're gonna help each other. You said you've never been a girlfriend, well, I've never had one either." It was his turn to sit back and feel a little uneasy at her laughter. "Yeah, yeah, fine. I've had sex, and fooled around enough, but it's always been just fooling around. Exciting, but over and done before it got serious."

Vicki blinked hard. "This is not supposed to get serious, Joel. That's not what I want at all."

"It's more serious than me picking you up at the bar and us going home for a few hours, isn't it?" Her slow nod helped clarify his thoughts. "You have things you need to accomplish, and so do I. If we spend the kind of time together over the next while we'll need to, it's going to be more than a casual thing. And that's okay. We can make this fun. I like the idea of having someone to call up who can come join me for...whatever. A movie, or a horseback ride, once you get comfortable, of course."

"We're going to bullshit ourselves as well as everyone else in town?" Vicki asked. "Gonna make us into some kind of *special friends forever?*"

She'd sat back on her heels, and Joel lifted a hand and brushed his knuckles along her cheek. "Who said it's bullshit? There are things about you I already admire. Like, man, the way you were ready to take Eric's head off in the café? Loved it."

"That was terrible. I need to get over the flame-ups I tend toward as well." She wrinkled her nose, and it was the cutest sight. "If I could trade in my temper for some cool horse sense, I'd do it in an instant."

"Take your energy and redirect it. It'll be fine." He finally let his gaze go where he'd been longing, taking in the swell of her breasts, the trim cut of her waist. She filled her jeans nicely, but she wasn't showing it off like...

He stopped and scratched his head to drag his thoughts away from the rest of the Hansol family and what they usually wore around town.

Okay, parts of this were going to be fun, and parts were going to be hellishly difficult. In the end, though, he would learn a few lessons, and so would she. With her leaving town in the spring, there was a solid deadline involved as well.

He could handle it. And enjoy it.

Vicki fidgeted where she perched on the bench. "Well, I suppose I should go. Let you think it over a little."

He caught her and again prevented her from escaping. "Nothing to think about. Just one more question." She stopped bouncing for long enough he rose to his feet and pointed at her motorbike. "Can I take her for a ride?"

All the sexual innuendo from their previous discussion left her confused for a moment as to what exactly Joel was asking. She didn't think he was going to simply lay her out in the grass and fuck her right then and there. If he tried, she would give him a violent reason to change his mind.

She might be naïve, but she wasn't an idiot.

45

She'd seen porn. Which, for the most part, seemed stupider and more hickish than she felt at times, but even they took a minute to move past the "bad cop pulls over the innocent-yet-way-too-busty miniskirt-clad speeder".

But when he ran a hand over the leather seat of her bike, her earlier amusement returned with a vengeance. "Typical guy. You only want me for my Harley."

Joel straightened from where he'd been examining the bike, his gaze coming down hard on her chest, lowering to between her thighs before rising back to her face. "Oh, darling, are you ever wrong."

A flash of anger struck, and she turned away to hide her reaction.

She'd asked for this. He'd done nothing wrong, and taking it out on him would be stupid and ignorant, not to mention screw everything up before they even began.

She needed a minute to figure out how to deal with her conflicting emotions. Vicki forced all the enthusiasm into her voice she could muster, that is, she lied her fucking ass off. "Why don't you take her for a spin. I'm going to hang out and relax for a minute."

"Vicki? You okay?"

"Hell, yeah, just—like I said, I've never been here before." She pointed down the riverbank. "I'm going for a walk. Take your time. You need a hand?"

Joel caved. There was no other reason her pathetic excuses worked, because he looked suspicious as hell. But he nodded and lifted the bike to vertical, rolling her out from under the tree and aiming her toward the main highway. "I'll just try her for a bit. Always wanted a bike, just never seemed to get around to buying one."

"She's nice on the highway. Take as long as you want." Vicki grabbed the helmet off the bars and pressed it to his side. "It's not going to fit great, but wear it anyway."

She waited until he'd cooperated, both of them real careful and polite. By the time Joel had mounted up, she was ready for him to be gone. She needed some space.

Vicki slipped down the bank before he even fired up the engine. The rush of water grew as the bike's motor faded. The farther Joel got away, the more her surroundings were nothing but wilderness. Birds chirping every now and then. Mostly the water, and this weird creaking sound she finally figured out were the trees themselves shifting in the wind.

She found a flat rock right at the water's edge and sat, a handful of pebbles at the ready.

Talk about an unexpected twist. Joel's help with the horses was awesome. His promise to help her get a better name in the community, and keep Jesse out of it— Well, the first part of the deal had been wholly dependent on the second. She couldn't get involved with two guys and make things anything but worse.

But being his actual girlfriend? Asking him to have sex with her?

My God, she'd slipped down the exact same path her sister and mother were walking. Using sex to get what she wanted. Only...

Only what she wanted *was* sex.

The first rock she tossed barely made a ripple. The current was strong enough the slight weight broke through the surface and vanished as if she hadn't even been there. Vicki stared at the remaining rocks resting in her palm.

What she'd said she wanted was true. A way out. Which meant a future to look forward to. A little redemption from her past, in terms of people seeing her with new eyes.

And a present filled with pleasure. What the hell was wrong with that?

She wasn't sure how long she'd sat there, stewing, tossing one stone after the other before a loud rumble sounded from the top of the ridge and Joel's face popped into view. Vicki rose and brushed the dirt from her hands, adjusting her T-shirt before she stepped up the narrow path to his side.

He wore a huge grin. "That was awesome. Come on, I want to show you something."

She took the helmet he offered. "Where are we going?"

He slipped forward on the seat. "Hop on. It's better seen than explained."

Chapter Five

For a moment, he wasn't sure she would cooperate. Stubborn was too light a word to describe what he'd already discovered about Vicki.

"You don't have a helmet," she pointed out, the one he'd returned dangling from her fingertips as she clutched the straps.

"I'll be real careful, and we're not leaving Six Pack land. Come on, trust me."

She slipped the helmet over her shining hair, and Joel twisted in the seat to let her hop on without him staring.

He wanted to stare. Oh my God, he wanted to strip her down and look his fill. He'd never thought before if he had a type. He'd loved the girls, and they loved him, and there hadn't been much thinking beyond the physical pleasure they shared.

But if he had a type? Vicki was it. Typical male he might be, but those tits of hers caught his eye. It was the whole package he really liked, though. How small the rest of her was, the way her eyes lit up when she got pissed.

This unexpected turn of events was becoming more interesting as the day progressed.

She nudged his foot. "I can't climb on without a boost."

He shifted his leg out of the way so she could use the footstep. She caught hold of his shoulders and swung her right leg over the bike, settling in behind. Her thighs wrapped around him, her crotch to his ass.

When she slid her arms off his shoulders and curled in tight to his back, something hot and wild raced through him.

It was only the start of physical contact between them, and already his cock had grown uncomfortable, confined by his jeans and the tight position on the bike. He shifted his hips slightly to ease the pressure, and her breasts rubbed his T-shirt.

Another jolt of fire hit hard.

Distraction needed, now. He revved the bike, speaking over his shoulder. "You ready?"

She gripped him tighter in response, fingernails digging into his chest. The tiny bit of pain shot straight to his dick like a bolt of lightning.

Sweet mercy, he was going to die.

Joel took off carefully to not lose his passenger, heading the bike down the dirt road for about a mile before swinging onto a horse trail. This section of land rose and fell in uneven waves, so the family had turned it into grazing land to avoid driving equipment over the hilly terrain. But for the animals, it was a beautiful retreat, with small, shallow coulees and oases of trees clustered in groups.

They crested a hill, and he slowed to allow Vicki to spot the herd. He didn't say a word, just pointed.

Her grip on him had loosened as they'd ridden, less of a death clasp, more staying safe and in control. Now she squeezed, a deliberate message she'd seen them. Joel headed for the trio of pines standing sentinel over the fields and turned the engine off, balancing the bike so she didn't have to move.

"Nice bunch of horses." Vicki leaned forward to look around. "How many are there?"

Joel ignored the pressure on his back from her breasts nudging him and focused on the question. "This is the specialized breeding herd. There are about twenty mares Jesse and my daddy are using to build up the stock. The rest of the herd is split onto other sections of the ranch."

Vicki crawled right off, her warmth vanishing and making him sad. "Breeding?"

"Means they're pregnant."

She glared. "I'm not a farm girl, but I'm not stupid. I know what breeding means. I meant when will they have the babies?"

"No insult intended. This herd should foal by next April. Well, except for Sable. The stud covered her late last fall, so Jesse figures she's gonna drop sometime in the next couple months, probably before Christmas."

Joel propped up the bike and followed Vicki to where she'd moved to get a better view of the animals. The herd wandered, grazing a little, but mostly relaxing.

"I'm such a wimp." Vicki wrinkled her nose. "They don't look so scary from this far away, but I'm still not keen on getting any closer."

"Hey, don't push it. It's only October, and you've...well you've got nearly as long to work this through as they have to wait to foal."

Vicki plopped to the ground and pulled off her helmet, her hair pouring over her shoulders. "Oh goody, it's a race. Me against the horse. May the least smelliest win."

Sarcasm dripped from every word, and Joel chuckled. He lowered himself beside her, careful to maintain a bit of distance and not crowd her the way he'd like. "It's a target. You'll take shots and get closer to the bull's-eye all the time."

She flashed him a smile, that one she'd surprised him with back in the café the other day. "So hitting the target at all is a win in the beginning?"

"Yeah."

Vicki nodded. "Okay. I can do that. When should the *I love horsies* lessons start?"

Joel moved with deliberate slowness, casually placing his hand next to hers. She was leaning back on her arms, hands planted in the grass. Their fingers weren't touching, not yet, but damn close. "You free tomorrow? Around the ranch we try to take things a little slower on the weekend. Just the daily chores for the animals and not a ton more. So if you come to the barns, I'll show you around."

She shivered as she observed the herd. "Go slow with me, okay?"

Hell, yeah. Slow in more ways than one, although it might

kill him.

Joel adjusted position. Again, a tiny move.

He was back in junior high, trying to convince Suzie James to join him under the bleachers for a few stolen kisses. He was in the back-row seats of the darkened science classroom during a movie, him and Tara Koloskis tossing furtive glances at each other as they stumbled around making the next move.

No. This was no flashback to his early days of sexual exploration. He was right freaking there, right fucking now. On the side of a hill, too old to play these kid games, but there you had it. Vicki leaned forward and her fingers slipped over his. She would have jerked away, but he didn't let her. Instead, he trapped her hand and held her in place with his palm resting over hers.

It was barely holding hands. Barely touching, and she could have been naked and riding him for how hard he'd gotten at the simple touch.

He glanced at her profile as she maintained a fixed lock on the horses, steadfastly refusing to look his way. She wasn't trying to pull herself free though, that was good.

Blood pounded through him harder than had any right. Joel stared over the herd as well and once again considered the day a bit of a turning point.

Whatever else the next months brought, life wasn't going to be boring.

He was holding her hand.

Vicki didn't move. Scarcely breathed.

She would have liked to blame the *not breathing* part on the fact he'd suggested she drop in at the barns the next day, but oh. My. God.

How was it possible that holding hands could cause more violent reactions than her most recent self-induced orgasm?

"There are a couple of mares I'm keeping a special eye on." Joel sat straighter as he lifted his left hand and pointed. "I've got favourites, I guess. Buttercup over there is a first-time mom, and Sable is the daughter of my first horse."

"Makes—makes sense." God. She'd had to stop and clear her throat to get past the block in her way.

She tugged their linked hands experimentally, and Joel eased off enough to adjust his grip. Now his fingers were completely enveloping hers.

Giant knuckles, thick fingers. The rougher skin of his finger pads caressing her softly. It felt too damn amazing to want him to stop. Add in the naughty images of him stroking her entire body, and she didn't want to stop that train of thought either.

But...*shit.* "We really gonna do this, Joel?"

Another rub, this time with his thumb over the back of her hand. His fingers moving oh-so-slowly, but still more than enough of an impact considering the pounding in her throat. She honestly felt her heartbeat there. Another first, it seemed.

"Are we gonna hold hands? Hell, yeah. Seems like a good place to start."

She dropped the idea of crawling into his lap and rubbing all over him like a lovesick cat. "It's nice."

Joel chuckled. Such a dark, rich sound for something that should show his amusement, but when she glanced at his eyes, there was far more there than merely fun. Full dark pupils pinned her in place. "It's a *start*, Vicki. You sure you want me to teach you everything? Because, goddamn, I'm eager. But every bit of it is worth doing right."

"I'm sure." Holy hell, she was sure. If a little thumb rubbing got her aching between her legs and longing for more, she'd done this perfectly in terms of asking for help. "Only don't go too slow, okay? I'm not gonna break."

She didn't see him move. Somehow, though, she hit the ground and he was over her. His elbows were braced on either side of her head, and his knees must have been on the ground, because otherwise she would have been crushed beneath him.

Instead, she was caught between the solid ground and his rock-solid body. Just the lightest of contact between them, mostly heat.

Oh God, though, the *heat*, especially at her core where a thick ridge pressed...

His cock, *Vicki. Think the damn word. You're going to get a close-up view at some point, so use the big-girl words.*

She forced herself to acknowledge the truth. Where his *cock* made contact, need and excitement roared though her. Her mouth went dry as she stared into his face, wondering what he would do next. All thoughts of stopping him had vanished.

If he stripped her right then and there, she'd willingly get grass stains on her ass.

He wasn't breathing too smoothly himself. The hot stroke of his jagged gasps rushed past her cheek, and she braced herself for the next first. He was going to kiss her. She was sure of it. Crushing her lips beneath his, taking her by storm. That had to come next.

She debated closing her eyes, but he held her trapped with his gaze.

A long, low rumble issued out, his chest moving slightly as he spoke. "You might not be breakable, but I already said it. This is worthwhile doing right."

He lowered his head, his cheek brushing past her hair. She swore he took a deep breath before he rose. All the muscular length of him towering over her.

Vicki lay in the grass, the cool blue of the October sky framing the big cowboy. She took her time looking him over as the rush of whatever he'd triggered buzzed through her system. "How long is it gonna take before my heart rate goes back to normal?"

"Hell if I know. That's good, though. Tells me I'm not the only one turned on like crazy right now."

She tried not to stare at his hard-on. "You aren't the only one. Fuck, no."

He grinned and held out his hand. "Tomorrow, come to the small barn around ten and we'll get started."

The sexual tension between them deflated, at least on her

part. The first thing she thought of was the terror of the horses, but she hid it under the other fear. "Jesse?"

Joel pulled her to vertical. "He won't be home until late afternoon. We'll be done morning chores, so Blake and Matt won't be around. Trust me."

She wanted to, but saying and doing were two different things. She'd already opened up a can of worms starting this entire thing. "That's gonna take more time."

He snorted. And didn't let go of her fingers. "Come on. Walk with me for a minute."

It was a good thing he led her to the level section at the top of the hill, because hanging on to his hand was more distracting than she'd thought possible. He didn't let her loose, as if there were a delicate iron band around her wrist, holding her to his side.

She didn't want to let go.

"You still looking for a job?" he asked, deep voice smoothing over her like butter.

Vicki shook her head to clear the cobwebs. "What's that? Oh, no, I got on at the shop. I start full-time on Monday, thanks to you."

"None of my doing. You going to miss the café?"

She sighed. "Yeah, I love cooking. But the shop is a safer place to work. Less chance of breaking people's heads, that kind of thing."

Joel paced steadily, guiding her along. He was probably itching to ask her about Eric, or was her guilty conscience making everything all about her? No matter. Some secrets were not coming out today. Not ever, if she had her choice.

So she tried to return the distraction. "You enjoy ranching?"

Joel pulled her to a stop and looked over the land. She liked that he took a moment to think her question through before answering. Made it seem less some practiced comment, more from the heart.

"I can't imagine living anywhere else. Even being the couple hours away for school while Jesse and I went to college was brutal. I wanted to wake up in the spring and hear frogs. Let the roosters be my alarm instead of some tinny music pounding through the walls of the dorm from my neighbour's room."

"I bet there's an app for that."

Joel chuckled. "I bet there is."

She wasn't sure why it was suddenly so important to have him...well, like her. Oh, she was sure he wanted her, but like her? As in actually *like* the Hansol bad girl?

He'd said he admired her spirit, but most of that was impulsive. Spur of the moment. She'd rarely set out and done things to get them done. And now? Having Joel Coleman actually *like* her became an important part of the plan.

Although with every new thing she added to it, the damn to-do list was getting as full as she'd ever had it in her entire life.

"Tell me about...?" She scrambled back through the sexual cloud for the details he'd shared. "Sable. What was her mom's name? And how do you say that properly, because talking about a horse's great granddaughters probably follows some secret rancher's code, like breeding and mares and other stuff."

Joel glanced down, adjusting his grip on her fingers to curl his entire hand around hers. "You want to know all the terms?"

"All about horses. Tell me everything."

"I bet there's an app for that," Joel deadpanned.

"You're better than an app. You can hold my hand while you teach me." She gave him a smile, hoping this was the right thing to do, willing him to accept her offering.

Willing herself to be brave enough to take this adventure and stick it out to the end, because the potential for something wonderful was incredible.

Past, present and future. It all hinged on the here and now. If she could make it through the next months and learn to handle horses. If Joel was smart enough to help her.

If the town could just stay out of their business for a little while.

They stood there for a minute. She wasn't sure what came next. "I guess we should get back."

"I guess we should." Joel didn't let go of her fingers until they were at the bike, then he lifted her hand to his mouth and pressed his lips against her fingers briefly. "Give me a ride back to my truck?"

She wasn't sure if she should go *awww* for him being a gentleman, or kick him for leaving her aching with anticipation. "You don't want to drive?"

"Your bike. Let's see how you handle it." He handed her the helmet and waited until she'd mounted. Then he stepped over the back and curled an arm around her belly, and all the wild fantasies she'd shoved into a corner sprang up.

Hard-as-nails muscles pressed against her, bands of iron holding her steady.

The dry mouth she'd suffered from vanished, and she swallowed hard to stop from drooling. "I think it's better if you drive. I don't think I can balance her with your weight in the back."

She escaped from the circle of his arms. Not because she didn't want him holding her, but because she wanted it too badly.

Joel seemed to accept her excuse. "It's a bigger bike than you should have, isn't it?"

"I'll trade down someday. It was cheap."

He slipped into position and waited for her to mount. Wrapping her arms around him didn't seem nearly as dangerous, but the control she clung to was an illusion. Because in spite of the drive back to the truck, the time it took for him to dismount, in spite of all that, she was still horny as all get out from having her inner thighs rubbing his fine ass.

She wanted him between her thighs for real, and while it seemed she'd get her wish eventually, going slow was the order of the day.

Not even a goodbye kiss.

Joel hauled open his truck door. "I need to get back. I'll see you at ten outside the red door."

He started his engine, rolling down the window so he could finish talking to her. Like he was putting a barrier between them. Vicki adjusted position and turned the bike for the road. "Ten then. I'll call you if I can't make it for some reason."

Although what reason could she have other than avoiding the horses of hell?

He pointed sternly, a cross between a frown and mischief on his face. "You show up or I'll track you down."

Drat.

There really wasn't any answer for that, and if she stayed around any longer things would get more awkward. So she took off, her body still buzzing with need, her head filled with images of pregnant Six Pack mares, and Joel Coleman pinning her to the ground.

She was totally going to get off tonight on the memories of him covering her, and she wasn't even a bit ashamed.

Chapter Six

Joel gave her room to leave, not wanting to crowd her as she somehow got the massive bike back onto the highway. He pulled over, ready to turn down the narrow drive leading to the trailer he shared with Jesse, then changed his mind.

He needed help on this one, and his options were limited as to who he could ask. Frankly, his dad was the one he'd normally go to for the horse advice he required, or Karen, but they were both out of the question for obvious reasons.

Instead he headed toward town and his closest brother. Daniel might not have the twin-speak advantage there'd always been between him and Jesse, but in some ways, that made him a better sounding board.

They got each other. Understood the motivation to do something a little different.

Pulling up in front of Daniel and Beth's home in town felt a touch strange, though. Jesse had been right. His older brothers were settling down, which was normal, but changed the dynamics like crazy.

As did the wild new family additions who rushed his truck.

"Uncle J, Uncle J." Little boys shrieked as he stepped onto the lawn, allowing his three nephews to tackle him to the ground.

"Hey, guys. You ready for it? Three, two, one." The game Daniel's adopted boys had created of *Guess the Uncle* hadn't gotten old yet, so he and Jesse still went along with it.

"Joel," two of them shouted.

"Jesse," the littlest of the three, Robbie, insisted.

"That's Joel's truck, you dum-dum." Lance poked his brother. "Jesse only drives it sometimes."

Robbie tilted his eight-year-old head to the side and stared hard into Joel's eyes. "You sure you're not Jesse?"

"Sorry, short stuff. Uncle Joel at your service."

Nathan didn't care who it was dropping in unannounced. "You gonna take us fishing? Riding? To visit—"

"Whoa, rein it in. I'm here to visit your mom and dad, and you for a bit, I guess. What you up to?"

"Playing."

The front door opened, and Daniel stuck his head out. "Lunch time."

The three short people vanished as if they'd never been there. Joel pushed himself off the grass and wiped at his jeans. "You got extra for me?" he called.

Daniel leaned on the doorframe. "Don't know. You planning on teaching my kids any more bad habits like proposing another 'who can shove the most hard-boiled eggs in their mouths at one time' contest?"

"That was Jesse." Still he couldn't help but smile as he headed in and patted his brother on the back. "Also, I seem to remember you won."

"Shh, no getting me in trouble." Daniel grinned at him. "Good to see you. Got something other than a free lunch on your mind?"

"That transparent?"

They walked toward the kitchen and the noise level rose exponentially.

"You're always welcome, but there's not much excitement around here for a single guy, egg-eating contests exempted. Also?" Daniel paused in the doorway and spoke softer. "I saw you last night at Traders. You were distracted. Let me feed you, and once the horde is full we can take them outside and talk."

Joel nodded, but felt a bit of a fool. "Is Beth around? I kinda have a question for her first."

Daniel raised a brow. "Sure. You can take lunch into her office."

He passed over a plate filled with finger foods and pointed

down the hall.

"It's nothing bad," Joel started, but Daniel waved him down.

"Don't be stupid. You want to talk to Beth, talk to her. I don't need to know the details ahead of time. Ass."

"Daddy. You're not supposed to call your brother an ass. Mummy said so." Robbie was all wide-eyed as he worked on the sandwich he held in a two-handed death grip.

"You're not supposed to call your brothers an ass until they are adults. Then you can pick the best words for the occasion, okay?"

The older two nephews snickered as the littlest one puzzled over that explanation.

Daniel pushed Joel down the hallway. "Go, before you get me in more trouble."

The continued spirited conversation behind him regarding the use of the words *ass*, *jackass* and *butt* had Joel chuckling by the time he knocked on the office door.

"Yes?"

"Lunch delivery by Six Pack Express."

The door swung open and his sister-in-law Beth appeared, her dark curls more tousled than usual, as if she'd been dragging a hand through them or something. "Hi, Joel. Good to see you. Again."

"I know, it's been less than twenty-four hours. I'm a terrible burden."

"Oh, stop it, you're family." She took the plate from him and returned to her chair, pointing across from her to a recliner tucked into the corner. "Sit. I'm nearly done, to be honest, but sometimes it's better to stick to the routine so the boys stay on track."

Joel glanced around, noting the piles of organized paper on the desk and side table. "Marking for school?"

Beth nodded. "And planning. I used to ignore everything until late Sunday night, and dread it all weekend. Daniel finally convinced me it would be better to get the work out of the way, so we have a lazy Saturday breakfast then he and the boys take care of things until I'm done sometime after lunch."

"Sounds like a plan."

She leaned forward and whispered. "Once? I finished early and read a book for a bit. It was heavenly."

He loved his nephews but, yeah, a break from their wild energy every now and then could be a good thing. "I won't say a word."

She picked up a carrot stick and waved it. "So, what's up?"

"Since last night?" Holy hell. How to answer that question? The last twelve hours had been mind blowing. "Mostly, I wanted to ask you something as a teacher."

"Really? Sure."

"What's the best way to teach someone something new?"

A laugh burst from her. "Summarize four years of schooling? Nice one, Joel."

"Okay, maybe not quite that. I mean, I remember how the teachers at college and high school covered stuff, but frankly? Most of it was..." He paused. *Boring* wasn't a great word to say to a teacher, was it? Not when he was looking for a favour.

"Dry?" Beth suggested.

He nodded reluctantly. "The only reason some of the information was interesting was that I was interested. The actual way they taught was painful, most of them. I had this awesome teacher back in fourth grade, and I can still tell you the longest rivers in the world according to length, but that's too far back to remember how he did it."

"Ahhh, okay. Now I have an idea. Teaching 101. You ready?"

"You want me to take notes?"

Beth shook her head. "I think you'll get this. Joel, most people have a learning style that works best for them. Some people read for information, some listen, some have to do it. The best teachers use all the methods. The class you remember so well must have hit your style. Boom, you retained it better."

That kind of made sense. "So some doing, some talking, a

mix of stuff. What else?"

She smiled. "Start at the beginning and make sure the basics are there. Even if you don't remember learning to read, what do you think you learned first?"

"ABCs and basic words."

"Right, and I teach math, so the kids learn number order, adding, subtracting. Each next step builds on the previous skills." She took a bite of her sandwich before continuing. "Is this helping?"

God, the ideas racing through his brain. "Yes. Anything more?"

"Last thing that leaps to mind. Celebrate your successes."

He picked up the pad of stickers from the desktop, the ones with neon stars. "No farm creatures saying 'Way to Go'? I loved those."

"I teach high school, but yeah, stickers still go over surprisingly well. But use praise, or even a pat on the back. When you do break something down it's tempting to rush through the easy steps, but learning often works best when you do a little, celebrate, and then do it all over. Build in the information until it becomes instinctive. Or set a goal reward, like once you learn the times tables you get a new book."

His abstract plans for teaching Vicki how to love horses suddenly didn't seem nearly as far-fetched.

Add in the last of Beth's suggestions and, well hell, they gave him *ideas*.

Rewards? Setting goals? This could work.

He rose to his feet and came around the desk to hug her. "You're brilliant. I'm so glad you're one of us."

"Glad I could help. And if you need anything while you're going along with your teaching assignment, whatever it is, let me know."

She was gloating. He resisted sticking out his tongue. "You'll find out eventually."

"Of course I will. Keeping secrets around the Coleman clan? Good luck. And Joel?" She pointed at his face. "You totally have a secret. It's written all over you."

"Dammit..."

"Your poker face sucks. Sorry to tell you this, but it's true."

"Be nice, or I'll tell them you're done for the day."

She mock-glared. "Out. And not a word."

He ducked from the room and rejoined the male side of the equation. Through the rough-and-tumble happiness of the next couple hours, he enjoyed the change of pace. Hide and seek with the boys, good-natured teasing with Daniel.

The entire time his brain popped with plans for teaching Vicki all sorts of lessons.

Tired. Scared. Hungry. It was like the most wretched trio of sensations, and all of them had arrived in spades this morning. Awesome way to start the adventure.

Vicki stared at the red barn doors before her and considered making a mad dash home. She could crawl back into bed and pretend none of this had ever happened. That she didn't have a chance to escape Rocky. That Joel had never touched her hand in such an innocent way, and caused such an erotic response...

And that's where the damn thing fell apart. She physically ached to experience more, and desire had gotten her tired ass out of bed and brought her back to the ranch only a day after setting up the stupid deal with Joel.

The doors blocking her path were the first challenge. Vicki grabbed the large iron loop attached to the right side and tugged.

Nothing happened.

She pulled harder.

Nothing budged. Not when she put her full weight behind it and leaned back.

"Vicki?"

She jerked upright so fast she had to scramble to find solid footing. Joel stood eight feet to her left, a much smaller man door open at his back.

She smoothed her T-shirt and pretended she'd just been hanging out as she managed to join him without tripping over her still-uncoordinated self. "Hey. How are you today?"

"Great." There was laughter in his voice. "You ever open a set of barn doors before, darling?"

She refused to apologize for her ignorance. He knew he was getting a raw recruit. She lifted her chin and batted her lashes. "Nope."

He turned and led her back to the dratted handle she'd been whaling on.

"Man doors open like doors. These? Slide sideways." He took her hand and placed it back on the handle. "Try again."

The tug she gave sent the wood flying so hard Joel rushed to catch it.

"Shit, sorry. You got that thing well lubricated."

Oh. My. God.

Okay, all the dirty images from the past night had to come rushing in right then, didn't they? It seemed she was not going to be able to win this contest and get anything done the easy way.

Only when she risked a peek upward, he wasn't leering, just casually closing the doors.

"It's tough to keep them moving with all the dust around here, but my dad thinks it's important, in case there's ever a need to get the animals out quick. So we do regular maintenance on the glide system."

He wasn't even joking. And when he guided her toward the man door, his big hand placed against her lower back, Vicki had to make another mental adjustment.

"You're taking this seriously, aren't you?" she asked. "This teaching me all about animals and ranching and shit?"

Joel stopped a pace inside the building and nodded. "You have a good reason to want to learn, so we'll do it right."

That's when it struck her. She was inside a goddamn barn.

There were horses in this place, and she was about to have to climb on the back of one.

Her stomach clenched. "Oh, shit..."

"You okay?" Joel leaned down and peered at her. "You're this weird shade of green. Breakfast not agreeing with you?"

"Didn't eat anything," she confessed. "I was afraid I'd lose it."

He swore. "It's ten o'clock, and you haven't eaten?"

She wondered at the annoyance in his voice. It was just a meal. "Trust me, it's not the first time I've gone without breakfast. I'll live."

He examined her closer, top to bottom, and she tried not to wiggle. His examination wasn't sexual, but damn if she didn't want it to be. At least when his gaze was rolling over her, she could put hell horses on the backburner and ignore part of what she was there for.

He finished his nonsexual, but still stimulating perusal by staring at her feet. He shook his head. "You don't have any cowboy boots, do you?"

She snorted. "Umm, no."

"Fine. Today you can wear these, but we'll have to get you some real boots."

Right. She'd checked before. Not because of the horse thing, but because she liked how they looked. Too expensive for her pocketbook. "I'll poke around."

Maybe there would be some used ones at the thrift store. Salvation Army or somewhere.

That's when she finally registered what he was holding out. "Rubber boots?"

He twisted his feet forward to show off the pair he wore. "The finest bit of footwear on any ranch."

She eyed the black monstrosities suspiciously. "To ride a horse?"

He shook his head. "You're not riding today."

"Oh, thank God."

The words burst free about the time his laughter surrounded her, and he led her back to a bench, squatting to pull off her runners. He held the floppy tops of the rubber boots open. "Nope, you don't have to worry about the big smelly beasts for today. So relax, and enjoy your lesson, okay?"

Now she wished she'd eaten breakfast.

It was more than a little distracting to have him kneeling in front of her. Another opportunity to have their heads at about the same height. He was this enormous mass of a man, and the stroke of his hand over her sole as he straightened her damn sock shouldn't have felt so good. The way the back of his knuckles rubbed her calf as he held the boot steady and she pushed her foot in was downright sinful.

She leaned forward on the second boot, her hand on his shoulder for balance, close enough his scent surrounded her.

Wow. Putting on rubber boots with Joel Coleman was making her motor run. Was she pathetic or what?

But stupid? She didn't want to be that. So instead of kicking herself in the ass for being a little too fast off the starting gate with her hormones, she decided to enjoy it. He smelt good as she took a deep breath, the scent of soap fading, the masculine aroma of a man who'd been moving all morning rising. He hadn't reached the sweaty stage yet, just smelt like Joel.

She resisted licking his neck. That was good.

Joel broke the easy silence between them. "Ready for your first lesson?"

"If there's no actual riding involved, I'm as ready as I can get."

"You'll be happy to know there's no actual horses involved either." Joel stood and held out his hand.

No horses? She was nearly distracted enough by his words to miss that first second of slipping her hand into his.

Nearly, but not quite. She'd spent too much time last night fantasizing about his hands to ignore it entirely. Her fingers vanished into his hand as he curled tight around hers and tugged her down the hall. "We're gonna start at the beginning. Welcome to day one."

He stopped beside a boxlike space, one of about ten in a row. Each had a gate at the front made of wooden slats, openings between them. Wood shavings littered the floor and off to one side was an unmistakable pile of crap that stank to high heaven.

Joel let her fingers go to grab something leaning up against the next gate.

The pleased expression on his face when he turned back was the only thing that stopped her from kicking him into tomorrow. Especially when he held out the mystery object—a shovel—and announced, "Lesson one. Cleaning stalls."

Chapter Seven

Maybe he should have worn a cup. The flash of rage in her eyes shocked him with its intensity.

Then, in the next breath, all was calm. She stared at the floor, her shoulders shaking slightly. "I'll shovel shit forever to avoid the actual horses."

Joel grabbed his own shovel. "Well, it might not be the method they'd use at some fancy training school, but you said to teach you what I know. I've hung out in these barns since I was little, following my dad and brothers. Taking care of the animals and doing chores. I didn't start with the big smelly beasts."

She lifted her head and smiled as she clung to the shovel handle, using it to hold herself vertical. "You gonna call them that all the time now, just to tease me?"

He grinned his answer. "For the next while we'll take it easy. You got until May to get ready, so there's no rush, right?"

She eyed the line of stalls warily. "I'm gonna be working full time. I can't be over here doing your chores every spare moment I get."

"No, you're not. 'Cause you and me are also going on the town. Plus spending other time together." Her pulse quickened—he saw it in the curve of where her neck and shoulder met. Hell yeah, his body tightened as he considered what was coming in the days ahead. "You're going to get used to the animals slowly, and every time you accomplish the next task, you get a reward."

His sister-in-law had been right. Everyone liked an incentive, and by the way her eyes lit up, it seemed Vicki was no different.

"What kind of things you got in mind?"

"We'll make some of them up as we go along. Today? You get this task done and I'll give you a surprise."

"You're not even going to tell me what it is?" Her lower lip was out, and it was so damn adorable he nearly reconsidered.

"I can tell you you'll like it." He hoped she'd like it. This part of the planning was worse than figuring out what lesson to give her with the horses.

He wanted to lift her to the top of the railing and consume her like a feast. Kiss her until she gasped for air, hold her squirming self to his body and let her rub all over until his cock gave up aching.

Going slow was necessary for dealing with the horses, but hell if going slow sexually wasn't going to kill him.

Her nose wrinkled. "Okay, teach me, but don't try to tell me this doesn't stink."

"I wouldn't dream of it." Joel showed her where to find the latch to open the gate. He moved a wheelbarrow into position. "Just think. When you go home after a long day of work, wouldn't it be nice to have a clean bed and a cool drink waiting for you?"

"You got French-maid fantasies. Nice."

He laughed. "While you're missing the French-maid costume, you do get to make beds."

He showed her how to clean the mess into the wheelbarrow, then he pushed it outside for her the first time.

"Oh, *man.*" Vicki fanned a hand in front of her face.

"Come on." He left the full barrow for a moment and walked her around to the garden side of the manure pile. "This part doesn't smell as much. It's wonderful compost now that it's aged. We turn it over in the fall and by the spring it'll be ready to be worked into the garden."

Vicki raised a brow before a full-fledged snicker broke free.

"What?"

She clutched her hands over her chest dramatically and stared into the sky. "Be still, my beating heart, for I am a-swoon with delight. My new boyfriend showed me a compost pile."

Joel smirked. "It's one of the 'little things' you've always wanted to experience, admit it."

Her eyes sparkled. "It's been on the list *forevah.* What other secrets you gonna share while we toil with the behind-the-scenes shit?"

"Ha ha. Watch and learn, my young Padawan."

Joel helped her empty the heavy wheelbarrow, then took her to the pile of shavings to fill up a load. She tipped the bedding to the floor in her cleared stall, but barely got the oversized contraption back to vertical.

"I don't suppose you have any junior-sized barrows?"

Joel shook his head.

She spread the shavings with the pitchfork, a little awkward with the length of the shaft compared to her arm reach, but she didn't complain. Joel watched her for a minute to make sure she had it, but cleaning stalls wasn't rocket science, so he went back to work as well.

They continued at their tasks, chatting over the stall walls. Joel had a good time working alongside her. For a novice, she did a decent job. Never complained, didn't take breaks or try to shortcut. She put her back to the task, wrinkled-nose expression firmly in place, and got it done.

She'd gone quiet in the past ten minutes. Still bouncing, but her energy directed toward finishing. And the expression on her face when he caught a glimpse was no longer as if she were holding her breath, but more as if she was having fun.

Well, what do you know?

They finished about the same time. Joel stepped behind her as Vicki laid a hand on the sidewall of the stall and leaned in. She breathed deeply, and he laughed.

Vicki twisted. "Fucking hell, can we put a bell on you or something?"

"I must be seeing things, because I coulda swore you just sniffed the wall."

She gave him a hesitant smile. "Okay, it doesn't stink so

bad anymore, so I was, you know, curious. How can it make that much difference we hauled the shit out and, voila, everything is roses?"

"It's the new bedding. We replaced one scent with another." He took the pitchfork from her and put it aside. "Admit it. It smells good now."

"I'm not going to go that far." Vicki shook her head. "If you bottled *eau de barn*, I doubt it would be a big seller."

"You'd be surprised."

"Speaking of surprises..." Vicki held up a hand to put her work on display. "I finished, boss. What do I get?"

He tugged on her sweatshirt sleeve. "Take this off."

Eyes going wide, Vicki grabbed the bottom and lifted it over her head without a word. As her tank top came into view, Joel decided life was damn good. This might be a reward for her, but he was going to enjoy it too.

He tilted his head toward the stall where they stored extra hay to have it conveniently on hand. The pile was running low, leaving only a few bales, which was exactly what he needed right now. He'd placed a thick horse blanket over the pokey surface. "Have a seat."

She hesitated for a second before dropping to the bale and facing him. He reached to the top of the post where earlier he'd placed the jar of cream.

"What's the surprise, Joel? You're making me nervous."

"Trust me. You'll like it."

Vicki muttered under her breath, but let him step behind her without any more questions. He straddled the bale, scooped up a couple fingers worth of cream and rubbed his hands together. "Pull your hair out of the way," he ordered.

She gathered it together and hauled the long strands forward, and once again he got caught in her freckles. He slipped his hands over her neck and shoulders, distributing the cream evenly before going back and working it in, using his thumbs to add pressure.

"Oh God, a massage? Yes, of course I'll clean your horse

poop for a massage." She groaned, tilting her neck forward. "You should have told me. I'd have done your share of the work as well."

Good firm muscles flexed in her arms and shoulders. Real strength, not fashion-thin soft arms. "You worked hard, I don't want you to be sore tomorrow."

She fell silent for a bit, well, not noiseless, but no words. Plenty of sounds, though. Moans and groans and little exhalations of pleasure, and right on schedule, Joel's hard-on arrived. He ignored it best he could. Figured he was going to spend a lot of the next month or so jerking off in the shower after he'd finished spending time with Vicki.

He traced a finger along her spine, softer now, wanting to feel her reactions. Get her accustomed to his touch. She leaned back when he lifted his hand away, as if attempting to stay in contact.

"Turn and face me." It was asking for trouble, but what the hell. *Live dangerously.*

Vicki twisted on the spot, her legs tucked in front of her like she was unsure where to put them. Joel reloaded with cream before he reached for one arm. "Drape your legs over my thighs. I want to do your arms."

She shrugged and opened her legs, arranging herself over him. Only her head went down, and they lost eye contact.

Damn. He'd embarrassed her. Still, he didn't stop. Just smoothed his hands down her arm until she relaxed once more.

It was all about getting comfortable. In the barn, around him. Didn't need to be explained, just experienced. Every minute now would help stop her from freaking as much when actual horses were involved.

And once he had her naked, she'd already be used to him touching her all over. At least that was the plan. If he could hold out long enough to put his grand scheme into effect.

She was halfway onto his lap, body totally open. The sweet scents of the barn, which he did find attractive, surrounded them. As he massaged her hand slowly, adding pressure to the pads of her fingers, she sighed. "You're good."

"One of the things I picked up over the years."

"Hmmm. It's nice."

"You get to learn how as well." Her eyes popped open. "Hey, trust me on this. Any guy you meet who you like? Give him a massage, and he'll be hooked."

"Yeah, because what guy doesn't want a girl touching his naked body?"

"That too." Joel returned her grin. "Seriously, though. It's not always about sex."

"Bullshit."

"Not bull."

Her right brow rose. "Don't guys spend ninety percent of their time thinking about sex?"

"Only the ninety percent of the time we're not having sex. While we're having sex, we're not doing much thinking at all."

She laughed out loud before considering him closer. "You're okay, Joel Coleman."

"Thanks. So are you."

She surprised him then, catching hold of his hand before he could let her go. "Your turn. Take off your shirt."

"I didn't mean today," he protested.

"I don't care. You got to touch me, I get to touch you. Only seems fair."

Oh hell. Joel didn't think fair should be involved in this discussion at all. Fair was going to change his hard-on from something he could ignore into something that made him crazy.

She didn't accept no for an answer, though, scrambling to her knees and tugging at his shirtfront. "As much as I like flannel, off with it."

Fine. He undid his buttons, enjoying the way her gaze stayed pinned to his body as he removed his outer layer.

"Damn it, Joel. A T-shirt? You cold or something?" She bounced on her knees. "Off," she ordered again.

He stopped himself from asking if she'd done this before

because there was no way that would come out right. She wasn't shy like he'd expected, or least she wasn't until he lifted his shirt over his head and dropped it on the bale beside them.

Now the expression in her eyes was less confident than a moment before. "You want me to stop? Back up? We going too fast, or too far?"

She swallowed hard. "You're just so. Damn. Big. Kinda blows my mind."

"You need to eat more and get bigger yourself."

Vicki leaned forward to grab the cream jar. "Nothing doing. I'm not getting any taller, and I don't want to get wider, so what you see is what you get."

Which was totally fine by him. What he saw, he liked plenty. Joel was more and more confident this deal between the two of them was going to work out well.

Especially when she rose, walked behind him and put her hot little hands on his back.

She had to hide behind him, because if she'd stayed in front for any longer she was sure he'd know every damn one of her secrets. Those blue eyes of his looked straight through her, and there wasn't much she could do in defense.

Except hide, which is why she now faced the daunting task of giving her first massage, and holy hell, all she wanted to do was strip down to nothing and rub the cream on his body with her own.

Perhaps later.

For now, she tried to imitate what he'd done. Smoothing a layer of the thick cream over his shoulders before steadily rubbing it in.

"That's nice. Use your thumbs more. There you go. *Yeah.* Here, start here." Joel reached up and caught her fingers, dragging them to the back of his neck. "Push down with your fingertips—you feel that muscle?"

She squeezed lightly, but she could see the damn muscle without touching. "Yeah?"

"Drag your fingers out and follow it. If there're any knots you'll find them and, fuck—*there*. That feels great."

Hmm, this wasn't as tough as she'd thought it would be. "You've got a ball under the muscle. Is it supposed to be like that?"

"No, so work it out. Dig in with your fingers."

"Dig in? What if I hurt you?"

He twisted his head to the side. "Trust me, it would take a lot to cause me any damage. Just add pressure, and if it gets too hard, I'll warn you."

She was so into what she was doing the sexual innuendo of the comment skipped over her head as she followed his directions. It was only after she'd pulled a *hell yeah* from his lips it registered. "Does everything you say have two meanings? Like a regular one and sexual one?"

"I'm a guy. Remember earlier about the *all sex, all the time* comment?"

She laughed, but kept rubbing. The broad expanse before her was heavenly to touch, and she was getting turned on. It wasn't enough to make her call things off, but damn, touching Joel wasn't a hardship.

Or having him touch her.

"You know this would be easier if you were lying down."

He nodded. "We'll do that later. Any time you want to give me a massage you just offer, darling. You have wonderful hands."

Vicki screwed up her courage and stepped back in front of him. "You want me to do your arms?"

He held out a hand. "All yours."

She knelt on the hay bale. He rested his hand on his thigh, but the positioning was awkward. "I can't get at you easily. Everything is in the way."

He settled his fingers on her hip, and they both paused.

It was like an elaborate dance. One set of touching, retreat. Another caress, then a move away from each other. Only the longer they touched, the longer she stroked those muscles in his biceps, and the more she traced her fingertips over the dusting of golden hair on his tanned arms, the more the ache between her legs grew.

His fingers on her hip tightened briefly before he tugged her tank top free from her jeans.

"Joel? What—?"

"Shhh, it's okay. I'm not gonna rush you. Just want to touch skin."

He slipped his fingers under the fabric and held on, and holy fuck, she wanted him to rush. If he'd sent electrical charges flipping through her yesterday when he'd held her hand, this was like being in direct contact with a power plant.

She forced herself to finish the massage. To imitate all the careful caresses he'd given her, but it wasn't about working kinks out of muscles anymore.

It was about touch. About skin. About the new awareness between them that had nothing to do with horses and everything to do with her wanting to taste the half-naked body in front of her.

She lifted her gaze to meet his. The blue of his eyes had faded to a thin ribbon as his pupils dilated, centers darkened with...desire?

"Am I doing this right?" she breathed quietly.

His fingers stroked her hip. A minute motion that had blood pulsing through her hard. "You're doing everything perfectly."

Go slow. Go slow. The words repeated themselves in her head, but her brain wasn't listening. She wanted something more than what they were doing even though she wasn't quite sure what. "Joel?"

"Yeah?" The word escaped him nearly as breathless sounding as hers had.

"Can I...?" Damn it. Asking seemed stupid, so she interrupted herself and knelt upright, bringing herself right between his legs. "I'm going to touch you."

He nodded slowly. "Okay."

She rested her hands on his shoulders, like she'd done at the start of the massage. This time it wasn't about copying anymore, but exploring. She stroked one hand down his chest, the heat under his skin warming her fingers. The fine curls on his chest tickled her, the bulk of muscles giving her lots of lovely terrain to tease.

She took her time, smoothing over shoulders, down his sides. His ragged breaths gusted past her cheek as she stared mesmerized by his body.

When she touched his abdomen he sucked in a quick gasp, wrapping his fingers around her wrist and trapping her in position. "I think that's enough touching for today."

Damn. "But I wasn't done," she complained.

"Trust me, you're done."

The husky tone of his voice made her lift her eyes, staring from under her lashes. They gazed at each other for a moment, and all of it hit real hard.

They were going to have sex. Not that minute, but sometime. And she was okay with the idea. Like, oh-so ready for the experience.

"Damn it, Vicki."

"What?"

He cupped his hand around the back of her head and pulled her forward, holding her in place when she would have lifted her head and brought their lips together. He stopped them inches apart to lean his forehead against hers. "Damn it that I'm not doing this right. I was going to wait. Go slow, but hell if I can stop from wanting a taste of you."

"I'm okay with it. Really."

He smiled, wicked lips curling at the corners. "You are so fucking sexy, you have no idea."

"Does that mean you're gonna kiss—?"

It seemed it did. Because he did. Kiss her, that is. Soft, brief. Pressed his lips to hers and retreated before she'd gotten to wallow in the sensation.

This horrid noise escaped her. Most people would have

called it a whimper. She just knew she wanted more. She slid her hands back up to his shoulders and held on tight as he came in for another pass. This time he stroked her lips with his tongue causing an instant shiver.

"Oh..."

The moment she opened her mouth, he slipped his tongue inside. Teasing. Fleeting. Soft and careful, yet sending every one of her nerves to high alert. She couldn't press closer. His hand at the back of her head held her in one spot. She couldn't rub against him. His hand at her hip locked her the precise distance away so there was only their mouths. Only the soft, sweet, intoxicating sensation of the kiss.

She pulled in her courage and met him halfway, darting her tongue out to make contact with his before retreating. He hummed approvingly and kissed her again, open lips closing as he worked his way to the corner of her mouth, planting tiny kisses as he moved.

Oh *God*, this was good. He nipped her lower lip, and she sucked in air, the shot of pure pleasure taking her by surprise. Another stroke of his tongue followed, easing the throb of pain in her lip, but doing nothing to ease the throbbing elsewhere.

"Ahem."

A rush of adrenaline hit, overpowering even the lust in her veins. Vicki's head snapped to the right where Joel's dad, Mike Coleman, stood casually examining the rafters.

"Fuck." Joel exhaled the word under his breath as they attempted to untangle themselves. Somehow her fingers had become buried in his hair, and his hand under her shirt didn't slip out as easily as it had gone in. "Excuse us, Dad."

"No worries, just wanted you to know you aren't alone anymore."

Mike stepped past the stalls and out of their line of vision. His footsteps were replaced by the sound of light tapping from the far corner of the barn.

Her heart pounded in time with the banging. "You in shit?" she asked.

Joel chuckled, shaking out her sweatshirt and passing it back. "Hell, no. Just surprised, that's all. I was enjoying myself."

Well, yeah.

He cradled her chin in his hand and brushed his thumb over her lower lip. "I like kissing you."

"I liked it too."

Their soft whispers made it seem more real. Like a real kiss between them as boyfriend/girlfriend. God, even if this was just fooling around and helping each other out, her first kiss had more than met her expectations.

Joel sighed. "As good a time to end the lesson as any. I'll call you this week, okay?"

She nodded as she stood and knocked the loose bits of hay from her jeans. "Hey, Joel?"

He finished pulling his T-shirt over his head before turning those gorgeous eyes on her. "Yeah?"

"You're an awesome teacher. Thanks."

Between the brilliant smile on his face and the memory of their kiss, she was good for a few days. And a lot more eager to return for lesson number two than she thought possible.

Chapter Eight

Joel watched until Vicki was back on the highway before returning to the barn. He had a feeling a few questions would be coming his way, and he wanted this done without his mama overhearing.

He wasn't sure what his dad's reaction would be. He hoped it wasn't going to be an issue.

Stepping back into the barn was stepping into familiar territory, though. The peaceful atmosphere settled the concern in his belly. It wasn't as if his parents ran his life, but their family was close-knit enough that if they disapproved he wanted to hear it.

Didn't mean he would change his mind about being involved with Vicki. Just meant he'd know off the bat exactly how difficult this deal would be.

Mike Coleman was easy to find, tapping away on a small display shelf his mama usually had hanging in the living room.

"Need any help?" Joel offered.

His father glanced up. "You done with your earlier project already?"

Joel stifled his laughter. "And Mom wonders where us boys got our sense of humour from."

Mike laid down his tools and turned to face him full on. "You're a grown-up. You make the choices who you spend time with. But you're still my son, and if you want to talk about anything, I'm here."

"Is that dad-speak for 'what the hell are you doing with Vicki Hansol'?"

"Well I'm not blind, so I pretty much already know what you were doing with the girl."

"Dad." Joel was thirteen again, caught necking behind the barn. Only that time his father hadn't walked away. He'd stayed and watched until Joel and the girl he'd been kissing had separated and returned to the school picnic being hosted on the ranch.

His father grinned. "Look, I'm not some saint. I see why she caught your eye. Just..."

Joel waited. Leaned back on the nearest wall and let his hands hang by his sides. Kept his body language open. "Whatever you've got to say, I want to hear it. I respect you."

Mike sighed, his lips tightening into a thin line. "You're too old for me to be warning you about safe sex. If you haven't got the message by now, you ain't never gonna learn it. And I don't know Vicki other than hearsay. Never liked the type of man who assumed, because a lot of the time, they're wrong."

"Her family isn't the best in town," Joel admitted.

"I'm not talking about her family. I'm worried about you in the long run. All I'm gonna say is be careful."

Joel could hear the wheels spinning. The things his father was trying to say without saying them. "You are the fairest man I know."

"I'm still human. I want what's best for my own first and foremost, and right now I'll admit I don't know what to say to you." Mike shook his head. "Dammit. Raising you boys was easier when you were all trying to kill yourselves building tree forts on rotten limbs instead of getting involved with people I have no control over."

"She helped me clean stalls today." Joel had no idea why that bit of information popped out. "Just talked, mostly. She's fun to be around. Easy to talk to."

"Easy to kiss as well."

Joel nodded. "Hell, yeah."

Mike shrugged. "You make your decisions. I'm not about to turn into some fool of a tyrant, since laying down the law and ordering you to stay away from her would probably be the stupidest thing I could do, right?"

"You've never interfered before."

"Exactly. I don't know what brought you two together more than she's a pretty little thing, and I doubt she minds looking at you either. It's not my business. Only I hope you trust me enough to say there are warning signs here. Be careful. Don't let your dick lead you into trouble."

Joel bit down on his lip and swallowed his laughter. "Yes, sir."

Mike flipped the shelf over and pounded in another nail. "You bringing her to Thanksgiving dinner next week?"

Oh hell. He'd forgotten. Suddenly the entire *Vicki as girlfriend* was rolling along way faster than he'd expected. "Not sure. She welcome?"

Mike tossed him a glare. "Don't be an ass. If you're going out with the girl, bring her home to our table. If you don't want to bring her home, then you're not dating her, you're fucking her. And if that's all you're doing, I don't want to know the details, but I'd be hell of disappointed in you."

The fact he was doing Vicki a secret favour eased the flash of guilt at his father's words. "I'm not fucking around. For once."

"Smart ass."

Joel chuckled. "Well, I'm not."

The pause that followed was long enough to get Joel wondering. Mike crossed his arms in front of him and refused to break eye contact as he asked, "Jesse fooling around with her as well—?"

"No." The word burst out like a shotgun blast. "And whoa on this conversation continuing."

"Why?" Mike asked. "Because you think I don't know about some of the games you and your brother play? I'm not stupid. Don't treat me like I am."

His dad wanted blunt, Joel could give him blunt. Even though his cheeks were burning. "No, Jesse's not invited to play any games with me and Vicki. Not anymore. They were fun at the time, but they're done."

At that, his father looked him over carefully before nodding. "Maybe you are growing up then. Damn good job I'm doing with you boys, if I do say so myself."

Joel snorted. "Nothing to do with Ma, right?"

"Hell, no, it's all my work setting a shining example that's coming to the foreground." Mike glanced around the barn. "Although if you repeat that to your mother, I'll deny I ever said it."

They stood quietly for a minute, Joel thinking everything through. He wanted to reassure his father, but without breaking confidences he was caught. Which pretty much meant his father was right. He was growing up. Thinking of more than himself and his pleasure for the first time in his life.

Still, his family deserved something for all they'd given over the years. "It's going to be a good thing, me and Vicki. Really."

Mike nodded. "Thanks for that. You know where to find me if you need a butt kicking. Or a shoulder. Or whatever. You're my son, and that'll always be true, no matter what."

Mike patted him on the back, which was about as close as his father got to saying *I love you* to his sons. Joel grinned and went in for a hug.

Masculine back pounding ensued before they broke apart, Mike to return to his repairs and Joel to head home.

He was pulling into his driveway before his twin's truck reminded him he had another set of explanations coming. He wasn't looking forward to lying to Jesse at all.

Vicki was still buzzing when she pulled up to her apartment complex, lips tingling from the memory of his kisses. The oh-my-God-goodness of touching him. Being touched. The fact she'd spent a couple hours doing chores with the guy was totally forgiven because there'd been no actual horses involved—poop didn't count.

She might have been a little light-headed from the sheer hormone overload. When her key twisted in the stubborn door lock far easier than usual, it took a second for her to realize why.

She'd already swung the door open as it registered. The door had been unlocked already. *Fuck.*

Vicki froze on the spot. Released the handle and prepared to back away and call the RCMP. She wasn't about to be one of those too-stupid-for-words women who wandered in on a thief and got killed for her troubles.

Only the room was small enough she'd already spotted her intruder, squatted down and rummaging through the bottom drawer of her dresser. The recently bleached silver-white hair was a dead giveaway, and Vicki stormed in, fury rising to replace all the happy thoughts she'd been swimming in for most of the morning.

"Sarah? What the fuck are you doing?"

Her sister blinked in surprise, snatching her hand away as she shot to her feet. Just as quickly, Sarah relaxed, hip sliding out to the side, head tossed back. "Hey, sis. Good to see you."

Bullshit. "Why are you here?"

Sarah clicked her tongue. "That's so sweet. You're always so nice to your family, aren't you, baby? Too bad Mom never taught you any manners."

Goddamn hypocrite. Vicki bent to see what Sarah had been going through, but it was only T-shirts and shorts. All too plain and simple to be interesting to Sarah for the most part. "Going through other people's things is manners? God, don't even start with me."

Sarah shrugged and headed to the lone chair by the table, pulling it out and sitting like she planned to stay a while. "I thought you might still have that sweater you borrowed. I want it for a party next weekend."

Vicki looked her sister over closer. Sarah's hair was perfect, held in place by more hairspray than Vicki had used in her life. Her sister's flashy new hair colour was a welcome change— there was always hope that now that they didn't look so much alike the gossipmongers would stop treating them alike. The

Vivian Arend

rest of the package was typical Sarah. Her low-cut V-neck T-shirt emphasized her chest, tight faded jeans clung to her ass. Boots that rose up high and hugged her narrow calves. Vicki admitted it; her sister was attractive. If only she'd stop selling her wares so cheap.

"Next weekend is Thanksgiving. Mom's not doing something for us?"

Sarah snorted. "Mom's got a new boyfriend. They're going to Jasper for the weekend. Just you and me, sis, and since the last time I invited you over for a meal you said you'd prefer to starve, I've made other plans."

Okay, Vicki wasn't proud of that loss of temper, but damn it. "You weren't cooking. You were opening cans and heating them in the microwave. Which, fine, if that's what you want to eat, but when you fed the lasagna I brought to the damn dog, I got pissed."

"Whatever. Make your own plans because we're all busy. You can stay in this hole and cook whatever fancy crap you want."

It wasn't late enough in the day to start drinking, but hell if the thought of a couple of shots to numb her right then and there didn't seem attractive. "Okay, Sarah. I haven't borrowed anything from you for years. There's nothing here you need."

Sarah slowly gazed around the room, taking in the tiny space, the uncluttered bookshelf and counter.

Uncluttered, because Vicki didn't own a hell of a lot of stuff. And that was fine. It was going to make it much easier when she finally did get to take off and get free. Nothing to weigh her down. Nothing to hold her back.

"You know, there's room for you at the house." Sarah sniffed lightly. "I still don't see why you rushed to move out in the first place. Now that my old roommate is gone, it would be nice to have some company."

Yeah, right. Like Sarah really wanted the company. She wanted someone to help pay the rent. Her sister also knew why Vicki had moved out. Listening to Sarah having loud sex with random guys was not something Vicki ever wanted to

86

experience again, along with other issues. "I'm good here."

Sarah rose and headed toward the door, pausing at the picture of their middle sister. "Lynn call you lately?"

Lynn didn't keep in touch very often, but when she did, it was with Vicki. "She's doing well."

Sarah snorted. "I bet. Mom's still pissed at you for contacting social services."

"Well, she can stay pissed. It's been four fucking years already. Lynn is happy, and that's what counts." Happy and safe. Vicki suddenly felt way older than twenty. "You know Lynn needed to be in the special education program earlier, and Mom didn't follow through. The group home is exactly the kind of—"

Her sister cut her off. "Whatever. If Lynn's happy, that's great. Just don't expect Mom to ever welcome you with open arms, not after you pulled that fast one. Got the authorities on her ass and all."

Another conversation that didn't need to continue, because it was going nowhere but old paths. "You planning on hanging around for a while?"

Sarah rolled her eyes. "Nah. I guess not. If you ever decide to get that stick out of your ass and have a good time, call me. Otherwise, I'll see you round."

No wave. No hug. Nothing but back as Sarah left without another word.

First things first. Vicki was getting the damn locks changed on this place. She didn't think she'd ever given Sarah a key, but obviously, she'd gotten one from somewhere.

Her plans for the following weekend were now easier. No need to go through the motions of being an all-loving family. Mom would be out, Sarah would be partying. Lynn would be celebrating with the caring people in her life, thank God.

Vicki would be the one sitting at home and staring at the walls. Or not. Maybe she'd go for a long ride into the mountains. Pack a picnic lunch and stare at the wilderness for a while.

Tomorrow she'd make arrangements for the locks to get

changed. Sometime this week Joel and her would get together for another lesson. A bright shiny spot to look forward to.

It was like wiping away the grime after a long time of not cleaning. It wasn't going to be easy, making changes. Getting the hell out from where she was trapped. But with the memory of Joel Coleman kissing her senseless, the feel of his tongue over her lips—

Okay, life was looking up. She would cling to that truth for all she was worth.

Of course, when she decided to go grab a few extra bucks to put in her purse, and the cash she kept stashed in the top dresser drawer was gone, she wasn't really surprised. Guess Sarah had found what she'd been looking for after all.

Vicki sighed.

Clinging to hope for the future didn't change the fucked-up life she still had to live today.

Chapter Nine

Jesse sprawled on the couch in front of the television, the screen turned on, the volume at zero. It only took a moment for Joel to put two and two together. Jesse was hungover. Which, since it was past noon, meant he was royally hungover.

The temptation to make loud noises was childish, instantaneous and nearly impossible to fight.

Joel dropped into the recliner and grinned, speaking louder than normal. "Had a good time?"

Jesse narrowed his eyes. "Don't make me come over there and kill you."

"Moments like this I wish I'd taken trumpet in band class. Or drums. Or—"

"Fuck off and die."

Joel waited for Jesse to relax back on the couch, his head cradled on the cushions, blood-shot eyes watching the screen without focusing. "It was a good party, I take it."

"Brutally fun. I don't think Travis is ever coming home."

"Right."

"No shit. He and Ashley were all over each other the entire weekend. I swear I couldn't see daylight between them most of the time."

After years of Travis constantly going with someone new, the feisty Ashley was the first in a long time to last more than a week. "I thought Travis said she couldn't go. Had to hit the States for some meetings."

"Got moved to next weekend. Trust me, she and Travis were a definite item."

"He'll be back." Joel was more concerned about how to explain what he'd been doing all weekend. Maybe if Jesse had found someone interesting... "You have fun with anyone in particular?"

Jesse shook his head then cringed. "Fuck. No one I'd want to see again, but I had a great time. You should have come, jackass."

"I enjoyed staying here, thanks. Also, don't make plans for next weekend. Or not for Sunday. Family dinner, remember?"

Joel breathed out slowly. "Oh, yeah. I can handle Thanksgiving with all the trimmings. Mom's and Jaxi's cooking? Damn, I can totally go for that."

"We have to bring something to contribute. You remember that part as well?"

Jesse waved a hand. "I'll pick up more chicken wings."

Joel laughed. "You would too. That could get you killed."

His twin wiggled to a more vertical position and stared across the room. "What's up?"

"What?"

Jesse frowned. "You're not telling me something."

Damn twin connection. "You're not letting me get a word in edgewise. I had a good weekend as well."

"Stuck around here and found someone to play with, did you?"

Oh hell, yeah. "Surprisingly, yes."

Jesse waited expectantly. "Come on, spill."

Joel went for broke. "I'm seeing Vicki."

"You shit."

Not the reaction he'd expected. "What?"

"If I weren't ready to die, I'd come over there and beat the crap out of you. You said you weren't interested in anything other than ogling her tits."

"Hey, that's enough."

"What? You telling me you weren't ogling them the other day in the café? Sure the hell looked like it to me."

"She's got more than tits, okay?"

Jesse leered. "She's got a whacking hot bod and a

reputation for putting out."

And that's where this stopped. "She and I are going out, so cut the trash talk. Do me a favour, and assume I'm smarter than you and know what I'm doing."

"Hell, I know what you're doing." Jesse wouldn't let it go. "Was the sex good?"

"God, you are such a shithead. We didn't have sex. We only started dating."

Jesse leaned forward on his elbows, upper body swaying. "You're serious. You took out one of the Hansol girls, and it didn't end in bed?"

"No. Not yet. It might get there eventually—"

"My God, you've been taken over by a pod person or something. What the fuck are you up to?"

Joel looked past the crude words and at the actual concern on his brother's face. "Vicki's okay. She's not like her family, at least not as far as I can tell."

"If the date didn't end with her asking you for some cash, I'd say yeah, she is different." Jesse blinked hard. "I'm still too damn drunk to find a way to say this other than straight out. The Hansol family is known for using sex to get what they want. You really thought about this?"

"Yeah." It was all he was willing to share.

"Use a goddamn condom. And bring them with you. Don't use one of hers."

Joel froze for a second. "What the hell are you... Oh fuck. You're not suggesting she's going to get knocked up or something?"

"I'm saying I hope the girl is different, and you're not usually an idiot, so fuck around with her if you want, but don't take any chances." Jesse's glassy eyes had finally focused; concern chasing more of the liquor from his system.

"You're such a bastard."

"Takes one to know one."

They glared at each other until Joel gave in.

Jesse's snide but real concern forced Joel to stop and consider. It wouldn't be the first time a girl had gotten herself out of a bad place by accidentally getting pregnant. But *fuck...*

Even having to think about it made him crazy, and guilty, because now he was judging her just like everyone else. Definitely showed him, though, part of what Vicki put up with every damn day.

He gave in a little. "I'll be careful. But in the meantime, you'll be polite. I think she's different, and you're not going to come on to her, or offer to fool around with us, or..."

"Stop it." Jesse rose to his feet. "You already gave me hell for butting in on your party a couple months ago with what's her name...Sue. I was a shit, okay? I didn't think you meant it, but you don't have to hit me over the goddamn head anymore. Even if you think Vicki is different, I don't want to be sticking my dick in some girl that half the town's already had." Jesse walked to the fridge and poured himself a big glass of orange juice, downing half of it before turning back. "You want some?"

Joel shook his head. Having this discussion with Jesse while his brother was hungover meant he wasn't sure if Jesse was trying hard to be extra rude or simply acting his normal self.

The snarky asshole with attitude wasn't a side of his twin Joel liked very much.

"Tell me, who have you heard boasting they made it with Vicki? Because I know talk is hot and heavy about her sister—"

"—and her mom." Jesse made a face. "God. Why does that seem even worse than her sister being fast? You really going to go out with her?"

"I'm seeing Vicki, not her mom. Answer the damn question."

Jesse returned to the couch. "Honestly, the only person I remember talking about doing Vicki was back in high school."

"Eric Tell, right?"

"Right." Jesse grinned. "Hate that asshole, but still. And didn't she break his arm at one point, or something majorly fucked up?"

"I can't remember the details. Jaxi might know. She knows all that gossip."

"Other than that, you're right. I haven't heard anyone boasting or complaining about Vicki." Jesse examined his glass of juice, holding it up to the light. "Maybe you aren't as stupid as I thought."

"Thanks for the vote of confidence." Enough of this. Joel was ready to move on. "I told Dad, I'll tell you. I think she's nice."

Jesse snorted in disbelief. "You already talked to Dad about her? Wow, you are moving fast. I was only gone for two nights."

Joel cleared his throat. "He caught us necking in the barn today."

"Ha." Jesse put his empty glass on the coffee table before collapsing. "Damn, I need a nap." He cracked one eye open for a second. "If you're done all your true confessions, and shit."

"Fuck off."

"Love you too, bro."

Jesse was asleep in under a minute, or faking it well. Joel made his way back to his bedroom to mull over the chaos of the day.

He was fully committed to the plan as long as Vicki didn't chicken out. Although that option didn't seem likely.

There were more bits of mystery to the whole thing than he'd originally thought, and with the secrets she remained hush about, and the ones he had promised to keep, finding out the truth would take some careful questioning.

But the figuring it out could be fun.

When he called her Wednesday night, Vicki was already headed for bed.

"Hey, Joel."

"Hey. You sound tired."

She ached. "Hauling boxes all day takes different muscles than working in a café. Plus, I'm now on opening shift. I have to be up at five."

He hummed. "I hear you. I've had early chores this week and this is the first chance I've had to breathe."

"Good thing we've got until May, right?"

"Yeah, but I do want to see you again. Soon."

The sudden rush of pleasure through her eased some of her exhaustion. "For our next horse lesson."

"That, and to make sure everyone in town knows we're dating. It's going to take time for people to cut us a break, so the sooner we set up as a couple, the better."

The disappointment that struck wasn't easy to define. This was all a ploy. One that she completely agreed with.

Still felt a twinge of sadness he wasn't calling her for real.

She put on her best act. "You want to come over for a while? Now or tomorrow. I'm home by two o'clock."

"If I come over, people will assume we're…"

God. Couldn't he even say it? "Don't be shy, no one else would be. They'll assume we're fucking each other, right?"

"Yeah," he admitted, reluctance in his voice. "So let's blow their minds and go for a coffee in public."

"As if that's going to stop them from assuming we're fooling around."

Joel damn near growled, and a shiver raced over her skin in response. "You know what? I don't give a shit what people say. We know the truth, so fuck them all. For the next six months before you leave town, we're going to date, and the details are none of their business. We'll do what we want, and in the end, they can believe or not."

Wow. "I feel like waving a flag or something. That was totally hot."

He laughed. "It's true, though. People can be jerks. Screw them."

Vicki breathed out slowly. "Okay. I'll try."

"Also, I talked to Jesse. He promises to not be an ass. Well, not more than usual."

This time a definite conflict of emotions hit. Relief and panic. "Did he give you hell for...hooking up with me?"

Joel hesitated. Long enough for her to notice, but his honest words soothed the sting. "He's my brother, and I'd have done the same thing to him. But I kept your secrets, and he's not going to bother us. We can move forward, okay?"

"Sure." Focus on the things she needed. Horses. That was first priority.

"So. Vicki."

"Yeah?"

"Can I buy you a coffee tomorrow?"

"Goof," she laughed.

Joel joined in, the deep rumble of his laughter heating her from the inside out. "I can take a break for a few hours. You want me to pick you up from work or meet you at the café?"

"The café? Oh God, you are a glutton for punishment. Gossip will spread like wildfire throughout all of Rocky before we even get the cheque."

"Good. Let's get this thing started. Also..." He cleared his throat. "Head's up. You're invited to Thanksgiving dinner on Sunday."

"Whoa, seriously?" That was heading past fun into freaking-out territory. "You want to do that already?"

"I'm sure." Solidly spoken. "Although you're going to kick my ass for this part. Everyone is supposed to bring something to contribute."

Maybe he felt guilty, but she grabbed at the opportunity with both hands. "Awesome. I don't mind at all. What do you want me to make?"

"How about you come over here on Saturday and we can bake a pie."

She snorted. It couldn't be stopped. "Is that what they're calling it these days?"

"Smart ass. I meant a real pie, after we're done your horse lessons."

She'd been thinking about those. "It's going to be tough to keep the lessons secret, aren't they? I mean, your dad just dropping in, that kind of thing."

"Don't worry. Remember, if we're dating no one is going to think anything of you hanging out at the ranch. It'll work okay."

She'd just have to trust him on that. "You really got what I need to make a pie at your place?"

Silence on the other end of the line.

Vicki figured as much. "Do you even have plates in your bachelor pad? Or do you use paper?"

"Hey, we have plates. And a pot. And a hell of a big frying pan. I can cook. Some."

"Right. We'll bake pies over here, after the lessons at your place."

"But first tomorrow. Our date."

They organized time and place, and Vicki hung up the phone with a blurry blend of happiness and fear simmering through her veins.

There was a faint bit inside her that hoped he actually did want to spend time with her. That all these elaborate arrangements were more than her forcing him into doing something he didn't want.

She was tired enough to decide he was a big boy, and yeah, if he didn't want to help, he'd have told her to fuck off. By the time she fell exhausted into bed, she'd pushed aside her doubts and focused instead on the next first.

Tomorrow was her first official date. How cool was that?

Chapter Ten

The date was anticlimactic. They had coffee, she got stared at.

The only thing that changed was she had company for the staring part. She sat in a booth and gazed into Joel's blue eyes. She smiled at his jokes, sipped her drink and ignored the people around them.

She didn't feel the urge to beat anyone up. As a first date it was rather ordinary.

...and that was rather okay.

He asked if she wanted to stop in at Traders with him on Friday evening, but while hitting the local pub would have been fun, it wasn't meant to be. Between the early-morning start at her job and dealing with a shipment they had to shelve, she was exhausted enough to call off and crawl into bed before eight.

It was Saturday before they met in the Coleman barn, throwing her back into unfamiliar territory. Weirdly, the buzz of borderline nausea and adrenaline in her belly was getting addictive.

The barn was empty. "Where is everyone?"

Joel shrugged. "Here and there. If any of them do show up, it's not the end of the world. We're just hanging out in the barn."

"Necking, right?"

"As good an excuse as any if we need it, but chances are no one's going to stop in. Dad was a surprise. You don't usually spend extra time hanging out where you work."

Vicki nodded. She sniffed, less afraid than last week, but still cautious. "The horses aren't here, are they?"

He shook his head. "We had them in for a few days to

check them over, but now they'll be out until the snow flies. It's only during the coldest snaps they need to be sheltered anyway, but my dad likes to coddle them."

"And Sable? Does she get treated different since she's further along?"

Joel grinned. "Yeah, I'll be bringing her inside in the next couple weeks. I'm a softy."

Wow. "Which means this is lesson two, and I still don't have to deal with the beasts. Nice."

"You'll be pleased to hear there's no manure involved this time."

She copied his grin. "Well, aren't you the gentleman? What're we doing, riding stick ponies?"

He blinked hard. "Actually, kinda."

Joel caught her by the hand and led her deeper into the barn. They passed the stalls they'd worked on a week ago before entering a smaller room. Two walls were lined with leather straps, ropes and various horse stuff, saddles organized along another. The entire place had a rich heady scent to it, of leather and the outdoors.

"Hmm, this lesson smells better than last week's."

He nodded. "Addictive. Being in here brings up all kinds of good memories for me with the smell of the leather. I think they call that association, but it's almost like it helps me relax."

Oh boy. "Let's hope you can pass that on to me, because I can use it."

He tapped the double-wide sawhorse in the middle of the room. A thick quilt-like blanket was draped over the top of it. "Come meet your horse."

"Really?" She laughed as he nodded. "I do have a stick horse. Cool!" Vicki stepped up and patted one end. "Nice horsie. You're about my speed."

"That's his ass, not his head."

Vicki jolted upright then glared at Joel.

He grinned. "Okay, fine, until there's a saddle down you can pick which end is which. Although, patting a horse on the rump is as good as on the head. Lets them know you're there."

"So they can kick you into tomorrow..." she muttered.

Joel placed a saddle on the sawhorse. "One step at a time, darling. This horse is guaranteed not to kick anyone, anywhere. Now watch. You want to learn it all, you get to start from the ground up."

He led her through saddling her "horse". She nearly got caught staring at his ass when he stood sooner than she expected from showing her how to tighten the cinch. She laughed when he somehow attached a set of reins to the wooden frame, draping the loose ends over the raised part of the saddle.

When he stepped back and watched her expectantly, though, she had no idea what was going on. "What?"

He gestured. "Mount up."

"Seriously?"

"Why not? You're scared of horses, right? Not their saddles."

"Jerk."

Joel flashed his smile, the one she'd started to recognize as his truly happy expression. It hit her that she was having fun. Relaxed and looking forward to whatever reward was coming at the end of this lesson.

She hoped it was more kisses.

"Fine." Vicki stepped forward, then paused. "I thought that sawhorse was taller than usual so I could learn how to tighten the straps without bending too low but, hell, how do you expect me to get up on Goliath?"

"Same way you get on that oversized bike of yours." He pointed to a loop of leather hanging from the saddle. "Stirrup. Put your foot in there and hop on."

Maybe it should have been more awkward, acting like a kid and climbing on board her pretend horse, but the situation was right. The expression on his face when she pressed herself up and tossed her leg over the back of the saddle, settling into place—

Like he was proud of her. Of getting on a damn sawhorse.

She would totally take it. "How did I do, boss?"

Joel stepped beside her, and suddenly it wasn't only a flash of pride at having climbed into the saddle making her flush. He planted his hands on her ass and rearranged her, sliding his fingers down one thigh and placing the other hand on her lower back.

Touching her? *Yes, please.*

"You want to sit comfy, which means not slouching too much. When the horse walks let your body stay loose and react to him swaying. That's it." Joel paused, and she noted with her perched this high, his eyes were only slightly below hers. "How's that feel?"

His palm rested on her lower back, and she wiggled slightly, enjoying the rub. "Damn good."

Far too breathy a response, but whatever.

He carried on the lesson, handing her reins. "You need to know how to use them, but guiding a horse should be more about body messages than yanking them around by the head."

Okay, now he had to be lying. "Bullshit."

"Not."

She gave him a dirty look.

"I'm serious, Vicki. You don't need reins at all with a good horse. Gentle nudges with your knees, a few words every now and then. They're smart."

"Great." She shivered involuntarily. "Just what I need, an animal that's smarter than me."

Joel leaned in front of her and caught her chin in his fingers. "Stop getting yourself all tangled in knots."

Too late. "Is it time for a reward, because I could go for one right about now."

He stroked her cheek with his thumb. "You think you've already earned a reward?"

"Hell, yeah."

She wasn't going to be shy. If these were double lessons,

she wanted to keep moving forward with the boyfriend stuff as well.

He leaned in, and she leaned over, and their mouths made contact. Easygoing at first as he kept the exchange gentle. Although, having the advantage of height allowed her more control. Reins abandoned, she slipped her hands to his face and held him in one spot so she could enjoy his touch. His tongue swept along hers, followed by light bites that made soft, heady noises escape from both their lips. None of the rest of their bodies made contact, but she felt that kiss in every single bit as if she was pushed up against him, naked.

When they broke apart far too early, she protested.

Joel smiled. "More later. You have to finish your lesson first."

"More?" She wasn't going to pout too hard then. At least this hadn't involved as much physical work as last time. "What else?"

He had her get off Goliath—*dismount*—then go through and take the straps off. Coil the reins and hang them up. She eyed the saddle. "If you expect me to move that sucker, try again. I'm not sure I can lift it."

Joel picked it up easily, returning the saddle to its spot along the wall. "Like anything else, you'll work up to it. You're going to practice this every time we have a lesson, and eventually you'll find it's not a problem."

Vicki eyed the space optimistically. "We're all cleaned up. Does this mean the lesson is over and we can get back to kissing?"

He laughed like she'd hoped he would before dashing her hopes. "Not yet. You're not done."

"Really?"

"Really. I told you a good horse doesn't need reins, and I'm going to prove it."

Instant heart in throat. "You're taking me to a real horse?"

Joel turned his back on her and squatted. "Hell no, you're going to ride me. Hop on."

He glanced over his shoulder in time to see her expression change. From that edge of fear to disbelief to amusement.

"Seriously, you're going to give me a piggyback ride?"

He faked a horse nicker, soft and low, and she giggled, right before she crawled on his back and wrapped her arms around his neck.

Crazy as it was, he was having the best time with her.

Joel stood carefully, adjusting her slight weight to make her sit a little higher. "You need to eat more."

"Be quiet, horse. Now, how do I do this? How do I direct you without using reins?"

"Squeeze your legs. Harder on the side you want to turn. Lean forward to go ahead, and squeeze both legs to slow down."

"And if I dig my heels into your sides?" She gave an evil laugh.

Joel glanced back at her. "I'll trot."

Her eyes widened. "Sounds scary."

He faced the door and waited for her first command. Of course, her leaning forward meant she pressed her chest hard against his back, which was a lovely start. He stepped in a straight line, which took them out the open door of the tack room.

"Whoa," Vicki shouted, her arms around his neck tightening in a death grip.

He jerked to a halt an inch from the wall.

She slapped his shoulder. "Stupid horse. Don't you know not to walk into immovable objects?"

"You didn't tell me to stop," he pointed out.

"Yeah, well, you said horses were smart. I didn't think you'd do a face-plant into the wood."

Joel shoved down his laughter. "Waiting."

She squeezed, and he twisted to the left. Moved forward when she pressed to his back. Slowly at first, then with more confidence, she guided him through the barn. They went around the stalls, in and out of the various rooms.

Vicki had him back in the clear, facing down the hallway when she chuckled.

And dug in her heels.

"Oh, darling, you didn't do that."

She kicked lightly again, so he held onto her legs and took off, bouncing as he imitated a trot.

Vicki shrieked in delight and clutched him tighter, fingers digging into his shoulders. Her body rubbed his with every motion. She was laughing so hard he was worried she might fall off, but the grip of her thighs stayed solid throughout.

Joel went back for another pass of the hall when a deep voice boomed from beside them.

"I'm not even going to ask..."

Vicki sucked in a gasp, Joel twirled. His brother Blake stood in the doorway shaking his head.

Vicki tucked her face against Joel's shoulder and laughed and laughed, her body quivering as he held her in position.

"Hi, Blake." Joel jiggled Vicki. "Hey, come on down, and say hello."

"No," she whispered into his neck between gasps. "Oh my God, I don't know which is worse. Last week your dad catching us necking, or this."

Now he was laughing as well. "Vicki, dismount."

Blake snorted, but otherwise held his tongue.

She released her death grip and lowered her legs, helpless giggles still escaping. "I'm so going to kill you," she warned.

Joel pulled her against his side and took a deep breath, finally meeting Blake's gaze. "You know Vicki? Vicki, this is my big brother Blake."

Blake tipped his head. "Nice form, only you lose points on the dismount if the horse has to tell you to get off."

Vicki snickered. "Good thing not many horses can talk, then."

"Vicki will be joining us tomorrow for dinner," Joel added.

"You guys need us to swing by and help bring over anything?"

Blake examined Vicki, not so much a once-over to judge, but a curious glance of admiration. "That would be great. Between the food Jaxi's got made, and the girls, extra hands are always welcome."

"We're going to make pies this afternoon," Vicki announced. "You have any favourites?"

Approval lit his face. "Ma's got pumpkin covered, and Jaxi's made an apple, but if you know how to make pecan, I'd be sold."

Vicki nodded, then surprised Joel to pieces by twisting to face him. Her head tilted to the side in this adorable way as she poked him lightly in the chest. "Hey, you never said what your favourite is. We should make one of them as well."

"Strawberry rhubarb. Don't think we can do that right now, but anything we make will be fine."

"Deal."

Her smile was real, and he slipped his fingers around hers without much planning, loving how her eyes brightened.

When they both turned back to face Blake, his big brother was eyeing them even more suspiciously.

"If you're serious about helping, stop by around eleven. Ma likes us to show up in plenty of time to talk before we sit down and start stuffing ourselves." Blake nodded at Vicki, winked at Joel. "I'll see you later."

He slipped out the door, and Vicki collapsed against Joel's side, laughing again. "Oh God, your family will think I'm insane."

"My family will think you fit in fine." He adjusted her so he could lift her chin, their eyes making contact. "Well done on your lesson, by the way."

"You are a fun guy."

"Why, thank you." Joel tilted his head toward the door. "You ready to teach me how to bake pies?"

It was a good thing she nodded and pulled him from the barn. The steady stream of conversation between them all the way out to where she'd parked her bike stopped him from hauling her against his body, face to face this time, for more physical contact.

He wanted to be rubbing them together in a way that was a whole lot less wholesome than a laughter-filled piggyback ride.

They'd get there. But for now, he had to make sure this didn't go too far, too fast.

Chapter Eleven

Joel was too slow to get around in time to open the door for Vicki. She met him at the front of the truck, rubbing her palms against her thighs while she stared at the big old ranch house Blake and Jaxi lived in as if she were facing a firing squad.

"You okay?" he asked.

The crease between her eyes smoothed a little as she pasted on a smile. "Just wondering how this is going to go over. I've never been to a family meal that didn't end with shouting or some kind of argument."

Well, hell. "That sucks."

She shrugged. "It's life, but I'd hate to bring my special brand of joy into your world."

"Oh no, don't you go thinking my family is perfect. We fight plenty." Joel held out his hand, and she slipped her fingers into his and clung on tight. "Six boys? You think there's never been shouting at our table, you're not thinking too hard."

"Yeah, well..." She blew out a steady breath then lifted her pretty eyes to meet his. "Thanks. For everything. You like to live dangerously, and I appreciate it."

"Hey, remember, you're helping me as well," Joel pointed out. "Come on, Blake and Jaxi will wonder what we're doing in the yard."

Her obvious fears made him more aware, though. They stepped into the house and were greeted by his brother and sister-in-law. Blake's smile was a little tighter than the day before, and Jaxi was...not typical Jaxi.

Normally she was all welcoming and the perfect hostess. Now she stood quietly, waiting for Joel and Vicki to join them in the kitchen.

Screw it, his family would have to get used to this. There was no harm being done, and he'd have to make that extra clear.

"Hey, Jaxi, you know Vicki?"

The two women eyed each other like cats meeting on unfamiliar territory.

"Hi." Jaxi nabbed one of the toddler girls racing under foot and settled the child on her hip. The wide expansive of her pregnant belly didn't give a ton of room for the little one's legs to wrap around. "Thanks for offering the extra arms. You can see we need them."

Vicki nodded, sliding up to the table. "You've been busy."

"I'll say." Joel chose to ignore the awkwardness and instead gave his approval to the load of food on the table. "Did you let anyone else cook this year?"

Jaxi pulled a face. "I went overboard a little, but whatever. You bottomless pits will have no problem finishing it."

Joel picked up a cardboard box, smiling at Vicki. "I'll take this to the truck. Back in a minute."

She nodded, stepping out of his way.

Blake joined him. They were slipping their loads into the truck cab when Blake cleared his throat. "What are you up to?"

Joel pulled back until he could see Blake's face. "What?"

"Jaxi told me who Vicki is. I had no idea when I met you in the barn. Why are you going out with her?"

Sheesh. "So, when you met us in the barn you thought I was having fun with some great girl and you had no problem with it, but now suddenly you do?"

Blake raised his hands in protest. "Hey, all I know is Jaxi went real quiet when I mentioned Vicki's name, and she wasn't too happy about hearing you were tangled up together."

"Don't worry. And don't you dare be rude to Vicki. She's alright, and we're having fun, and that's all you need to know." Joel stomped back toward the house. Good grief. Jaxi was the first one to make trouble? He hadn't expected that.

Inside though, the women seemed to be getting along fine.

107

Jaxi was adding more food to yet another box. Vicki was tying shoes on the twin toddlers, Rebecca and Rachel, both little girls chattering a million miles an hour at the newcomer.

Jaxi poked the box he'd picked up. "Put that down for a minute, there are things we need from the cold room. Let me show you."

Eight months pregnant, and she still had enough leverage to haul him down the hall toward the basement. He went willingly enough, at least until she got him into the confined space, whirled on him and crossed her arms. She spoke softly but loud enough he got that she was pissed. "What the hell are you up to, Joel Coleman?"

God. "Getting pickles, I assume."

She lifted a finger and shook it in his face. "Don't even try it, mister. If it had been Jesse showing up with Vicki, I could have bought this as some kind of twisted joke, but you? You don't usually think with your dick."

"Fuck, Jaxi, why don't you tell me what your opinion is? I'm not sure I'm clear." Joel leaned on the wall and stared down, thankful for the final growth spurt that allowed him to tower over her, because she was a force of nature without being the same size as him.

"You want it explained? The Hansol family is not who I expected to see you hanging out with."

"And I'm not." Joel held up a finger in imitation of her early motion. "I'm seeing Vicki, who is one of the family, but she's not her family."

She wasn't impressed. "I thought you had more sense."

"I thought you knew how to mind your own business. Oh, wait. No, I knew you wouldn't do that. But I hoped you'd do better than to jump to conclusions."

"She's not good enough for you," Jaxi snapped.

"Not your decision," Joel tossed back.

She continued to give him the evil eye, her breathing sharp and tight. Then she exhaled slowly. "I'm worried, okay?"

He nodded. "I get it. But I'm a big boy, and this thing

between me and Vicki is between me and Vicki. Not trying to be rude, but it's true."

She snorted. "Except, it's not just between you. You're bringing her to the family table. You're mixing her in with our group. It's not a private event anymore, and so I want to know if you've thought this through."

Oh fucking hell, *no*. She wasn't going to go there. He wasn't going to let her.

"You might want to stop now before you really put your foot in your mouth," Joel warned. "I love you to pieces, but you're not the head of this family. And while I respect you for the many things you've done to make the Coleman clan better over the years, if you're trying to dictate who I can date, you're going too far. You're not going to be that kind of woman, are you?"

She stuttered to a stop, eyes wide. Speechless.

Joel felt like a shit. He wanted to tell Jaxi everything would be fine, but this was the first of many battles. He'd made a commitment to Vicki to help her, and if he couldn't convince his own family to give the girl a chance, they were fucked.

For a moment he wondered if it was worth it. If sticking with the plan was the right thing to do.

Then he remembered the sound of Vicki's laughter the day before, and how she'd been so patient later teaching him to roll piecrust. How they'd just talked, and none of it had been awkward, or dirty.

And yet she put up with this kind of crap all the time? The judging, and being cast aside? He was amazed Vicki hadn't simply up and left town years ago.

He lowered his voice and put every bit of sincerity into it he could. "You're very special to me, Jaxi, and we go way, way back. I love that you care about me, but Vicki deserves to be judged on her own merits. That's all I'm asking, okay?"

Jaxi had bit down on her bottom lip, body tight with frustration. But she nodded slowly. "I...can do that. And I get what you're saying, but I hope to hell you know what you're doing."

"I do. Trust me." Joel stepped in and wrapped his arms around his sister-in-law and squeezed her carefully.

She hugged him back for a minute, sighing heavily again.

"You okay?"

"Yeah, just feel a bit of a fool."

He chuckled. "Welcome to my world."

Jaxi pushed him away. "While you're down here, we may as well grab some stuff. You and Jesse need any canning?"

Joel shook his head. "Later. Let's get over to Mom and Dad's before they send out search crews."

They were talking about her. Vicki concentrated harder on the task Mrs. Coleman had assigned, but it wasn't as if laying silverware on the table was going to distract her from noticing.

Interestingly, though, the Colemans didn't do their gossiping out in public, like most folks. No, they took it out of the room, which meant there were little excursions of duos and trios casually hauling Joel outside or to the basement or even behind the massive swinging door leading to the kitchen.

Vicki straightened the knife she'd laid on the linen tablecloth and tried not to mind. At least they weren't being *in her face* rude.

"Can I help?"

She looked up to find Beth Coleman smiling at her. "Nearly done."

Beth nodded. "Good, then I'll get you a drink, and we can visit until dinner is ready."

"Just water for me, thanks." Because she needed to keep her wits about her.

Vicki ended up sitting by the fireplace, glass of ice water in her hand and wondering if this was the start of the inquisition. Only what followed was nothing like she'd expected.

"You live in town, right?" Beth asked.

"Dresh Apartments."

Beth laughed. "Really? That's one of the places I tried to get into when we moved into Rocky, but it was booked solid."

"It's not a bad complex. I have a bachelor suite."

Little-boy hands tugged at hers until her lap was clear and someone short crawled up and settled in like he owned her. "But you're a girl. You can't live in a place for bachelors."

"Robbie is very concerned with using proper words," Beth explained. "Honey, in this case it means a certain kind of apartment, not that it's for bachelors only."

He frowned, seriously considering it all. Vicki thought he was about the most adorable thing. "Your mom is right. It means I have everything in one room. Well, except the bathroom, that's separate, but the rest is one big open space."

The ensuing conversation about apartments that slipped into discussing shops in Rocky versus Beth's experiences back in Calgary was so comfortable and easy that Vicki relaxed. Joel finally escaped the interrogation crew and joined them, curling up at her feet where he was immediately piled on by another little boy and one of Jaxi's girls.

It was peaceful, pleasant and just about every picture-perfect situation she'd ever seen on television.

Of course, it was bound to blow up in her face.

"Ten minutes until we're ready." The warning shot out, and Vicki wiggled herself free of little people and Joel's hand that had somehow landed on her knee.

"I need to wash my hands. I'll be right back."

She escaped to the bathroom off the hall, patting her face with water and wondering if anyone would notice if she hid there for the rest of the day. So far the gathering hadn't been terrible, but this was about when things had to go to hell.

One pace into the hall she jerked to a stop. The man blocking her path had a familiar face, with the same intensely blue irises Joel possessed, but unless he'd changed clothes in the last five minutes, this had to be Jesse looming over her.

She took an uneasy step backward.

He frowned. "Now what the hell was that for?"

Vicki caught her fingers together and measured the distance between him and the wall, calculating if she could slip through the tiny gap. "What are you talking about?"

Jesse leaned to the side, blocking her escape route. "Honey, that look of panic in your eyes just now? That's not the way to make me feel all cozy and warm."

She didn't want him to feel cozy and warm around her, but hell if she'd say that. "You surprised me. Didn't expect anyone to be waiting in the hall."

Jesse examined her slowly, his gaze far less sexual than she'd anticipated. "I thought I should say hello before we get herded to the table. Joel says you're alright, and he likes you, so I'm going to give you a break."

Her temper flashed. "Oh, are you now?"

"Yeah." He grinned, and she got even more pissed off.

Funny how his expression didn't give her goose bumps of desire, not when the smile wasn't real, when it didn't reach his eyes the way it did with Joel. She figured even as identical twins, she could spot who was who if Jesse kept that stick up his butt.

"Maybe I don't need you to give me a break. Maybe I just need you to step aside so I can join my boyfriend at the table."

Jesse's expression slipped to a scowl. "Don't push it, honey. You're being watched, closely, and the first thing you do that steps over the line, I'll make sure you're out on your ass."

God. Like he was one to judge her? Vicki's nails dug into her palms as she fought to keep from tossing words in his cocky face. Or worse, tossing her fists into his gut to remove that self-righteous attitude. "Fuck off, Jesse, and get the hell out of my way."

"Don't start a war you can't win, little girl."

She lost her meager control. Stomped forward and slammed her heel down on his instep. When he swore and jerked his leg out of her way, she shot past his bulk and popped through the doorway to the main room, heart pounding like a drum.

If her purse had been somewhere other than on the coffee table, she would have left right then and there. Walked to the highway and all the way into town if necessary.

But Joel rose and came toward her, the smile on his face turning to concern.

"What's up?" he whispered as he slipped her fingers into his.

Escape was impossible. She'd make the best of it and then never again agree to attend one of these events. "Nothing. Everything. Just...let's sit down."

"I saved you a seat by me," Robbie called out.

Joel had her by the hand and wasn't letting go. "Sorry, short stuff. She's my date, so she's sitting beside me."

Robbie pouted until Gramma asked him to ring the bell to call everyone to the table. While he happily raced off, Joel tugged her in close and leaned down to speak quietly. "You okay?"

She took a deep breath, wishing she could lean her forehead on his chest for a while and hide. "This being-your-girlfriend thing isn't working too well."

He snorted. "Yeah, it's been interesting on my side as well. We'll compare notes after dinner. In the meantime, stick it out. I think the toughest part is over."

"*God*, it better be."

He squeezed her fingers as the dinner bell rang, and people pulled out chairs and settled children into place. Joel led her toward the middle of the table where she discovered to her delight Beth was seated across from them.

There was hope for survival. Especially when the food arrived. And continued to arrive.

Obviously, this was one of those households she'd heard about where food equaled love. Not like the family where she'd grown up. She examined the bounty of the home-cooked meal and compared it to the one year her mom had bothered to notice the holiday by prodding her current lover to pick up a bucket of Kentucky Fried Chicken.

This was a different setting, a different environment altogether, and suddenly even Jesse being a jerk she could understand. They were guarding their own. Protecting the family from an outsider, and she could hardly fault them for circling the wagons.

She didn't like it, but she could see why it was happening.

Vicki got lost in the passing of platters, gravy bowls and side dishes. She avoided looking at Jesse who fortunately was on the same side of the table as her and at the extreme end.

The longer the meal went on, the less tense the situation got. There was still the occasional time she looked up to see someone glance away, but more often instead the person smiled.

And offered more food.

"You want the mashed potatoes?" Travis held out the bowl. "I did the honours, and I am the king of mashing them."

"King of eating them as well," Joel joked. "You sure you can't put the rest of what's in the bowl on your plate?"

"I'm being a gentleman and offering our guest a spoonful before I claim the remains." Travis shook the bowl. "Go on, you know you want some."

"I'm going to explode." Vicki turned down the offer. "You go ahead."

More talk. More laughter. More food. She really was getting uncomfortable. She never ate this much. Platters were removed, bowls were nearly empty when Mike spoke from the head of the table. "You know, I think this is the biggest Six Pack-only gathering we've had yet."

Vicki quickly counted heads. Seventeen. Three single Coleman boys and five kids. Three couples, four counting Joel's folks.

Her cheeks flushed. *Five* couples counting her and Joel.

Weird. And hugely uncomfortable.

Mike pushed his chair back and rose to his feet. Silvery-grey painted his temples, and a dusting of lighter strands shot through the dark brown hair on his head, but he was obviously the sire of the six grown men gathered around the table. He cleared his throat.

A toast or something was coming. Vicki planted her hands in her lap to stop from fidgeting.

"When you boys were little, every Thanksgiving we'd go around the table and get you to tell us what you were the most thankful for."

"I remember that." Daniel pointed at Joel. "Especially the year Joel shared he was most thankful we hadn't been caught making rope swings in the barn like you'd told us not to."

Laughter rose to cover Joel's protest. "I was five. I was very thankful."

"Rope swings?" one of the little boys asked.

"Don't go getting any ideas, young man." Beth turned to her husband. "You want to let your dad finish speaking?"

Once the amusement died down, all eyes returned to Mike who was nodding, a contemplative expression softening the lines on his face. "I'm not going to get us to do that this year, mostly because there are so many of you if I let you get talking, we'll never get to dessert. But it did remind me. Every year I'd expect you to say one thing, and damned if nine times out of ten you didn't surprise me with something else. And you boys always seemed to focus on a different topic than your brothers."

His gaze trailed down the table as he spoke, lingering for a moment on each person before moving to the next.

"You might all be my sons, but you're all unique. Over the years you've brought different things to this family, both good and bad to be honest, but I'm glad of it all. It's made us have to band together, and it's made us learn. And now that there are others than just blood joining us, each of them brings something special with them as well. Things that can make this family stronger and richer because of who they are."

Vicki kept her chin in place as Mike met her eyes. She refused to turn away, hardly daring to think what it sounded like was true. That he was asking his family to give her a break.

That she was welcome in their midst...

"So as the head of this part of the Colemans, I'm going to give thanks for us all this year." Mike raised his glass and everyone scrambled to copy him. "To family. Whatever that looks like. Constantly growing, constantly changing, let's celebrate our strong roots even as the branches reach in new directions."

Vicki raised her glass, adding her "to family" more hesitantly than the others around her. Clinking glasses with Joel, with Beth. Turning to the other side and connecting with Travis and others farther down the table.

It was the strangest sensation ever. Like she'd stepped into a warm embrace when she'd expected to be slapped. Joel rested his hand on her thigh and squeezed softly, and her throat tightened a little with the sheer flood of emotion washing over her.

God, what she wouldn't give for her and Joel to be real. Guilt at pulling a fast one should have shaken her to her core, but all she could think of was how good it felt to experience this at least once in her goddamn life.

Fuck doing the right thing; she *ached* to have this kind of acceptance.

When she glanced at the head of the table and caught Mike smiling at her, she wasn't sure what to do. He lifted his glass and nodded briefly, then turned to his right and kissed his wife before loudly announcing it was time for dessert.

Vicki put her glass down and snuck her fingers into Joel's. His bright smile had a shot of surprise in it, but he didn't let go until they had to have two hands to deal with the plates of pie being passed along.

What a topsy-turvy day it had been.

Chapter Twelve

It had been two weeks since they'd set up their little deal, and the few times they'd gotten together Joel had made sure they hit the tack room for more practice in the saddle. Between her job and the rush of fall chores, there hadn't been any more date-dates since the family dinner.

Joel stood at the railing and waited. Vicki examined the currently empty corral as if she expected horses to magically sprout from the ground and overwhelm her.

"If you put one foot in front of the other and keep moving, it works better," he teased.

Vicki flashed him her middle finger, but she obeyed, stepping to his side. Her reluctant motion gave him plenty of time to look her over, which gave more than enough time for his body to tighten with need.

She still didn't have proper boots, but the rest of her wardrobe made that detail slip. Her jeans fit just right, low on her hips and tight enough he wanted to lay a hand on her and stroke until she whimpered with pleasure. She'd found a ladies-cut jean jacket somewhere, and the swell of her breasts pressing the material made him happy for things to come. For when he could get more up close and personal with her.

While they had time for the getting-to-like-horses part, Joel was eager to step up the physical side of the equation. Not just because she was sexy enough to melt his brain, but he liked her. Stubborn, feisty—what was there not to like?

He held out his hand and Vicki accepted it, tucking up against his body.

She tilted her head back to meet his gaze. "Hmm, okay, see you should have told me you were starting with this kind of thing. I would have been over here a lot faster."

"You need to trust me, remember?" He leaned down and kissed her, just because he could.

She wrapped her arms around his neck and responded eagerly, their tongues tangling as a rush of lust poured through his limbs. Her lips were soft under his, but she gave willingly as he demanded more, taking the kiss deeper, a little rougher. Her enthusiastic response, that strange blend of inexperience and fiery passion Vicki seemed to bring to everything she did, set his body on fire.

Joel grabbed her around the ass and lifted her, dragging their bodies together and swallowing her low groan of pleasure.

When he set her on the top railing and moved back a space, she sighed. "Damn, I like kissing you."

He tugged her forward until she was perched on the rail, more held by his body than anything else. "Good. Because today you get your reward first."

She eyed their surroundings. "We're gonna fool around right out in the open? You're just daring your family to catch us going at something, aren't you?"

Joel shrugged. "After last Sunday, I don't think any of them are going to give us shit whatever we do. My dad was pretty plain about that. But honestly, there's no one around. Everyone said they had things to do in town, so we're safe."

Vicki stared at their bodies, at the intimate position with him stepped up close between her spread thighs. "If you say so, but damn if this doesn't look like a compromising situation."

She had no idea. "Lift your head up, darling, and let me at those sweet lips."

Desire rushed between them, and while he longed for skin on skin, this wasn't a bad place to be. The late-fall sun tried its best, but mainly body heat kept them warm. Vicki opened her mouth as he caught her by the back of the neck. She slipped her tongue along his lower lip then put her teeth to it gently. All the little things he'd done to her the last times they'd kissed, she proved she'd learned damn well.

It was fun, but not where he was going with this lesson.

Joel dragged his lips from hers and worked to calm his breathing. "You're too tempting. Now turn around and stand on the second railing."

Vicki frowned but with his help squirmed her way into position. "What are you up to, Joel Coleman?"

"Hmmm, you'll see." He lowered his hand to her ass and squeezed. "Damn, I guessed right. You're the perfect height now."

Her words came out a touch breathless. "Perfect height for what?"

Joel stepped in closer, meshing their bodies together. "A little exploration."

He took off his hat and hung it on the post next to them. When he tucked his head down along her neckline he didn't have to concentrate on anything but her. On the way his cock pressed tight to her legs, on the taste of her skin as he licked her neck.

She shivered. "Okay, so far this lesson is going fine."

"This isn't the lesson." He nipped her ear lobe and she squeaked. "Here's the lesson. You tell me what's in front of you while I distract you."

"It's a contest?" She wiggled her ass, and he was the one to groan in frustration. "I like contests. Love winning even more."

"Don't count your chickens ahead of time, darling."

She leaned her head on his shoulder, their mouths only inches away. "I have to describe what I see? Not very challenging."

"Best out of three tries," Joel whispered. "You ready?"

"Do it." Vicki planted a quick kiss on his cheek before straightening and grabbing the top railing with both hands. She turned to the barn and started. "There's a fence around a dirt area. I'm standing on the railing, and the ends of the fence are attached to the north and south barn walls."

"Doing great. Keep going." Joel took a deep breath. Planted his hands on her hips and moved in for some fun.

Kissing her neck and the sweet spot behind her ear made

her voice tremble, but she kept talking. "There's another fenced area on the other side of this one, and beyond that are bales piled up. I never knew you could pile round bales, but somehow you guys have done it. They're wrapped in—*oh.* Um."

Joel circled his hands over her breasts again. "You were saying?"

She arched into his grasp as she took a deep breath. "I'm saying you surprised me, but now I'm ready for anything. Do your worst."

Oh hell, yeah. Joel stroked her belly en route back to her hips.

"Done already?" Her clear disappointment made him smile. "I was enjoying that."

"Me too. Don't you worry. You wanted me to up my game, so I am." He tugged her T-shirt free from her jeans and snuck his hands under the soft cotton. Stroked his fingertips across her skin until his palms rested on her stomach, his thumbs brushing the underside of her tits.

His reward was a full-body shiver. Her grip on the railing tightened. "I'll go on and talk about the tractors and how—oh my *God*, that feels good."

He kept circling, each time his thumbs rising higher until they teased her nipples, only the fabric was too thick to allow him to do more than feel the faintest bump of where the hardened tips must be. "Damn padded bra."

She snorted. "Trust me, it's not padded. That's all me in there."

"Lined, whatever. It's in my way. Should have told you to not wear it. Fuck." It only took a second for him to reach around her and one-handed unclip the hooks.

She laughed. "You did that way too quickly, Joel. What kind of practice hours have you put in?"

"Shut up and tell me about the yard." He shoved her bra aside and went for skin.

Vicki moaned her approval as he cupped her and returned to nibble on her ear at the same time. Making circles with his thumbs over her erect nipples, savouring the weight of her filling his hands.

"The tractors are green and yellow," Vicki whispered.

"Count them." Joel waited until she'd drawn in a breath to answer him then pinched lightly with thumb and forefinger.

She arched harder into his touch. "Who cares? Don't stop."

He wanted to strip her down so he could see what he was doing, but there was something to be said for feeling his way.

He had awesome follow-up plans, but the proverbial rock and hard place was starting to wear on him. His rock? The hard-on he was carrying that wouldn't last much longer if she kept writhing her tight ass against his aching lower body.

Vicki lifted her face to the sun, unsure which was heating her more. The distant rays or the incredible sensation of Joel feeling her up. He crowded close, the thick ridge of his cock pressed to her ass, but it was his hands that obsessed her.

His work-roughened fingertips teased deliciously, the light tugs to her nipples a world apart from when she touched herself. With her non-existent experience with real partners, she was no stranger to self-pleasure. It shocked her in a good way, how much it turned her on every time Joel slicked his palms over her flesh, how her skin grew more sensitive.

How there seemed to be a direct line between his hands and her aching center, although with him behind her, there was nothing to rub against to ease the want.

"Joel. Oh yeah, touch me. More..."

"You enjoying yourself, darling?" He sucked her earlobe into his mouth, hot tongue tracing around the sensitive skin of the opening as his words whispered past.

She rocked uneasily. His firm grip on her body continued but it wasn't enough. "I want your mouth on me."

"It is," he pointed out, licking again.

Fuck. "On my breasts. You're making me crazy."

"Hmm, not yet. You need to earn the next reward."

He was supporting her anyway, so Vicki let go of the railing with one hand. She snuck her fingers into her pants. If he wasn't going to help, then screw him. She'd do what she needed on her own. Like usual.

She hadn't reached her clit before his big mitt of a hand caught her, his fingers trapping hers under the waistband of her jeans.

"None of that. Cheater."

"Please..." Great, reduced to begging. "We're still right the hell out in the open, and all I can think of is you touching me."

"All you can think of?" He pulled her hand from her jeans and adjusted position until he cupped her. When he rubbed, moving the seam of her pants against her sensitive clit, she whimpered.

"Get me off, *please.*"

He had her in a tight grasp, her naked breast clasped in one hand, a slow torment between her legs caused by his other, his body surrounding her and caging her in. "I will. Close your eyes."

Vicki snapped them shut, grinding her pelvis into his hand, looking for a little more pressure.

"Shh, I'll give you what you need in a second. Trust me." His hand slipped from between her legs, and she bit her lip to stop the protests from escaping. He wrapped her fingers around the railing, adding pressure until she caught hold of the worn timbers. "Keep your eyes closed and count to twenty. I'll be right back."

Then he was gone. Nothing but cool air at her back, and aching sexual tension thrumming through her. She wanted to look so badly, but hell if she'd blow it right now. "God damn you, Joel. What the fuck are you playing at?"

"Count..." His voice came from farther away than she expected.

She growled her frustration but stayed where she'd been abandoned. "One, two, three... When I reach twenty I'm out of here. Jackass."

Her shouted count rose steadily, but by the time she hit fifteen he'd returned. Breathless, as if he'd been running.

"I'm back."

Vicki huffed, her eyes still closed tight. "Good for you. I'm not in the mood anymore."

He caught her chin in his hand and kissed her. Hard. Needy. Totally in control, unlike the earlier kisses where she got to explore and play. This was a rocking assault on her senses made all the more wicked as he wrapped his free arm around her and pinned her tight to his body.

Panting breaths escaped as they broke apart briefly before diving back in. He slid his hand down her throat, big fingers like a collar moving gently in contrast to the battering her lips were taking. He paused for a second before cupping her breast again, this time on the outside of her T-shirt, her bra bunched up over her chest awkwardly, but she didn't give a damn because he was touching her.

Finger and thumb trapped her nipple, rolling the fabric of her shirt over the tip in endless loops as his tongue thrust into her mouth. She moaned as he pulled her onto his thigh, resting her core on his leg. Renewed contact meant all the little hormones that had been fading leapt to attention again and demanded a response.

She abandoned the railing and caught hold of his head, dragging their lips apart and forcing him to look at her.

"You are driving me mad, Joel Coleman."

He grinned. "Ready for the lesson?"

The temptation to cause him bodily pain was huge. "I don't like you right now."

"You're gonna love what I'll do to you, though," he promised. "Grab the railing and close your eyes once more."

Vicki slapped her palms on the railing. "Bastard."

"Close them? There you go." He spun her and they were back in the position they'd been in before he'd left, his hands taking possession once more.

This time, though, he was under her jeans, fingertips

skimming downward. He paused to trace the edge of her panties, and she shivered.

"You okay with me going farther?" he asked.

"You stop, you die," she warned.

Joel laughed as he leaned in tight, his lips brushing her cheek. "I have no intention of stopping unless you tell me to."

He'd reached her curls. The top of her mound. The sensation of someone else's fingers slipping through her folds had her legs quivering. She adjusted her stance to give him more room.

His cheek rested on hers, their breathing nowhere near synchronized as she tried to suck in enough oxygen to fight the spinning in her brain. The tortuous touch to her breasts had resumed as well. Sensory overload, and yet not nearly enough.

Joel pressed a finger deeper into her core and hummed in approval. "You like this. You're hot and wet."

She didn't think that needed a response.

"I'm going to make you come, Vicki. All over my fingers. Your tight pussy is just waiting for me to play with you." That finger slid deeper still, and she softened around him.

"Feels so good."

"Gonna feel even better." He put the heel of his hand against her clit and rubbed.

An electric pulse raced up her spine. "Oh, yeah—that's what I like."

Joel touched his cheek to hers. "Lesson time. Your reward is I make you come."

Lesson? "What do I have to do?"

"You have to trust me. You're totally safe, and I'm going to make you come. Think about that, and open your eyes."

She couldn't help it. Every muscle tightened involuntarily. The only reason he'd mention *trust him* and her being safe was if...

"You didn't."

Increased pressure over her clit distracted her, as did him

sliding his finger all the way out of her body.

Damn it, *no*. She might not want to deal with horses, but he couldn't leave her hanging like this. "Joel..."

"Open your eyes, darling. You can do it."

"Fuck." She edged one eyelid up the smallest distance possible.

A horse stood at the far railing. Her heart pounded, but that was the moment Joel pressed two fingers into her core and she lost a bit of her mind.

"Sable's in the other yard," Joel whispered. "I opened the side door, and she can't get any closer than that railing, so relax, take a couple deep breaths, and you tell me when you deserve your reward."

Vicki fought the fear. Fought to calm her racing pulse that had leapt into high gear even though she knew the horse was nowhere near. Instead she focused on what was close. Joel, his big body wrapped around hers. His hands doing wonderfully wicked things.

The incredible sensation of him working his fingers in and out of her body.

She breathed out slowly, staring into his eyes. The blue became a place of refuge as he took her body higher. She wanted to freak out, but couldn't muster the energy to give a fuck.

Sable was far away, and Joel was right there. Caressing and rubbing, spreading her wider, keeping her needy. "Make me come, Joel."

He smiled. "You stare over there at the nice horse and let me do the rest."

She never would have believed it. Standing on a railing, time-smoothed wood under her fingers. She breathed in the scent of dirt and grass, of animals and distant fireplace smoke. Joel's hands were on her right out there in the open.

And across from them not even twenty meters away was a goddamn horse.

Sable ignored them, wandering her area of the yard, her

wide belly swaying as she moved. It was obvious Vicki and Joel's presence wasn't on her mind.

All the sights and sounds faded, though, as Joel pressed harder on Vicki's clit, piercing her body with his thick fingers, stroking her just right so the tension of her orgasm rose swiftly. Another squeeze to her breast, another nip with his teeth to her ear. Another thrust and she broke, her sex pulsing hard, clutching his fingers. Moisture rushed from her and allowed his final thrusts even deeper.

Vicki groaned, letting the aftershocks take her, hoping like hell Joel would continue to hold her because her legs were done. There was nothing left in them to support her, just this awesome total-body relaxation sweeping in.

Even looking across the yard at a horse had no impact. Stress? What was that?

Joel rocked his hard-on against her hip, breathing deep. "God, that was fun."

She laughed. "That's my line."

He pulled his fingers from her body slowly, tiny circles soothing his departure. "We both had a blast. Good for us. And you did awesome with your lesson."

Vicki glanced across the yard. "She's over there, I'm over here. I suppose we can be pen pals."

She turned and caught Joel by the neck, wrapped her legs around his body and clung on tight. "That was incredible. And I feel like a shit that you're still..."

Joel raised a brow. "What? Now that I've had my fingers in your pussy you're not going to use the big words anymore?"

"Screw that. I wasn't sure if I'm supposed to offer to help you with your hard-on. I'd love to help you with your hard-on."

He paused to put his hat back on then walked them toward the barn. "Next time. Now I'm afraid if we keep going there's bound to be an interruption. We've about used all our good luck in terms of the family staying away. Let's not push it."

Vicki nodded.

He carried her all the way to where she'd parked her bike.

"How long before I see you again?" he asked.

"Things are slowing down at the shop now that we're done inventory. I'm still on the early shift, but any afternoon you want to get together, I'm game."

Joel nodded. "I'll call you. If nothing else, let's make sure we hit Traders on Friday night, okay?"

Goody. More time in public, although it had to be done. "Sounds fine."

He handed over her helmet, leaning back and stretching that long strong body of his. "You're doing great, Vicki."

He kissed her briefly before winking and turning back toward the barn, his whistle cheerful and loud in spite of the bulge still pressing the front of his jeans.

Chapter Thirteen

The walls needed a fresh coat of paint, but other than that Vicki's apartment building appeared decent enough. Joel scrutinized the carpets as he waited for her to answer his knock. He startled as the door behind him creaked opened and an oversized middle-aged man wearing dirty jeans and a wife-beater peered out.

The stranger eyed Joel up and down once then grunted before shutting his door.

What the hell was that about?

Vicki didn't keep him standing in the hallway long. The door swung open to reveal her petite form wrapped in a pretty purple dress, her hair loose over her shoulders instead of pulled back into a ponytail.

Joel whistled in appreciation. "Well now, don't you look nice?"

"Is it too fancy? I don't usually wear stuff like this, but I spotted it at the..." She paused then shrugged. "I was looking for boots to wear while dealing with the evil horses of hell. I struck out on footwear, but this dress was at the thrift shop, and I thought I may as well go for it."

Joel closed the door behind him. "Vicki, don't apologize for shopping at the thrift store. There's no shame in it, and it makes a ton of sense."

She leaned back on the wall. "I'm not ashamed. It's not something I talk about. Ever. So it feels weird."

Joel paused, glancing around at her tiny apartment. Like the last time he'd been here, he was shocked by how little she had, and yet impressed by how everything was still very obviously hers. The few personal items she had on display seemed extra special because they were so scarce.

"You don't talk about clothes or you don't talk about shopping, or what?"

Vicki sighed. "Are we going to Traders tonight?"

"Stop avoiding the conversation and answer the question." Joel sat in the lone chair by the small table. "We'll get to Traders when we get there."

"Stubborn ass."

"You bet. Now spill."

Vicki stroked the sleeves of the pale purple dress, the sheer lace over the solid fabric very pretty and very modest. She was covered up a lot more than many of the women Joel had gone out with over the years. The neckline wasn't too low either, but bar her wearing a puffy winter coat, nothing would hide her chest.

"I don't talk about clothes or shopping. First because I rarely shop, and second, who am I gonna talk to? The guys at work?"

Joel opened his mouth to ask about her girlfriends, and closed it just as fast. Over the past couple weeks she'd never mentioned going out with the girls, ever.

She lifted a brow. "Yeah?"

He went for honest, although on a different tangent. "I don't talk about clothes much either. Or shopping. What the hell. It's a pretty dress and it looks good on you. That's all we need to worry about."

Her smile warmed, sunshine spreading across her face. "You're a slick one, Joel Coleman."

"Just enjoying the view." He took a leisurely gaze down her body, lingering on her legs, sad that her knees barely showed. "Although the skirt is longer than it needs to be. I'm kinda pissed we started seeing each other so late in the season. I bet you do Daisy Duke shorts well."

Vicki peeled herself off the wall and paced forward, skirt flaring around her hips nicely. "I don't do Daisy Dukes at all. But for you? Sure."

He opened his arms and she walked all the way against him, and Joel got reminded all over how much he'd been wanting her. Fooling around and kissing wasn't going to be enough for much longer, not when she rubbed her torso over his as the kiss continued languidly.

He held her loosely, avoiding the temptation to run his hands up her thighs and under that flimsy skirt.

Pulling their mouths apart was tough, damn tough. "We'd better get going or we're gonna end up—"

Joel stopped dead.

Vicki backed away, her eyes full of fire. Her words husky as she spoke. "Or we're gonna end up *what*, Joel? You afraid to use the big words?"

He shook his head. "I'm not going to deny I want to take you to bed, darling. But not now. Not yet."

They stared at each other for a minute before Vicki sighed heavily. "Damn you."

He nodded. "Soon, okay?"

Vicki slipped on her shoes. "Don't know what we're waiting for, though. Like you want some signal the time is right?"

Hell. "Maybe."

There was something, though. Something held him back from making the next move, and Joel knew enough to trust his gut.

She was locking her door when the neighbour poked his head out again. Joel couldn't believe it as the man basically stripped Vicki with his gaze. Joel stepped between them and glared daggers.

The stranger's door shut a hell of a lot quicker than it had opened.

They were down on the street headed for his truck when she hesitated. "You want to walk?" Vicki asked. "It's only a couple blocks."

"If it's not too cold for you." He checked her shoes, but they were more practical than fancy. He held out his arm, and she slipped her fingers over his elbow, cuddling close as they made their way down the sidewalk. "Who's your nosy neighbour?"

Vicki made a disgruntled sound. "He's a pain in the ass, that's who he is. Moved in a couple months ago, and I swear every time I hit the landing he's staring at me."

"Have you complained to the manager?"

Vicki snorted. "Right, what am I supposed to complain about? That my neighbour opens his door? Joel, no one gives a shit."

He fell silent for a bit. "I give a shit."

She offered him a smile. "Yeah, you. Thanks, but it's okay. I make sure I have my keys ready when I get home, and he's never really bothered me."

The more he thought about it, the less he liked it. "If you ever get worried, let me know, okay?"

She squeezed his arm then pointed across the street to a window decorated for Halloween, and talk turned to more general things.

A rush of heat and sound hit them as they walked into Traders. Joel took her coat, then her hand and led her toward where the family usually gathered.

Vicki stayed close to his side, her warmth like a gentle connection between them. "I am drinking tonight, just so you know."

"You mean a drink, right?" He laughed at her sudden jab to his arm. "Well, if body weight has anything on it, half a glass of wine should make you wasted."

"I can hold my liquor," she insisted. Her gaze stopped on someone in the room, and she swore. "Hide me."

He followed her line of vision to spot Eric Tell and a group of his cronies gathered around a table. Joel pressed his hand to her back and guided her forward. "Ignore him. Not worth the energy to spit."

"Oh, I don't know about that. A nice direct hit, right between the eyes would be fun." Vicki made a face. "Tell me again this is a good idea."

"This is a great idea. Come on."

Thirty seconds later they had chairs in the Coleman section of the bar. Tonight the group was smaller, but just as loud as usual. Pool tables and drinks, conversation and teasing.

Jesse looked up from the pool table where he was taking a shot. His gaze leapt to Vicki, then returned to Joel. His wink didn't bother Joel as much as he expected. It was more a hello, and less like his twin was actually looking Vicki over.

He turned to settle Vicki in her seat. "Vicki, you know my cousins, Tamara and Lisa."

Vicki nodded. "Hi."

Tamara smiled back tentatively. "I heard you two were dating. Nice you finally made it out."

Joel lifted his hands in protest. "Finally? Damn, you're demanding."

"Hey, the clan expects instant updates at all times," Lisa teased, her expression still questioning as she peeked at Vicki, at Joel, and over both their shoulders at Jesse.

Ahhh, *shit.* The tension was thick enough to cut with a knife. Vicki wiggled in her chair, and he draped his arm around her, trying to reassure her and protect her at the same time.

It was about as awkward as the evening Travis had showed up with one woman after forgetting he'd already invited another to meet him at the bar. Joel twisted to eyeball the pool game, hoping it would be over soon and the guys would join them. And yet he didn't really want Jesse to come over and hang around Vicki either.

He'd fucked up. Big time. Or more to the point, he hadn't realized how bad the situation was going to be. Setting them up as a couple meant being in public, but this was damn painful.

Vicki answered a couple questions, but pretty much sat silently as the girls attempted to keep a conversation flowing, and the rest of the people in the bar found reasons to wander past and gawk.

The girls turned to watch something at the other end of the bar, and Joel leaned down to whisper in Vicki's ear. "You okay? Want to stay or want to go?"

She caught his shirtfront, turning until her lips brushed his earlobe. "Staying here is like a negative twenty. Top of the list is going back to my place and having sex. And somewhere in the middle is getting you drunk enough you agree to teach me how to give you a blow job."

Joel's body tightened—everywhere—her words slamming into him and taking this way off the comfortable chart and into dangerous territory. "Don't push me, darling."

"I'm not, I'm trying to tempt you."

Temptation was there, that was true. Joel wavered, because for a tiny package, Vicki was dragging him to the very limits of his control. And right now, he couldn't blame her. Getting away and getting naked was way more attractive than the current option.

Vicki squirmed, the heavy sensation of being stared at worse than ever.

Well, wasn't this a ton of fun?

She glanced around the room and counted how many people's gazes darted away as she skimmed past them. Maybe the whole idea of breaking through her bad-girl rep was stupid. Awkward for sure. And this time she'd hauled Joel along into her unique brand of torment.

Brilliant. Way to go.

The idea of leaving was very appealing, so when Joel rose, hope rose with him. He caught her by the hand, tugging her to her feet. "Come on."

Thank God. "My jacket..."

She reached for it, but he shook his head. "Not leaving. Let's dance."

Okaaaay.

He led her around the divider between the two halves of the bar. On one side of Traders were the pool tables, dartboards, and seating for the get-away-from-it-all crowd who wanted to relax and shoot the breeze. On the other was the dance floor, where tall standing-room-only tables lined the edges to entice drinkers to watch and mingle.

Vicki could count on one hand the number of times she'd been in the bar. Not only did she tend to avoid places where the ridicule got worse, she'd lied her ass off to Joel—she couldn't drink at all.

But as the music volume increased, she focused less on the people around them and more on the man holding her hand as he guided her through the maze of bodies.

He turned and took her in his arms. She relaxed, resting her cheek against his chest as they moved to the slow music.

He chuckled, his body vibrating under her. "That was pretty terrible, wasn't it?"

Vicki tilted her head as his fingers touched under her chin. "Let's not talk about it. If we pretend it's not there, it'll go away."

"Actually..." he nodded, "...it will. So let's have some fun."

The floor was only partway full. Joel's older brother Matt was dancing with his fiancée Hope, and the two of them smiled as they caught sight of Vicki.

"Remind me never to get on the wrong side of your dad, okay?"

Joel frowned. "What makes you say that?"

She pointed to Matt and Hope. "After his *rah rah* speech the other day, your immediate kin seem to have calmed down about me being around. He put the fear in them I guess."

"Hope's a damn good woman. She's got pain-in-the-ass family as well. I think she can empathize, and so can Matt since the *pain in the ass* is his ex."

"Right." Vicki glanced their way again, a rush of sympathy hitting. Hope's older sister was back in town, and her strange behavior continued to light up the gossip circles as bright as the tales regarding Vicki's family.

Maybe it was stupid to feel a connection—having family who wasn't much family—but somehow Vicki felt it. Real or not, for the first time since they'd walked into the bar, she got her mind off herself and the damn town gossip, and focused on someone else.

"You ever double date with them? Or, you know, hang out?"

"With Matt and Hope?"

"Yeah."

Joel tucked his hand against her lower back and pulled her in tighter. "Sometimes. Usually do more with Jesse and Travis, but..."

Yeah, she'd put the kibosh on that option. "Not a big deal."

With his hands spread on her body, the smooth slide of his touch as he stroked her suggested how they could spend their time once they left the bar.

Joel interrupted her dirty daydreams. "I think Matt said something about camping out for a weekend before the snow flies. You want to join them?"

"Camping? Like, in a tent?" Vicki laughed. "I've never been. Other than at the cabins for the kids' camp."

"Then you're in for a treat. Baked beans and hotdogs over a fire. S'mores. Coffee in the morning strong enough to wake the dead."

"Jumping in the creek for a bath?"

His expression twisted into sheer mischief. "Dare ya."

Bastard. "Now, that's cheating."

Joel's grin increased. "So I have figured out the way to motivate you. Awesome. I'll get the gear together, and you can help with the food. It'll be fun."

The music tempo increased, and they slipped apart, more gyrating and hip shaking going on than up close and personal. The floor got crowded enough they bumped and connected, Joel inserting his big body between her and the others.

She'd never really been protected like that before, and it felt kinda awesome.

A loud cheer went up, and the crowd pressed aside, giving more room to a couple who was using the music way too vigourously for her to match. Joel tucked her against him and retreated farther, ending up close to where Travis had a firm grip on a blonde in a skintight outfit.

Travis rocked his lady, his fingers splayed over her hipbones as she nestled her back to his front. He raised his voice to be heard over the pulsing music. "Joel, Vicki. You know Ashley, right?"

Vicki recognized her, but didn't know her. "Hey."

Something about the way Ashley checked her out didn't bite like the stares of the rest of the crowd, especially since she gave Joel that same once-over. It was less judgmental, more sensual. Her lips curled into a smile that somehow looked hungry. "Well, damn, don't you two look hot together?"

Travis swatted her ass. "Be nice, Ash."

"I am," Ashley protested. "If I'm not allowed to admire a good-looking couple while you've got your hands on me, you need to work on your self-esteem." Her gaze returned to Vicki even as she rocked her hips against Travis. There was no doubt that the two of them were more than first-time dance partners.

The move screamed intimacy, and heat pulsed inside Vicki. She moved closer to Joel, looking for more of the passion between them, because, damn, watching Travis and Ashley rub together was making her hot.

Something flashed in Ashley's face, as if she'd read Vicki's mind. Vicki's cheeks flushed, but she refused to look away. Refused to draw back from Joel who had her by the hips, one leg slipped between hers, brushing her core on his thigh.

It was crowded enough there was a reason for her to be riding him, but not enough reason for her to lose her mind and forget herself completely. She and Joel were supposed to be setting a new direction, not becoming the talk of the town for doing it on the dance floor.

The woman gave her a wicked smile. "We got the best guys in the house, sweetheart. What say we make everyone jealous?"

"*Shh.*" Travis spun Ashley and squeezed her against his body, hands capturing her ass and keeping the motion of their hips going. "Behave. Joel and Vicki aren't looking for your kind of mischief, sweetheart."

Joel chuckled. "No, but don't let that stop you."

Vicki glanced around the place, enjoying having Joel holding her tight, relishing the way the energy of the room seemed for once to be working with her and not against her. People still stared, but for the most part they were engrossed in their partners, bodies undulating in time with dance, with the music. She wasn't experienced enough as a dancer to try anything fancy, content to make touching the connection between her and Joel.

Compared to the couples around them, they must have looked prim and proper, but she didn't care, barely noticed. An organic flow to everything took her, and she ignored the dirty dancing, lifted her chin and focused on Joel.

His hands circled her waist. The wide grasp made her feel delicate and fragile, even as his expression said ravishment was rising on the agenda. Vicki trailed her fingers up his chest until she caught hold of his neck, nothing but fabric separating them.

His pupils dilated, his breathing increased in tempo. It wasn't just the dancing, wasn't the energy around them feeding the demand. Vicki felt it, needed it. Needed *something* with an urgency she'd never experienced before.

I want you. The words were there in her brain, yet she kept her lips from forming them. Not in public, not with their plans.

He seemed to have heard her anyway, his nostrils flaring. If he'd dragged her from the dance floor in that moment, she wouldn't have been surprised, the tension thick enough to make her want to throw caution aside.

Good thing one of them was in control, because she seemed to have lost it, and this time it wasn't her temper making her careless and foolhardy, it was the fire in her veins that called for his touch. For more than public glances and caresses.

The music broke, switching to another slow song. But instead of taking advantage of it, Joel found them a spot at one of the tables and tucked her against his side. "I need a drink."

So did she. Ice water, to pour on her head. "Okay."

Travis and Ashley joined them. Matt and Hope. In the time they'd been on the dance floor, more of the Coleman clan had switched to the dance side, and suddenly the space around them was filled with Joel's family. Another couple of the older guy cousins who Vicki only knew vaguely stepped closer. Tamara was there with a lean, dark-haired man. It was a totally overwhelming and complete surrounding.

Only, this time the atmosphere changed subtly. No one focused on her alone. No one checked her and Joel and Jesse to see if something kinky was about to start.

Especially since Jesse had found someone to dance with, and the two were wrapped around each other on the floor. He'd as good as put up an *I'm not interested in Vicki* sign, and she couldn't be happier.

Maybe this evening hadn't been a mistake after all. Glancing up at Joel and the wicked promise in his eyes, the evening wasn't over either.

Vicki reluctantly untangled herself from his embrace. "Got to hit the washroom."

She needed a moment alone to cool off. She patted water on her face when she was done, trying to soothe her heated cheeks, but there was no hiding the sparkle in her eyes.

She hadn't felt this alive in forever. Being with Joel and his family was a different world. Hope for the future gave her a reckless courage. This relationship was only going to last for the next six months, but she was going to enjoy every minute of it.

She was headed out of the bathroom when the door opened. Vicki moved aside to let a group enter when one of them blocked her path.

The woman gasped indignantly. "I can't believe you have the guts to show yourself in public."

Without any warning she raised her hand and slapped Vicki in the face.

Chapter Fourteen

Vicki fell back, hands rising in defense, her cheek burning as she attempted to escape her attacker. She found her balance only after she slammed into a stall door.

"What the hell are you doing? Stop it." She swung at the hands reaching for her.

The blur of bodies in the small space made it difficult to focus on faces. The air filled with noise, and one single voice called out above the rest in anger. "Bitch. Get out of here, you whore."

Fingers caught her dress, the fabric ripping as she was shoved out the main door. She stumbled over her feet and ended up in a heap against the opposite wall. Anger flared along with a healthy dose of fear. *Fight or flight* was kicking in, but she wasn't stupid enough to head back into a confined space to face her attackers. Nor did she want to end up brawling in the hallway.

For once logic swept away the urge to swing her fists, and she scrambled upright and headed toward the main room and the protection of the crowd.

Cool air brushed her side, and she stared in disbelief at the wide gap in her dress, the seam torn in two from her rib cage to her hip. Even pulling the fabric together didn't help, as holes gaped on either side of her white-knuckled grip, leaving her bra and underwear exposed.

She couldn't go into the main room like this. And she couldn't stay in the hall—the group that had assaulted her could be out at any moment.

Frustration and anger flared, this time at the unfairness of it all. Everything had been going well, and yet her usual luck had caught her again.

She turned and headed for the emergency exit, hoping it wasn't wired to set off alarms.

The tears that threatened to rise were shoved away by sheer determination and the rush of cold air that greeted her. Cigarette smoke carried from the sitting area to the north, a far-enough distance from the main doors to meet provincial regulations.

Vicki glanced to check she was safe, but the few people huddled together within the smoky haze scarcely looked her way before returning to their conversation and beers.

One arm wrapped around her waist to hold herself together, she pulled her phone from her purse and dialed Joel.

The noise in the background was deafening loud, but the confusion as he answered was still audible. "Vicki?"

"Can you grab my coat? I'm outside. We need to go."

"I'll be right there."

Thank God he didn't ask any questions. She tucked her phone away, keeping alert as she hid in the darkest section of the area. It seemed only safe to stay out of sight from anyone driving by.

She was shivering by the time Joel rounded the corner, but hell if she'd let this break her. Although running and jumping into his arms was what she wanted, she simply stepped forward.

He was at her side in a moment, wrapping her coat around her shoulders, looking her over. "Damn it, Vicki, what the hell is up?"

"Someone—"

What did she say when she wasn't sure, other than it had to have something to do with her family?

"Fuck." Joel lifted her chin and turned her face to the side, brushing his fingers tenderly over her cheek. "Who hit you?"

He was furious. She played it down. "Let's go home. I'm cold."

He might have ignored her request if a full-body shiver hadn't shaken her. Joel had her against his side and headed toward her apartment without another word.

She didn't need revenge right now, didn't need his anger. He was there, and that was enough. Made it easier to put aside some of the confusion, and a lot of the frustration, and just accept his arm around her, the heat of his body brushing hers.

The couple of blocks passed quickly, and they were out on the landing as her fingers shook on the keys.

Joel wrapped his hand over hers and helped her, turning to snarl wordlessly at the man in the next apartment who'd opened his door to snoop, this time classily dressed in nothing but boxers.

"Fucking bastard. I'm talking to your landlord tomorrow."

Vicki dropped her purse on the table beside the door, too wound up to protest. She kicked off her shoes and stumbled to the edge of the daybed. "Thank you for taking care of me."

"If I'd taken care of you properly, you wouldn't have ended up standing outside in the cold." He was on his knees in front of her examining her cheek again. He swore, his knuckles whisper-soft over where the strike still pounded. "What happened, darling? You went to the bathroom, and next thing I know it looks as if you've been beaten up."

"Someone called me a whore." The words burst out. So much for keeping her cool. The hopelessness she felt was clear even in her own ears. "I didn't do anything, Joel, I swear I've never done anything to—"

Her voice broke. Staying strong when he was looking at her with such tenderness in his eyes was impossible. She caught him by the shirtfront, leaned closer to soak in the comfort of his body, and gave in to the tears.

Emotionally he'd been yo-yoing all night. The slow changeover in attitude from those around them once they'd hit the dance floor had reassured him there was hope. The blazing heat rising between him and Vicki made the rest of their deal that much more attractive as well. With a few plans falling into place for the future, like spending time with Matt and Travis and their partners, things were looking up.

But the confusion of having her call him, and the sight of her stepping from the shadows so forlorn and broken had torn something inside him apart.

The truth finally sank in. It wasn't rumours and innuendo Vicki had to put up with. It wasn't laughing jokes or snide comments like he and Jesse had been fielding. To be physically hurt by someone pushed her life into territory he'd never experienced.

The asshole across the hall was just one more example of a dangerous situation she daily disregarded because there was no choice for her than to ignore it. How long did she have to put up with this insanity, until it was too late? Until she was seriously hurt or raped?

His safe, small town showed a different face in that moment, and Joel Coleman grew up in a hell of a hurry.

While Vicki wept in his arms, Joel's heart ached. He held her tight and let her have it out. Didn't try to reassure her everything would be all right, didn't give her any platitudes, because there was so much wrong here that he didn't know how to fix.

She released his shirtfront, slid her hands around his torso and squeezed him tight. "Thanks for being there."

Joel slipped his hands around her and was shocked to discover naked skin. He leaned away to figure out what the devil he was touching. "God damn it, what happened to your dress?"

"That's why I had to go outside. I don't think they meant to rip anything." Vicki took a stuttering breath as she lifted her fingers to touch her cheek.

"And that handprint was an accident as well, I suppose." Joel caught her gaze. "You should press charges."

Her expression tightened. "I don't even know who they are."

Which made it worse, not better. "No one should be able to attack you for no reason, Vicki."

"They had a reason, only I'm not the one to blame. I told

you, the woman who hit me called me a whore. Said she was surprised to see me in public."

Joel's anger wasn't cooling, if anything it was getting worse. "You think they got you and your sister mixed up?"

Vicki broke her gaze away, and Joel wanted to hit something. Yeah, that didn't make the attack any better at all.

Screw it. Joel sat on the bed beside her and pulled her into his lap, cradling her close. "What do you want to do?"

She wiped her eyes then rested her cheek on his chest. She was so still he thought she might be holding her breath. Then she brought one hand up to trace the buttons on his shirt, and all the tension in the room flipped the corner, his body stupidly tightening with need.

Vicki spoke clearly, without a waver. "I want to forget the last thirty minutes happened and go back to you being as hot for me as you were on the dance floor."

"*God*, Vicki."

She lifted her face. "I mean it. I was having the time of my life until, like everything else in my world, the fun and the laughter got torn away. And that sucks. So if you really want an answer, I want you."

Her hand cupped his face, fingers so soft as she stroked his skin.

"Darling—"

"If you still want me." The words whispered out as she buried her fingers in his hair and broke his remaining protests.

To deny his desire would be another slap in the face.

Joel let his gaze shift down her body. Watched her chest rise and fall far too rapidly for how calm and cool she pretended to be. The pulse at the base of her neck fluttered.

Ignore the past thirty minutes? He couldn't do that. He'd never be able to get what he'd just learned out of his soul.

But he could give her what she needed right now. What they both needed. To feel alive and in control.

"Let's see what happens, okay?"

Something lit in her eyes and she swallowed hard. "You mean it? We're gonna...?"

He leaned her over to reach her lips more easily, pressing her onto the bed. He spoke against her mouth as he smoothed back the long strands of hair that fell between them. "We're gonna see what happens."

Gentle kisses followed. Fleeting. Tender.

It wasn't time to wait anymore, but there was no need to rush.

"You have a whole lot of things you haven't experienced, remember?" Joel adjusted her until she lay flat on the bed, easy to touch and pet and stroke.

"You mean I get my blowjob lessons?" She smiled so earnestly before breaking into a grin of sheer mischief.

"We'll leave that one for a bit later. Now shut up and let me kiss you."

He cupped her face carefully to avoid bumping where the imprint remained. She'd likely have a bruise by the morning, and he didn't want to remind her of the stupid cruelty of others.

He laid his mouth over hers and kissed her. Used his tongue on her lips until she cracked them apart and he could slip inside. Gentle. Delicate. Still intoxicating enough that their breathing grew ragged and his body hardened.

He left her lips and glided lower, pressing another kiss to the throbbing pulse in her neck, drawing a finger down the neckline of her dress to one breast.

Vicki stared with wide eyes. "No padding this time either, I swear."

God, that she could joke? He wanted to wrap her up and protect her, and instead she was already forging ahead, dealing with what life had handed her. Damn brave, so much to admire.

So he followed her lead and teased right back. "Then you'd better prove it. Let's get that pretty dress off you. I want to hit second base properly this time."

Vicki shot upright, reaching behind her for the zipper.

"Not so fast. That's my job."

Getting a woman out of her clothes for the first time wasn't something to be rushed. Joel kissed her, tangling his fingers in her hair. Letting her set the pace so he didn't take it too far, too fast. Vicki moaned into his mouth and pressed against him, eager in her response.

Joel caught the back of her head in one hand, twisting her hair to the side to expose the long zipper. He tugged downward until the shoulders of her dress loosened off and allowed the neckline to gape open.

Her bra was in the way, but there was still a lovely amount of bare flesh before him.

"You gonna stare down my top all night or take off my clothes?" Vicki teased.

"Both."

Zipper dealt with, Joel stroked from her neck outward, pushing aside fabric. He leaned over and kissed the newly exposed skin.

He repeated the motion on the other side, only this time when the material slipped from her shoulder, her top fell away, leaving her naked from the waist up except for the bra.

Vicki hesitated for a moment. "It's nothing fancy—"

"Your tits? They don't need to be fancy to turn me on."

She shook her head. "Joker."

He had to touch. Teasing her skin until she arched against his hands, little whimpers of need escaping from the back of her throat.

Joel paused. Once he got started, he wasn't going to be able to stop. So he planned ahead. Jerked his shirt free from his jeans and tore off both layers at the same time, discarding them to the side.

Vicki smiled, approval in her eyes. "Nice floor show so far. Don't stop."

"This is about you." Joel leaned forward, the heat of her skin brushing his as he reached behind her and undid her bra.

He peeled the final layer away and the urge to cover herself arrived. It didn't matter that he stared as if he were starving, heat and desire clear in his eyes. She'd never been naked in front of a man before, and Vicki clutched the bedding under her fingers to keep her hands in one place.

"Beautiful." Joel closed in, and she was sure he'd go straight for her breasts. She ached to have him touch her, the heavy sensation of want strange and yet perfect.

Only he moved forward until their entire upper bodies connected. Skin to skin, mouths together for another air-sucking kiss. Stars floated before her eyes as she took advantage of his nearness to run her hands over his naked shoulders.

The twist of his tongue playing with hers wasn't enough to distract her from the heady sensation of her breasts compressed to his wall of a chest. His fingertips on her shoulder spread electric pulses to her core as he inched lower, shifting sideways far enough that he could wrap his big hand over her breast.

Oh God, it felt good. "Don't stop."

"You have no idea..." His lips left hers and moved downward. Vicki took a deep breath in anticipation as he traced patterns on her collarbone with his tongue. The cooler room air hit the moisture and she shivered. Waiting. Wanting.

Another kiss, this time to the top of her breast. He still held her cradled in his palm and actually seeing his tongue sneak out to make contact with her nipple was overwhelming.

When he wrapped his lips around the peak, Vicki swore. Such a strange connection, that his lips tugging on her breast could create the same tug lower in her body. She smoothed her fingers through his hair, keeping him in place, loving the attention and the incredible pleasure.

When he switched to the other side, she wasn't sure she was going to last. "How can that feel so unbelievably good?"

"Hmm." Joel sucked harder then popped off the tip, leaving it shiny with moisture and achingly hard. "Don't try to figure it out, just enjoy."

Back and forth, as if he couldn't decide which side he liked better. Enjoying his caresses was one thing, but even his focused attention on her breasts wasn't enough. Vicki squirmed, looking for more pressure, something to counter the ache between her legs.

Joel pulled off, a light chuckle escaping him. "You're wiggling like a worm on a hook."

"Nice visual, but...oh *God*, Joel. I want more."

He laid her back on the bed and rose over her. "Hang in there, we've got all the time in the world."

"If you take that long, I'm going to change into some kind of zombie creature."

"Well, we can't have that." Joel smoothed his hands down to her naked waist, his gaze following his touch. When he stripped off her dress, he took her panties as well, and in less time than she thought possible she was flat-out butt-naked.

She'd been watching his face as he'd moved, and she was glad of it. There was no faking the hunger she saw. The pleasure he experienced as her body was revealed. His obvious desire was exactly what her soul needed after the chaos of the day.

Joel lifted his gaze to hers, shaking his head lightly. "I'm in heaven. You're so damn beautiful."

Vicki's cheeks heated at his compliment. "Touch me," she whispered.

"Everywhere."

He worked his way down her body, and for the first time in her life pleasure overwhelmed her. Joel used not only his hands but his mouth and seemingly his entire body. Unexpected, and oh so good. Like the sweet rasp of the stubble on his jaw as he rubbed against her belly. His tongue stroking the underside of her breast. The subtle caress of his forearm along her rib cage. She squeezed her eyes shut to concentrate on not jumping off the bed every time he fondled a new section of skin.

But when he pressed her legs apart, she involuntarily shot upright.

"Joel..."

He placed his hands on her thighs and stroked down to her knees. "Yes?"

"You're not gonna...?"

He opened her, lifting her knees into the air and inserting himself as a barrier so she couldn't close her legs. Couldn't hide.

"Of course I'm going to touch you here as well." Another slide of his hands, this time to her core. He stared intently, and as his thumbs slipped along her labia, Vicki shuddered with the pleasure of it.

It wasn't only him stroking her. His fingers nudging her clit, playing gently at the sensitive skin of her sex. It was all of it together. Watching, feeling, listening. His moans of approval, the sounds of pleasure that escaped her no matter how much she tried to contain them.

He lowered his head and covered her with his mouth.

When he'd used his hands to make her orgasm the other day, the difference had astonished her. How much richer and more powerful it was to have someone else take her over.

This was another step up the scale of pleasure. He slipped his tongue between her folds, teasing, tasting. Bringing her to the edge fast. All it took was him licking her clit and she trembled, ready to go over.

"*Joel.*" His name snuck out even though the last thing she wanted was to distract him.

She didn't need to worry. His concentration was absolute. She was the one losing it as her orgasm slammed in and broke, jolting her body with a wave of pleasure.

Joel hummed his approval but didn't stop. He moved away from her clit for a moment as he continued to play. He lifted her hips into the air and ate greedily, as if she were better than anything he'd ever tasted. Vicki caught his hair in her hands and clung, not sure if she wanted to drag him away or hold him in place until she'd experienced that incredible sensation all over.

The decision was wrenched from her as he covered her clit and sucked, pleasure flashing like a bright light from head to toe and shaking her boneless. This orgasm caught her by surprise, more focused and tight as desire took her mind and spun her in circles. She stroked his hair as he eased away, gentling his touch, every stroke of his clever tongue setting off mini-aftershocks.

Joel slipped off the bed, caressing her naked skin lightly as he crawled from between her legs. She protested, but he smiled. "I'm not going anywhere. Just try to get me to leave."

Chapter Fifteen

He popped open the button on his pants, and Vicki rolled so she could enjoy the view. Everything about him turned her on. The muscular spread of his chest, his narrower waist. That trail of hair leading downwards being revealed more and more as he lost his jeans and stripped off his briefs.

She pressed up on her elbows, scared and intrigued at the same time. Both of them finally naked, and unless she was mistaken, there was only one way this was ending.

Joel stroked his hard-on, a slow motion over the thick length. Every time he pulled his hand back to his body, the head of his cock thrust out from his fist, dark coloured and almost dangerous looking. Vicki tore her eyes off his hands, glancing up and over the whole huge package, wondering if she'd bit off more than she could chew this time.

The expression in his eyes saved her from getting scared. Patience was there along with the hunger, his gaze lingering on her pussy, her breasts, her face. Just long enough at each spot to make her want to preen.

The side of his mouth curled into this sexy smile. "You're looking mighty relaxed. Like the barn cats when they've had a good hunting session in the hayloft."

Vicki laughed out loud. "Some of your comparisons need a little work, but the rest of you is very talented. And gorgeous. God, Joel, why are you standing way over there?"

She shifted upright, smiling at the way his gaze automatically swung to her breasts. Strange how now that this was a sexual situation she wanted, his fascination with her chest turned her on instead of squicking her out like when strangers did it.

He leaned over without looking away, grabbing his jeans.

"Slide back on the bed and make room for me."

Now was time for regrets in terms of her sleeping arrangements. The delicate undersized couch-slash-bed was great for her. Not so great to imagine fooling around vigourously with a man Joel's size. "Maybe we should use the floor."

He dug into his wallet and pulled out a condom. "You might be right, but let's try this first."

He sat on the bed and tore open the package.

Vicki knelt behind him and peered over his shoulder, her naked chest to his heated skin. "Can I put that on you?"

His cock jerked. "Darling, if you want a chance in hell of me lasting, don't go putting images into my head right now of your hands on my cock."

She smiled and kissed his neck. Pressed tight to his back as she ran her fingers over his shoulder and down to his chest. Basically took every opportunity she got to savour her first chance to be totally naked with a guy.

"It's better than I thought," she confessed, watching him roll on the condom, fascinated with how easy Joel made this.

He adjusted his hips farther back on the bed and reached for her. "What's better?"

Joel had her by the waist and determinedly guided her where he wanted her. She ended up straddling his thighs, face to face with him. "Sex."

"Glad to hear it." He caught her around the back of the neck and drew her in for more kisses.

Each time she thought she knew what to expect, and each time he surprised her. He controlled her, taking charge and keeping her exactly where he wanted. She draped her arms over his shoulders and went along for the ride, the fire in her body rising back up.

A soft brush against her mound made her jerk, but his hand at her neck kept her from escaping his lips. Slow, even circles pressed over her clit and the dual sensations had her squirming for more.

He let her go, breathing heavily as he looked into her face.

151

"You still good?"

Maybe moaning wasn't a suitable response, but his talented finger or fingers, whatever he was using on her sex, had turned her mind to mush.

Then the teasing stopped as Joel lifted her slightly, hands firm on her hips, lining them up so her sex ground against his erection. "Come on, darling. Let's get you good and heated up."

"I'm hot already," she protested, but he didn't stop, rocking her over his length. She reached down with one hand to explore, touching herself, brushing her fingertips over his cock. She was somewhat embarrassed to find she was so wet, and every motion coated him more.

She stroked the side of his erection and Joel shook his head. "Troublemaker. You need to concentrate on what you're feeling, not on making me go off like a firework out of schedule."

He lifted her high enough her breasts lined up with his mouth and as his lips closed around one nipple, pleasure took over.

Every part of her, satisfied and happy from what he'd already given her. Every part aching for more.

"Joel, please." She trembled on the verge of another orgasm, and three was two more than her usual. She didn't want to waste this one. "I want to feel what it's like. I want to know."

He nodded, and lowered her carefully, his hand between her legs to guide the way. "Don't rush. Take your time. I know you might have heard otherwise, but trust me, okay?"

She wanted to rush, not to get the virgin thing over, but because she was so damn ready. "You've got me aching."

"I want to feel you around me too." He kissed the tip of her nose and flashed his suggestive grin. "Sexy, sexy woman."

The head of his cock slipped through her folds. Vicki held herself up, not sure what to expect. The near instant pressure wasn't it. "Umm..."

He supported her in place. "Slowly. Let yourself stretch a little."

She rolled her hips, trying not to lose him, but also not to drive him any farther in. "Joel?"

"Put your hands on my shoulders and wait."

Once he was sure she was braced, his hands went over her body. One to play with her breasts, the other back down to her clit. She took in a deep breath, but as soon as he began the rubbing motion, there was no way she could remain tense.

Vicki tried again to lower her hips, and this time it was different. It still hurt, but now the sensation of being pressed in two was somehow good. The pain almost a counter to the intense pleasure, and that contrast made her feel alive.

Joel swallowed hard, and she pressed her lips to his chin for a second. "Thank you for being patient."

He didn't answer. Didn't have to. She slid over him again and something gave, and this time her hips went all the way down. The initial jolt of pain made her gasp before the overriding sensation switched to fullness. Stretched to the maximum, Vicki was scared to move.

Her ass rested on his thighs, his cock fully inside her. She stilled and just took it in. As she waited for the pain to recede, she did a mental check, storing up every moment best she could. The newness, the wonderful bite and need Joel brought with his touch.

The stroke of his hands over her back and smoothing down her ass was amazing. She squirmed, adjusting position, pressure building in a new way now. Like an urgent requirement to move.

Vicki leaned back so she could look at where they joined. Lifted her hips and watched the shining wet length of his cock slowly appear. Lowered, and he disappeared, the wide crown pressing against the most incredible places.

She didn't hurt anymore. The pressure kicked up a notch. It made her want even more to explode with his cock inside to see how much different that would feel.

She straightened and found Joel had his eyes squeezed shut, his entire face crinkled as if he were in pain. "Joel?"

He dragged in a breath through his nose before opening his eyes. "How you doing?"

"I want to move."

Relief shuddered over his face. "Thank God."

Vicki appreciated him even more in that moment for taking her so gently. She stared into his eyes as, cautiously but with more vigour, she moved over him. He caught her by the hips when she was halfway up, adding his help. Lifting a little higher than she'd intended, bringing her down with a little more force.

The increased motion made her breasts swing, their bodies close enough her erect nipples brushed his chest. That need to burst free was there in her core, waiting, and she squeezed her inner muscles as an experiment.

"Fucking hell." Joel grimaced again. "God, I'm dying here. Don't send me over without you."

They were both panting, breath rushing out in gasps. She took a clue from his earlier actions and lowered her hand so she could play with her clit. Ran her fingers along the seam where they joined to grab moisture, savouring being able to touch him.

When she broke this time it was different. With her body pulsing around the rock-solid length of his shaft, the pleasure was so much more focused and intense. He worked in and out steadily, the incredible stroking on her constricting sex making her shake as repetitive rollers bore down on her.

"Oh, yes." Joel pulled her hard into his lap, thrusting upward as he rolled his pelvis and buried himself as deep as possible. Vicki stilled, trying to feel his release, to experience that as well.

His abdomen tightened, as did his grip on her body, one arm pressing her close. Slightly sweaty, both breathing hard. Full and yet empty...she'd lost all her stress in the past however long they'd been fooling around.

Joel kept her there, motionless for a couple of minutes as they came back down. He stroked her hair, caressed her body, but it was all the more intimate things that meant the world to her.

He didn't jump up and run off. He didn't start making small talk. Their breathing slowly got in synch, and he rubbed his cheek against her head. The quiet touches were what turned this from a fabulous experience into something she'd always remember.

She pulled back before he did.

Joel winked. "If that smile is any indication, I didn't blow it too badly for your first time."

Contentment poured over her. "Score. One hundred percent."

He cupped her face and kissed her one last time. Like a blessing, and a thank-you. Something for what they'd done and confirmation he couldn't wait to do it all over again.

Or maybe she was putting her own thoughts into his actions.

He leaned their heads together. "I don't want to get out of bed, but I have to."

Vicki collapsed lazily onto the mattress as he rose to his feet and dealt with the condom. "There are towels in the bathroom cabinet if you want a shower."

"I'm not going to be gone that long, darling, so quit hogging the covers."

He vanished into the bathroom for a minute, sink water running. Vicki found the energy to adjust the bedding and pull back the quilt. Half the pillows usually got shoved to the floor at night, so she rolled over to rearrange them.

The sight of blood made her swear. She'd forgotten. So much for simply rolling over and falling asleep.

Of course Joel returned at the exact instant she had a fist full of bloody quilt.

"I was coming to get you." He glanced at what she held, his smile fading but not to discomfiture, more to understanding. She was all ready to get embarrassed and shit, but he took her by the hand and helped her to her feet. Grabbed the quilt with his free hand and led her to the bathroom.

"Crawl in the tub," he ordered. "Shower or bath, whatever

you want."

He caught her under the chin and took her mouth again, catching her with her lips open in protest. She decided to simply enjoy the moment, whatever the hell he was up to.

Joel stepped back, his gaze dropping over her body. The self-satisfaction on his face made her happy. "I have no objections to washing you up if you'd like, but you tell me what you'd prefer. I'm not going asshole on you or do anything to make you uncomfortable."

Vicki glanced at the blood on her thighs. Jeez, how sexy was that? No, this one she wanted to be in charge of. She caught hold of the curtain, winking at him. "I totally want to fool around in a shower sometime, but right now? I won't be long."

He nodded, and she pulled the curtain across, flipped on the water and ducked from the first cold spray. By the time it warmed to tepid, she was impatient to get back for some cuddling. She hurriedly washed her legs, going carefully over the tender folds of her sex.

She hopped out and dried off, ignored the mirror and simply grabbed an elastic for her hair.

Strolling from the bathroom butt-naked took guts, but she figured what the hell, he'd already seen it all. Seen it, and enjoyed it.

Joel was smoothing the quilt on her bed, his taut ass flexing as he reached to the corner and tucked the material in.

Vicki could have stood there all night admiring the view.

"You ready to sleep?" He asked the question as he pivoted, and this time it was her turn to glance away from what she shouldn't have been staring at. Joel grinned. "Or at least, are you ready to crawl back into bed for a while?"

She eyed the quilt. "You get the...blood out okay?"

He did a Vanna White hand gesture over the surface. "You see anything? Don't worry. I have five brothers, remember? On any given day growing up we had to hide the evidence of us fighting from our ma, and knowing how to get out blood stains was vital."

She could see that. She could also see everything else about him, as he seemed comfortable being naked in front of her. Vicki stepped closer and pressed a hand to his chest.

"I never really got to touch you," Vicki protested. "Although I loved what I did get to touch very much."

Joel pulled the quilt back. "More touching is on the agenda, but we've got time. Come on, get in."

Vicki peeked down at her naked self. "Should I pull on anything?"

Joel's eyes widened. "Not for my sake. I think you're wearing exactly what you should to go to sleep."

She crawled on the bed and shuffled toward the wall. "You sleep in the buff all the time?"

"Saves on laundry." Joel joined her, somehow fitting his bulk next to her. "What are you doing way over there?"

"Yeah, right, this bed wasn't made—*oh*, for a person your size."

He'd caught her around the waist and pulled her tight to his body, tucking them together like two spoons. She wiggled but couldn't go far, not with the weight of his arm over her torso and the slight angle of his hips. He had her well and truly pinned in place, his breath caressing past her cheek.

She wanted to ask him all sorts of things, questions and ideas for other activities they could do sexually and otherwise.

But somehow the warmth of him wrapped so close shoved all her plans to a future agenda. "I had fun tonight, Joel."

And she had. Incredible fun. It wasn't until she was teetering over into sleep she remembered the entire evening hadn't been wonderful.

Amazing what good sex could erase. What a caring touch could move into the less-important list. And like he'd instructed her earlier in the evening, she didn't try to analyze it, just accepted it.

Vicki gave in to sleep, satisfied that the day had finished with far more highs than lows.

Chapter Sixteen

Vicki's breathing slowed as she drifted into sleep. Joel, on the other hand, was wired.

Physical satisfaction had calmed him for a moment, but now there was too much time to think through all the things he should have done differently. Like being far more careful as he took her virginity.

The other day when they'd fooled around he'd suspected she'd told him the truth, but he hadn't been hundred percent sure. Not until tonight. Not only the response of her body, but her face—part of him felt like a shit for taking her innocence.

Another part wanted to stand up and cheer because she'd said what she'd wanted, and he'd listened. That didn't seem to have happened very often in her life.

They had over five months to spend together, and at the end of it, he was sure they would be successful in changing some people's minds about Vicki's reputation. For those who refused to budge from their thinking, well, with her leaving town she could still feel successful.

Only how was he going to keep her safe until she left?

The light from the street lamps sent a dim glow into the small apartment, and he adjusted position until her face was visible. The shadows made it difficult to see if the blue mark on her cheek was a bruise or bad lighting. He'd be making a few inquiries regarding who the hell had been involved in attacking her. Maybe she didn't want to press charges, but knowing why it happened was one step in making sure it never happened again.

And she was never going to be unchaperoned in public around him.

The ass across the way was more difficult to deal with. Joel couldn't see anything that could be done. Getting her to move into his trailer was out. Jesse would never go for it even if it would defeat the purpose of setting a new path. No one would believe Vicki wasn't sleeping with them both.

She rolled, and the bed creaked forebodingly. Joel held his breath until she settled, one palm pressed to his chest. A happy sigh escaped her, and Joel gave up. For tonight there were no solutions, just the warmth and comfort of being there with her.

Tomorrow they'd deal with some of the chaos.

Or at least that was the plan. Unfortunately, morning arrived at about three a.m. He opened his eyes, not sure what had woken him.

It sounded again, metal on metal creaking ominously, and the bed quivered.

Shit.

He scooped Vicki up and attempted to roll to safety, but it was too late. They crashed downward, her body hitting into his with enough force a gasp escaped.

Vicki called out, sleep slowly shaking from her eyes as she blinked hard. "What...?"

The mattress lay at an awkward angle under him, Vicki cradled on top. "I think we broke your bed."

She planted her hands on his chest and pushed, and the final legs gave way, jolting them to the floor.

"Oh..." Vicki changed to a kneeling position, slipping to the side, "...fuck."

Joel sat up, now fully awake. He rolled off the mattress to examine the mess.

The legs had simply folded. Instead of a bed, she now had a mattress layered on top of a pile of twisted metal. "Umm, sorry."

Vicki tugged the blankets around her shoulder as a snort of laughter escaped her. "Don't worry about it."

Their eyes met and they grinned.

She patted the mattress. "I'm glad that didn't happen earlier while we were in the middle of fooling around."

"Me too." He rejoined her, the warmth of her naked skin waking up other parts of his body as well.

Only she yawned and rested her head on his chest, so he ignored his hard-on and held her as she fell back asleep.

Joel peeled himself away in the morning, somehow getting out of bed without taking her all over again.

She reached a hand over the empty spot left behind. "Joel?"

He squatted. Knelt on the floor, really, to reach her. "I've got chores. You come out to the ranch later for your lessons, okay?"

He pressed his lips to her temple, so sleep warm and soft— Damn, leaving her was tough. Now he understood better why Blake was a grumpy ass some mornings.

He dragged on his things from the night before, eyeing his watch on the drive to the ranch. He had enough time to grab a coffee and change so he didn't get his good clothes wrecked.

He slipped into the trailer and pulled to a stop. Jesse rotated from where he was holding up the kitchen counter, coffee pot bubbling away beside him.

His twin looked him over. "Walk of shame, eh?"

"Like you haven't come home wearing the same clothes before." Joel breathed in deep, the scent of caffeine nudging the back of his brain. "You make enough coffee for two?"

"Of course." Jesse cleared his throat. "Everything okay last night? You took off like a shotgun blast."

Joel grabbed the cream and sugar while he waited for the coffee to be ready. "Had a bit of trouble, but it worked out okay."

"Really."

They waited in silence, and it was the weirdest thing. Jesse didn't look too happy. Joel scrambled for a reason. "You pissed because I spent the night with her?"

Jesse shook his head. "I told you what I thought, you told

me. It's none of my business, right? Only..."

Dead silence again.

Awkward, and confusing. This wasn't how it was around Jesse, ever. They were both upfront and honest.

This tension between them was stupid. Joel chose to ignore it, looking instead for a few other answers. "Last night did you hear anyone talking about Vicki?"

Jesse snorted. "Um, yeah."

Asshole. "I don't mean the usual, I mean anything out of the norm." Maybe Vicki wouldn't appreciate him sharing this, but he had to know. "Someone hit her."

Jesse tensed. "Hit her? Like how?"

"Across the face. Some woman called her a whore. That's why I left so fast. She was pretty shaken up."

"Fuck." Jesse stared out the window. "Yeah, some of the guys were talking about the Hansols. Sarah got caught in Mike Lanhott's bed."

"And someone must have mistakenly pointed out Vicki as Sarah." Joel had been right. How the hell could he help Vicki when idiots like that decided to cause trouble? "Whoever it was needs a butt-kicking."

Jesse seemed to jerk himself to attention. He fiddled around as he filled two travel mugs and handed one over. "I asked you before if you knew what you're doing. I'll ask again. This seems like a crazy situation. You really want to get in the middle of it?"

"Damn it, Jesse, enough. I'm in the middle, there's no changing that."

Jesse literally backed off, pacing to the far side of the room. "Fine. Don't bite my head off more than you've been doing. It was just a—"

"What the hell does that mean?" Joel put his cup down and glared at his brother. "When did I bite your head off?"

"Lately? Every time I ask your plans. Or when I suggest we go do something."

"Bullshit."

"Not bullshit." Jesse grabbed his coat. "I'm starting chores. I'll meet you there."

The door slammed behind him as he left.

Joel thought through the past days as he got changed then headed over to the ranch. It was no use, though. He had no idea what the fuck Jesse was moaning about.

It was a couple hours later before he tracked him down, both of them working opposite sides of the chore list until finally meeting. Jesse's odd behavior aside, Joel was frustrated by the menial jobs today. Chores were far more boring when done alone, and he missed having someone to help pass the time. Not that they ever talked much, only there was a rhythm in two people doing familiar tasks.

He found Jesse in the feed room, loading sacks. "Way to hold a conversation there, bro. Walking out gets us to the bottom of things fast."

Jesse shrugged. "You didn't really want to talk. You want to drive to the back to check the breeding stock or deal the sheep?"

"Why don't we do them together?"

"Nope. Don't feel like wasting my entire morning with you."

What the hell? "You've got a mighty big chip on your shoulder, jerk."

Jesse dropped the bag he'd just tied, standing and glaring Joel's direction. "You want to lay off. Trust me on this one, *bro*."

"Tell me what's wrong, asshole."

"You're too busy." Jesse slammed out the door. Again.

What the fuck was his problem? Joel grabbed the sacks from the floor and surged after his twin. He tossed the load in the truck box, twisting to give the conversation another go. Jesse, however, was damn near pouting as he stared into space.

Good grief. "You seriously want to do chores alone?"

Jesse shrugged. "Been doing them that way a lot lately."

Joel thought hard to put that comment into perspective. Nope. He couldn't figure it out. He opened his mouth to find out more when Vicki's motorbike sounded in the distance.

Jesse made a big deal out of rolling his eyes. "Guess your girlfriend is coming to steal you away."

"Grow the hell up, Jesse, and stop being an ass."

"When you stop, I'll stop. How's that for a deal?" Jesse slammed the door of his truck and gunned the engine, heading out way faster than he should. Joel held his breath as Vicki pulled to stop just in time as Jesse shot off the gravel onto the highway ahead of her, cutting her off.

Fucking asshole. Joel grabbed his phone, but Jesse refused to pick up, his phone going to voice mail.

"You try something stupid like that again and I'll beat your head in. What the fuck were you thinking?" Joel jabbed the *end call* button and shoved his phone into his pocket as Vicki pulled to his side.

She caught the heavy bike and set the kickstand, swinging her leg over and jerking her helmet off. "What is his problem? Goddammit, he could have killed me."

A total body shiver took her, and Joel wrapped his arms around her. "I gave him hell. So sorry that happened."

"Not your fault."

But it seemed like it. Guilt smacked him upside the head. Jesse was in a mood, and it felt as if it was his responsibility to get his brother out of it. Just like in the old days.

Only, this wasn't his responsibility, not really. Jesse was acting up, and this time Joel refused to join him, rescue him or otherwise step in until the jerk confessed what the hell was wrong.

But Vicki he needed to take care of, and now. He caught her by the hand, rubbing her cold fingers. "You okay?"

Vicki flushed. "Umm, yeah?"

Their activities of the previous night rushed back in. He looked her over carefully, enjoying the view even as he was honestly concerned. "Sore?"

She cocked out a hip and planted her fists on her hips. "Gee, you should come right out and ask if my hoo-ha hurts. Yes, Joel, I'm a little tender, which is why I didn't appreciate having to basically can myself fighting with the bike as Jesse did his bat-out-of-hell imitation, but I'll live."

"Jesse is an ass."

"No arguments from me." She tugged him toward the barn. There was a first. They were around the corner before she seemed to remember where they were headed. "Umm, horses?"

"Only one," he promised. "Sable is here. Don't worry, we're not going to do any more than you feel comfortable with."

She wrinkled her nose. "Don't think you can distract me with your fingers in my pants today, either. Just saying."

"Oh, if I put my fingers in your pants? You'd be distracted, alright, but we have other plans."

His phone went off. Jesse willing to apologize already? He checked the display. Nope, another of the clan. "One second, Vicki."

She wandered to the nearest railing and crawled up as he answered, part of his mind on the call and the other part on how good her ass looked in those jeans. "Matt? What are you doing up already?"

"I was lying here, lazing in bed, and thought I'd call you."

Fucker. "You have early chores next weekend, asshole. I'll be sure to phone you when I'm in the middle of screaming hot sex…"

Vicki glared and he trailed off. He covered the mouthpiece. "Just kidding."

She didn't look happy, though.

Joel rushed to get off the line. "Matt, what's up? I've got something I need to take care of quickly."

Before Vicki learned where they kept the castrator.

"Hope and I were talking. We checked the weather forecast. If you were serious about wanting to go camping with us, we're heading out tomorrow for a night."

"That soon? I'm okay with it, but I'll have to ask Vicki."

"See if she can get the day off work. Hope's got the shop closed on Mondays, and it looks like this might be the last weekend before the snow flies."

"I'll call you back to get details," Joel promised.

"Much later, okay? Hope's naked and—"

Joel didn't bother to respond, just hung up on his brother and planned subtle revenge for down the road.

Vicki had turned around, elbows hanging over the top railing to hold herself in place. "What do you have to ask Vicki? If that's Jesse wanting me to stand in the middle of the road for a little more target practice, he can—"

Joel snorted. "Not Jesse, Matt. Remember we talked about camping?"

"Yeah?"

"How about tomorrow?"

Her eyes widened. "Umm, seriously?"

"Last chance this season."

She shrugged. "If they let me off at the shop, sure. Why not?"

Joel was surprised how much her quick agreement delighted him. "Awesome. If it works, I'll get the gear together this afternoon. You can help."

"You want me to cook? I can make some stuff up ahead of time."

Okay, now this was officially a good idea. "Definitely. I can pick up groceries with you."

They grinned, Jesse's stupid behavior pushed aside.

He held out his hand again. "Come on. Let's go see Sable."

She peered around the yard. Sable was in the far corral, and Joel had promised that's where the beast would stay, but right now? Vicki was still tired, she was pissed off at Jesse and more tender than she wanted to admit. The combination wasn't a good one. "Maybe we should skip the lesson today."

"Sure."

His instant capitulation made her look up with suspicion. "Really?"

Joel shrugged. "Hey, you've got time. Just, you know, no lesson, no reward."

Sad, how dangling that carrot in front of her nose made her pay attention. Only he'd forgotten one thing. "Well, let's see. Last night I got to experience your mouth on my breasts, oral sex and full-out sex. Maybe I'll be okay skipping the reward today."

He paused, probably going through the list she'd named. "Damn, you're right. I totally messed that up, didn't I?"

She laughed, catching him by the front of his shirt and pulling him closer. "You didn't mess anything up, and you know it."

Standing on the railing gave her enough height to meet him head-on, lips level with his. She slid her fingers into his hair, accidentally knocking his hat to the ground.

Joel moved in closer, pinning her to the rail with his body, careful as he slipped his thigh between her legs but pressing close enough she could enjoy the entire hard length of him.

Insane that a few kisses later she was feeling much better. After so long wanting to experience not just sex, but intimacy, there wasn't anything she could compare this to. Joel did everything so intensely. She loved it, taking his hungry kisses and returning them with enthusiasm.

Something nudged her ribs. She chuckled into his mouth. The man was insatiable, probably going for her boobs again. He'd seemed rather fixated on them the previous night.

Joel spoke in between kisses. "What's...got you...giggling?"

"You're tickling my ribs." She pulled back and glanced down, right at the moment when a blast of heat that shouldn't be there rolled along her arm.

She screamed, leapt off the railing and wrapped her arms around Joel's neck in a frantic attempt to get away from Sable, who had her damn enormous horse nose stuck through the railings, close enough she could have taken a huge bite out of them. Instant terror had Vicki's stomach clutched into a rock-hard knot the size of a football. Her blood raced, deafening her to everything, including whatever the hell Joel was saying.

She knew he was talking because his lips were moving, but the only thing audible other than the rush of blood were her own shrill cries.

He had her around the waist, still pinned to his body, only now he ran toward the barn and away from where Sable—*God*—stood with her head hanging over the railing right where she and Joel had been fooling around.

A huge hand covered her mouth, cutting off her involuntary shouts.

She fought for control, hands clutching him, as fear wiped away all her confidence, blurring the pleasures of the past twenty-four hours. She'd take being smacked around over how she felt at this moment, and that alone made her fight harder to calm herself.

Joel's voice finally broke through. He had her around the corner, out of sight from Sable. His hand covering her mouth slipped off as he knelt and wrapped himself close, his lips against her cheek. He shushed her gently with reassuring sounds that matched his hands moving over her body. Slow pets to her back, circular motions, easy and smooth.

Pulling in gasps of air was stupid, ridiculous, and yet the only thing she could do at this point.

At least she'd stopped screaming.

By the time the shaking calmed, mortification had risen higher than fear. She planted her palms on Joel's chest and pushed so she could escape. Or that was her plan, but the arms that had been gently cradling her turned to iron in a second.

"Don't try to rush away," Joel admonished. "I'm so damn sorry that happened. It was totally my fault, and I feel like a shit you got scared."

Vicki rested her head against him and took a deep, deep breath, letting it out as slowly as possible. "I'm sorry for screaming. What a girl, right?"

Joel shook his head, cupping her face in his big hands. "You have nothing to apologize for. Come on. I'll get you a drink, and we'll relax for a while. See if you can get hold of your boss to arrange a day off for the camping excursion."

Sounded like a good plan, but she didn't want to simply give up. "What about our lessons?"

Joel pressed his lips to her forehead, as if trying to give her something to think about other than demon horses appearing out of nowhere. "Later. We've got time. This is more important right now."

Vicki rose to her feet, reaching to tug him to vertical. Her offer was a token one—as if he needed her help—but he solemnly took her hand.

She leaned against his strong bulk to catch her balance, physically and mentally. It was a good thing spring wasn't just around the corner, because while she'd already mastered a few lessons?

The most important one, well, at that moment success seemed a woefully long way off.

Chapter Seventeen

Packing was done far too soon for Vicki's tastes. "You sure you have enough gear we're not going to freeze?"

Matt stepped past her and dropped a duffle bag into the truck bed. "What is it with you girls? You really think we'd take you into the backcountry and let you die of exposure?"

Hope crossed her arms. "I would say if it suited your plans, you would leave a few blankets behind and be all 'oh, we can share body heat to stay alive'. I know your type, Matt Coleman."

She winked at Vicki, though, before she moved forward to wrap her arms around her fiancé and kiss him thoroughly.

"Stop that. Focus on the task so we can hit the road." Joel transferred another cooler into the back of the truck. "Man, Vicki. It looks as if we'll be eating enough to stay warm, that's for sure."

"Hey, you made the list. I just cooked it."

The whole going-camping thing had rolled forward like a train. Her boss had okayed an extra day off from the shop, and suddenly she and Joel were joining Matt and Hope for a night in the mountains.

She stared at the sky, but it was anyone's guess if the snow would show up early or hold off until they were done this adventure. At least Joel had nixed the idea of using horses and camping on Coleman land as Matt had first suggested. Joel had convinced the others he wanted to hit a site farther from Rocky Mountain House, which meant using a truck.

One bullet dodged.

Getting there ended up rather comfortable and easy. Joel crawled into the back of the crew cab, tucked her to his side and held her hand as they shot the breeze with the two in the front. Matt and Hope made her feel welcome, and she appreciated that so much. Hope's dry sense of humour helped set Vicki at ease, and by the time they were setting up camp, her concerns had faded.

For everything except the actual camping.

She handed Joel items as he asked for them. "We're really going to sleep on something that thin?"

Joel laughed, tugging the air mattress from her fingers and pushing it in to the tent, arranging it carefully. "This from a girl who is currently sleeping on a mattress on the floor all the time?"

"Whose fault is that?" Vicki winked then dodged out of reach when he would have grabbed her.

"I didn't break your bed," Joel insisted.

There was a snort of disbelief from a few feet away where Matt was setting up a second tent.

"Stop listening," Joel called out to his brother.

Matt stood and shook his head. "First, I'm moving our tent farther from yours because you're too damn loud, and if I can hear you now, who knows what we'll be hearing tonight. And second? You broke her bed? Damn..."

"I didn't break her bed. Idiot." Joel threw a tent peg at his brother, but Matt had already grabbed his and Hope's tent by the sides and lifted it in the air.

Vicki knelt beside where Joel continued to work. "You're so bad."

"He's my older brother. It's in the rules I have to torment him on a regular basis." Joel caught her this time, tugging her into his lap. "But I'm glad they moved farther away. He's right. I don't want to listen to them fool around all night."

His hand smoothed upward, stroking along her throat until he held her chin captive, kissing her with lots of tongue thrown in for good measure. Vicki dug her fingers into his hair and went for broke. When he groaned in arousal, she smiled. From never having had a kiss to knowing how to drive him mad, she hadn't done poorly over the past month.

They separated just enough to draw in air. "Maybe they'll be happy not to listen to us all night as well," Vicki teased.

That delicious expression washed over his face, the one that said he had definite plans. "You not sore anymore?"

"Nope." His palm rested on top of her thighs, an innocent enough touch. She wanted him to shift his grasp a little and cup her sex. *Oh shoot.* "Did you bring a condom?"

"Hell, yeah, more than one." Joel glanced over his shoulder. "But stop talking about sex, or there's no way I'll last without dragging you into the tent right here and now."

The food coolers were still in the back of the truck, and neither Hope nor Matt was anywhere to be seen. "Umm, Joel? Where are the others?"

She and Joel fell silent for a bit until a loud laugh gave the answer. Joel grinned. "Damn, they're at it already."

Vicki wiggled her brows. "I think I'm going to like camping."

Only before Joel could haul her into their own tent, Hope popped up, her hair mussed, deep masculine laughter following her. She glanced their direction then rolled her eyes as she turned back to scold through the tent flaps. "Great. Now your brother and his girlfriend think we were fooling around. Nice going."

Matt's head poked out, an ear-to-ear grin shining on his face. "Pay no attention to the mad woman over here. She's in need of a little discipline."

"Matt," Hope snapped. "Behave."

He crowded out of the tent and went after her. "You're in trouble..."

Watching the two of them run and play made something break free in Vicki's heart.

That a couple could have a fun relationship as well as a sexual one—well, she knew about it, but to see it played out before her?

Magical.

A finger stroked her cheek. "What's got you smiling so sweetly?"

She went for honest, pointing across the campsite.

"It's good to see how much in love those two are. Makes me believe in positive things for down the road. That fairytales can come true. Maybe there's someone out there who will love me like that some day." She glanced up and was surprised to see his expression turn serious. "What's wrong?"

Joel shook his head. "Nothing. Just, yeah, you are right." He settled her to the ground and gazed after Hope and Matt. Matt had caught her in a close embrace, kissing her soundly with so much life and energy and sheer happiness in his attentions Vicki smiled even harder.

They got the fire going. It was cold enough even with the thing blazing, Vicki cuddled in tight to his side and still shivered.

"I hope our sleeping bags are good and thick." She shivered again, and he pulled her into his lap, wrapping the quilt around her tighter.

"You'll be warm tonight, I promise."

The way she looked at him with the promise of something else showing in her gaze made Joel have to focus on what they were about right now.

"Vicki, you did a super job with the dinner. Thanks." Hope and Matt were curled up to the right of them, the smoke from the fire drifting to the west away from where they were all huddled. Close enough to speak quietly, and yet not able to see exactly what was going on with the other couple unless they deliberately got up and looked.

"Matt and Joel made the list."

"You cooked. On short notice, I might add." Joel stroked her cheek. "I agree, everything was great."

"Better than the typical beans and hotdogs you told me about?" Vicki teased.

"I'll still make you coffee in the morning," Joel assured her.

Hope groaned. "No. Not Joel's campfire coffee."

"What? What's wrong with it?" Vicki asked.

Matt's laugh rumbled out. "Thick enough to paint the walls. But it'll wake you up."

Comfortable, easy. Such a contrast from the tension in the bar two nights earlier. Joel relaxed against the log they'd hauled over to use as a backrest.

"Well, I appreciate good cooking." Hope tossed a small stick into the fire, making sparks fly. "Funny how I got one of the so-called domestic skills—sewing—and totally missed the others."

"Hush," Matt chided. "You can cook just fine. And so can I. We're not going to starve."

Joel was having trouble concentrating while Vicki drew designs on his chest with her fingertips.

"I learned how to cook young. I hid out in the Home-Ec room during recess and lunch hours," Vicki shared.

She spoke so soft Joel wondered if the others had heard her.

"Did you have Mrs. Underwood for Home-Ec?" Hope asked.

"No. Well, not at first. This was back when Miss Graves was the teacher. I must have been about ten at the time." She spoke a little firmer. "The first couple of times I was...hiding. She was surprised to see me, but she made me a hot chocolate. I still remember that. It was so kind."

Joel sat motionless, willing Vicki to keep sharing. It was the first time she'd talked about something like this. A memory from her past. The total sum of what he knew about her, which wasn't a hell of a lot, hit him.

The girls carried on their conversation while Joel pondered.

"A good teacher makes a huge difference," Hope agreed. "Miss Graves taught me to sew."

"She wasn't even the teacher anymore when I hit Junior High and actually had Home-Ec classes, but she started bringing in little things for me to make during lunch hour, thank God, because there were times that—"

She jerked to a stop.

Times what?

Vicki took a deep breath before continuing. "It was one way to get something to eat for me and my sister Lynn. During the years she was there, Miss Graves probably fed us more than my mom did."

Joel's stomach tightened.

"Hope used to hang out at the boys and girl's club." Matt stared upward as he spoke. His words solemn, carefully chosen. Joel was grateful, because right now he was pretty speechless. "The first time that registered, I was in shock. Like, why had she hung out there instead of at home?"

He twisted to gaze at Vicki. "I hadn't much of a clue not everyone's family was like Joel's and mine. And I had no excuse for being so ignorant. I was involved with Helen at the time."

"Oh, family." Hope sighed. "Wait, let me adjust that ponderous comment. Oh, *my* family member who continues to drive me nuts."

"It's tough, right? Having family that's not family," Vicki whispered.

"Toughest thing in the world." Hope pressed a hand to Matt's face. "Then one day you get a taste of the other side, and figure out why people rave about it."

Silence fell. Joel wasn't sure what he would say, if he did speak up.

They hadn't actually come out and said Vicki's family was a pain. That Hope's family had been a disaster as well. The fact was there, though, hovering.

Joel wanted to apologize for his good fortune in having scored a family that knew something about sticking together, yet that impulse sucked. It was wrong. It wasn't right to try to cast off the good he'd had to make someone else's pain less.

That kind of attitude diminished what his dad and ma had worked for all these years. He appreciated his lot, never wanted to take it for granted, but the contrast—

With every breath it was clearer he had a good thing, and he'd never really noticed until now.

"Look, a shooting star." Vicki pointed skyward, and they all twisted to follow the trajectory.

A welcome peace floated over them, with nothing but the crackle of the fire carrying through the air.

"What did you wish for?" Matt asked Hope, his words soft but audible.

"Nothing doing. If I tell you, then my request won't come true." Hope stroked his smiling face to soften her denial.

"Maybe if you tell me, I can make sure all your dreams come true."

Oh, God. Vicki's heart fluttered at the sheer romanticism of the moment as Hope whispered *I love you* and kissed Matt, right then and there.

In so many ways, this camping trip had been more of a learning experience than Vicki had expected. She turned away from the other couple and gazed into the darkness. The cold wrapped around them, but Joel's arms were warm and gave her a sense of security, real or not.

Vicki hadn't been sure about sharing earlier, but it seemed right. The setting, the people, all of it worked together to make her want to open up. As if they wouldn't consider it a bid for sympathy, but more a statement of reality. Her reality.

She didn't often get to talk about what her life had been like.

Joel's lips nudged her temple. "You ready for bed?"

"What time is it?"

He chuckled. "Doesn't matter. It's dark, and the fire is burning low. We don't run on clocks while we're camping."

Nice. "You've obviously never been to a kids' camp, then. Trust me, you run on clocks."

"What, breakfast at eight, archery at nine? Sounds pretty cushy compared to getting up early in the dead of winter to do chores."

"Try waking at five to suck back a coffee before putting that breakfast together." Joel shuddered under her, and she nodded. "And don't forget, the worst part is after you're done? There's only four hours before lunch is served. Whoever put breakfast and lunch so close together should be shot."

"We'll have breakfast whenever we want it." Hope spoke as she rose to her feet. "Since I don't have to open the shop, I'm sleeping in as long as possible."

"As long as I'll let you..." Matt scrambled up, avoiding her halfhearted swing. "Come on, let's leave these two bed-breakers out here. If we're lucky, we can get to sleep before they start making too much noise."

Joel flashed a finger at his brother. "Whoever makes the most noise tonight gets to crawl out of their warm sleeping bags and make coffee in the morning."

Vicki hid her face for a moment. All this plain talk about having sex embarrassed her. She'd had dirty words and accusations hurled at her when they weren't true. She knew how to deal with that. This was a whole other matter.

Joel stroked her hair as *good nights* were shared, the night air sneaking past them cool and edging toward cold.

"If you'd like to sit by the fire for a while longer, I should add a couple of logs," Joel offered. "Otherwise, I'll put it out and we can call it a night."

If they sat up longer, she'd have to share more. Which wasn't high on her agenda right now. "I'm kind of sleepy."

Joel helped her find her feet. "Mountain air. You're about to get the best damn sleep of your life."

Vicki watched as he stirred the coals and put out the fire. "When I wasn't upset about the horses, or exhausted from the cooking schedule, I did sleep well at camp."

He rocked back on his heels and looked her over, something between sadness and confusion painting his expression. He didn't say anything. Just escorted her to the washhouse, the glow from his flashlight jumping ahead of them on the uneven ground.

By the time she'd brushed her teeth and washed up, she really was feeling sleepy. She pushed open the washhouse door to find Joel leaning on the railing, staring into the star-filled sky, his towel draped around his neck.

It was cold enough there were no bugs flying about the lights.

"By the way, thank you for picking a campground with flush toilets." Vicki accepted his hand, transferring her bag to her other shoulder.

"No problem. Roughing it is fun at times, but having an actual shower in the morning? Bonus. They'll be turning off the water in a couple of days, so we timed it just right."

Vicki nodded before she realized he couldn't see her response in the dark. A yawn escaped her, though, and he caught that.

"You really are tired, aren't you?"

She went for honest. "Tired, but still interested in fooling around. As long as it doesn't take too much energy."

Joel knelt and unzipped the tent fly, gesturing her inside. "I'm pretty sure I can muster up enough energy for the two of us."

Vicki squirmed her way to one side, attempting to make room for him, the swinging flashlight turning the space into a dance-floor lightshow before he clicked it off. "You sure this is a two-man tent?"

He laughed. "This is a four-man tent, darling. Feeling cozy?"

"Good thing I'm not claustrophobic." She slipped her pants off, pausing to wonder what exactly she should be stripping to. It was dark. Like hand-in-front-of-face-and-can't-see-it dark. "Joel?"

His hip bumped her. Or maybe it was an elbow. "Yes?"

She fought the giggles that wanted to escape. "I have no idea where my bag is or the sleeping bag or...anything."

"Hmm, then this could be a lot of fun." A hand brushed her arm, and he wrapped his fingers around her. "Feel your way."

Sounded fun indeed. Vicki stretched out her hands cautiously though. "If I poke you in the eye, it's your own damn fault."

His laughter rang loudly before he muffled it. "I promise not to poke you in the eye."

Oh *jeez.* "You're such a perv, Joel Coleman."

"Well you did offer to do something about my hard-on the other day."

That was enough. Vicki was mortified at the thought Matt and Hope could hear this conversation. "Use that mouth for something better than talk, mister."

He tugged the top of her shirt. "Give me something to sink my teeth into."

Her shirt vanished, her bra went next. She was sure he'd be all over her chest without any delay, but it seemed he had an agenda—*get Vicki naked.*

Which, *hello,* fine with her.

She was equally busy, shoving the fabric of his shirt up, the back of her hands dragging against his chest. Naked skin under her fingers—she couldn't get enough of it, couldn't get enough of him.

She'd just popped the button on his jeans, pausing to cup the heavy erection pressing the front of the material, when he picked her up and laid her on something soft.

Naked skin, cold night. Her nipples were tight from more than being turned on like crazy.

"Should I crawl under the covers?" Her teeth might have rattled.

Heat blanketed her, his breath brushing past her cheek. "I'll keep you plenty warm, darling."

Her lungs seemed impossible to fill. He wasn't crushing her with his weight, just overwhelming her with his presence as he lay over her. Skin to skin, his hips between her thighs.

Then it started. Delightful torment. A whirlwind of kisses to destroy her equilibrium, followed by physical devastation of the best kind.

He slipped away from her lips to nibble along her jaw. A kiss was pressed to the base of her throat before he sucked lightly and had her arching her back, begging without words for more.

Two nights ago she'd been able to see every move before he made it. The advance warning had been wonderful because of her lack of experience. It allowed her to consider, prepare, even anticipate. This was the opposite situation and still perfect. Without being able to see, her skin grew more sensitive, and each caress came out of nowhere, lighting her on fire.

Her breasts ached until he cupped one in his hand, plumping the mound and twirling his fingers over her nipple. If she expected a repeat performance on the opposite side, this time she'd have lost the bet, because it was his mouth she felt next. Or more specifically his tongue, circling in ever-tightening loops until he finally, *finally*, reached her nipple and drew it into his mouth.

Vicki used her hands as well, learning him as much as she could considering he insisted on moving. She dragged her fingers through his hair, caressed his shoulders. When she got creative and rubbed her foot along the nearest thing she could find, a growl-like groan was her reward.

Oh yeah, he had a nice ass, no matter what she stroked it with.

After his joking about blowjobs, she wondered if he would at least ask her to touch his cock this time, but again she was on the receiving end of intimate kisses. Joel rubbed his chin on her inner thigh, the rasp of his unshaven jaw leaving her craving.

And his mouth? Seriously addictive.

"Joel," Vicki whispered in desperation as she tugged his hair. He licked and lapped her closer to the point of no return. She was very aware they weren't alone in the campsite, no matter how far away Matt had moved their tent. "Oh hell, stop. Stop, or I'm going to come."

He dove in harder, ignoring her warning. The resulting pleasure was too much to resist, and her climax hit, a gasp floating from her lips as her limbs shook violently.

Before she'd finished, while her body was still squeezing, Joel shifted position. There was a crinkle of a condom wrapper briefly before his cock nudged between her thighs, just off-center. He adjusted and thrust in all the way.

"Joel." This time a shout escaped—*damn it.*

Once he'd filled her, though, he remained motionless, breathing heavily. When he'd slipped inside, he'd triggered a second wave of pleasure, and white spots floated in front of her eyes.

She didn't care how dark it was. At that moment Vicki swore she'd seen stars.

"Oh darling, that feels so good." A kiss landed on her cheek, his masculine scent twining around them and filling the enclosed space. "You happy?"

"So happy," she whispered back. She squeezed her muscles around his erection. "And you're still hard."

"I think I can do something about that pretty quick." A stroking touch slid up her side past the edge of her breast without stopping. He caught hold of her hand and carried it above her head. "Put your hands together."

She reached up, intending on linking her fingers. Instead he caught her wrists, both of them in one hand, and stretched her beneath him.

It was a different sensation, pinned in place, unable to shift away. Not that she wanted to escape, but the option was now removed. And when he rocked his hips, dragging his cock nearly all the way out, she held her breath.

Lost all the air as he drove forward hard.

Deep and fast he moved, taking her again and again. So different from their previous session of sex where he'd been careful and tender with her. This was a taking.

Pleasure unfurled through her body, the intimate strokes of his cock only one part. His chest rubbed hers, her nipples tightened and her breasts grew heavy with desire. Their breaths mingled, sharp gasps cutting off as they fought for air. Yet the need for each other overpowered basic essentials.

Another blistering kiss surprised her with the demand she open and give to him even as he gave in return. Yet another burst of pleasure was nearly on her, and when he added a twisting motion to his hips, she gasped his name.

He lowered his head to the mattress beside her, heavy breathing echoing in her ear as he slammed in once more then stilled. Inside her, his cock jerked, and she lifted her legs around him, pulling him deep as possible as his orgasm flashed.

Tangled like a pretzel around him, she couldn't find the energy to do anything at that moment. Not lower her legs, not pull her hands free. Just lay and let her racing heart slow, matching speed with the big man who somehow still balanced himself above her.

"Wow." She got the word out on an exhale. It was the only way she could speak.

"Hmm, yeah." His lips touched her cheek again, tender and soft. "I don't want to leave you."

"I'm not going anywhere." The absolute relaxation stealing through her limbs meant she wasn't even sure she had the energy to crawl under the covers properly.

"Give me a second, then we can cuddle up."

He was gone, stroking her arm as he pulled away. He must have dealt with the condom, but how and where—not only the dark but lethargy made it impossible for her to worry about details. She sighed when he rearranged her on the air mattress, tucked her against his body and covered them both with the sleeping bag.

"I think I like camping," Vicki admitted.

"You warm enough?"

She hummed contentedly, sleep sneaking up and dragging her off.

"Yeah, I figured." Joel stroked her stomach, the intimate caress so soft as he slipped his fingers over her skin. "Body heat for the win."

Chapter Eighteen

His nose was freezing.

Joel stared at the roof of the tent and wondered why the material was drooping so badly. Had one of the support poles broken during the night? It was only after reluctantly leaving Vicki's toasty warm body he realized what was up.

He nudged her hip. "Hey, look at the surprise."

She rolled, hair tousled around her head, sleep-filled eyes opening slowly. "If this is one of those kinky sex things, can we do it later?"

Joel lifted her into his lap and cuddled her close as he unzipped the tent fly. "Save the kink for another time. Look."

"Holy shit."

Vicki squirmed upright, her soft ass pressing his groin. Hmmm. Maybe he'd been too quick to say he wasn't going to bring the kink this morning.

She wiggled with excitement. "That's snow."

Everything outside the tent was blanketed with a couple inches of the white stuff. The tree branches were turned into picture-perfect Christmas-card decorations, the marker rocks around the edges of the campsite mushroom-capped.

Icy coldness poured in the door and wrapped around them. Vicki tugged the flannel material closer to her chest. "It snowed, and we're camping. Go us."

"A first time for everything." He kissed the top of her head and gently slipped her back into the sleeping bag. "Curl up for a while. I'll get coffee going, and the rest of breakfast."

She squirmed away, her gaze dropping over him, and he smiled at her expression. Nice to know he was appreciated.

She lifted her eyes, cheeks lightly flushed. "Can I help?"

"Relax. It'll take a while to get things going." Joel grabbed his clothes from where they were scattered around the tent, hauled them on and snuck out before all the heat escaped.

Other than having to brush snow off the picnic table and benches, the layer of white wasn't much of an inconvenience. It gave a fresh, clean feel to the morning, and soon the four of them were sipping coffee and eating the breakfast burritos Vicki'd prepared in foil so he could easily reheat them.

"It changes things, doesn't it?" Hope gestured around them. "Makes everything renewed, in a way. People always say springtime is the fresh start, but I love the snow."

"It's the good memories, that's why." Matt winked. "Come on, we have time for a walk before we head back to town."

Joel enjoyed every minute of it. Holding Vicki's hand as they tromped through the snow. Making snowballs and smacking Matt in the back of the head, as his brother and Hope rounded a corner in front of them.

By the time they were on the drive home, Joel was as relaxed as he'd been in days.

Hope twisted in the front seat to look at Vicki. She cleared her throat. "If it's not too weird, I have a question."

Under his arm, Vicki tensed. "What's up?"

Hope glanced at Matt, who nodded encouragingly. "I've got a bit of a problem, and I wondered if you might help me. You know there's an apartment over top of my quilt shop?"

"That's where you live, right?"

Hope nodded. "Well, I'm there less often than I should be these days. I tend to stay with Matt at his trailer, and yet I don't want to give up the apartment. I don't really want to have some stranger move in above the shop."

Joel held his breath. His little chat on the side a day earlier with Matt had resulted in a solution far quicker than he'd expected.

"I wondered if you'd be interested in taking the second bedroom in the apartment. That way someone will be around who I can trust, and..." Hope sighed heavily. "Okay, maybe it's stupid. Or mean, I don't know which. But to be honest, my sister Helen has been bugging me about wanting to move back into the place. I've told her no a dozen times, but she's not giving up."

Joel shook his head. "Why the hell would she think living with you is a good idea when you're marrying her ex?"

Hope shrugged. "I think we've established something is wrong with Helen. No, she doesn't see why it's impossible for her to move in with me. With us. And maybe this is a cop-out, but I figure it might shut her up if I tell her the room is filled."

Vicki nodded slowly. "I might be interested. It would depend what the rent is. If I can afford it."

Hope hesitated. "Also, I don't want to mess you up in terms of having a place to live. It's only a short-term thing because I'm looking at relocating the shop come the spring. Matt and I will live full time on Coleman land, and having a slightly bigger store is in the books."

"So you only need a roommate until the spring?"

Joel hid his smile. This would work out perfectly. Meant the creep across the hall from Vicki would no longer be a concern, and it was true, Helen was impossible at times. "You're damn patient with your sister."

Hope turned back to face the road. "What choice do I have? Ignore her? She's been better lately, except for this strange insistence she live with me."

Matt spoke up. "Vicki, think it over, but I'd be very grateful if moving doesn't put you out too much. I can help."

Vicki seemed to be holding her breath. "I'm not sure what to say. Thank you."

"We can look at the details when we get home, okay?" Hope rested her head on Matt's shoulder. "I'm too relaxed right now to talk money."

The snow disappeared as they drew closer to Rocky Mountain House and farther out of the mountains. By the time they were on Main Street there was nothing left except a wet slick on the ground.

"Fuck." Vicki jerked upright. "Stop the truck."

Matt pulled over before the next set of lights. "What's wrong?"

Joel stared out the window, trying to see what had her all riled up. "Vicki?"

She already had her door open. "Speaking of pain-in-the-ass family, Sarah just walked past. Or staggered past. Sorry, I need to go."

All the happiness on her face had vanished, her body tight as she slipped from the vehicle and headed down the sidewalk.

Joel tapped Matt on the shoulder. "If you want to—"

"Just go. We'll be here to help if you need it."

Joel scrambled out the door after Vicki, racing to close the distance between them.

Sarah was on her feet, but leaning unsteadily against a wall between shops. Definitely underdressed for the cool temperature, her makeup, which had probably been fancy and fine the night before, made her look more like a raccoon than a sexy woman.

Vicki had her coat off and around her sister's shoulders before Joel had time to react.

"What the hell are you doing?" Vicki planted her fists on her hips. "Don't you ever sleep in your own bed?"

Sarah looked over Vicki before running a gaze up and down Joel, speculation in her eyes. "Whose bed were you in last night, lil' sis? I don't think you slept alone. So get off your virginal high horse."

Joel pressed his coat over Vicki's shoulders, leaping forward to catch Sarah as she stumbled. The fumes coming off her were enough to make his head spin. "Had a few last night?"

Sarah clutched his arm, fingers wrapping around his biceps in far too friendly a manner. "Oh, well, now. Maybe I shouldn't tease my sister about taking you for a ride. You're a sweet cowboy, aren't you?"

"Sarah, you need to go home." Vicki glanced up the street, her teeth set into her bottom lip. "Joel, I hate to ask, but do you think Matt...?"

"Of course." He slipped an arm around Sarah's body to help her to the truck.

Only she didn't go willingly. Or maybe too willing as she pressed herself to his chest and draped her arms over his neck. "I like cowboys."

He turned his face to the side to avoid breathing her in. "Sarah, we're taking you home."

"You can take me home anytime."

Vicki snapped. "You really have no problem making a play for my boyfriend? I mean, shit, Sarah, have at least a little class."

Joel half carried, half dragged Sarah toward Matt's truck as Sarah struggled to get away. "Oh, that's rich, coming from you. You're the original boyfriend stealer in the family."

"Shut up. You're drunk, and you don't want to talk about this right now."

Sarah, however, wanted to do exactly that. "Poor Lynn was devastated when you stole her boyfriend. Silly girl never had anyone before, and you ruined it."

They were at the truck, Sarah continuing to ramble.

"You always fuck things up for Lynn. Got her sent away. Ruined her chances to find a decent guy. You're just a jealous bitch."

Joel was tempted to suggest they drop the woman in a heap and leave her there.

Only Vicki was opening the back door. "Matt, sorry, but can you drive to my sister's place?"

Maybe it was uncharitable, but he was grateful when Sarah passed out completely. Unconsciousness stopped her from groping him, and stopped the steady stream of foul accusations flung at Vicki.

Somehow they got Sarah's limp body into the truck and at the other end of the journey, up the stairs and into her apartment.

Joel carried Sarah as he followed Vicki, the chaos of the

room making his eyes bulge. "Crap, I thought guys were pigs." Oops. "Sorry."

Vicki thrust open a door and swept clothes off the bed to the floor. "Don't apologize to me. I agree completely. Put her down and we can go."

She pulled a garbage can closer to the side of the bed and jerked a cover over Sarah who was already snoring.

"You want to take her shoes off or anything?" Joel asked.

Vicki grabbed him by the hand and physically pulled him from the room. "The only reason we stopped is if she'd collapsed in some back alley and died after I'd seen her I would have felt guilty. What happens from here on is none of my business. Or yours, so just...let's go."

Matt and Hope were silent when they returned to the truck. Matt took them to Vicki's apartment, the ride far more subdued than the happy hours they'd shared that morning.

Vicki sniffed, her face blank as she blinked away tears.

Joel stepped out to help her with her things, but it was Hope who surprised them both. She waited until Vicki's small pile of camping gear was inside the apartment doors, then she swept in and wrapped her arms around Vicki, squeezing her tight.

Vicki stood stiffly for a moment before accepting the hug, her eyes bright with moisture. "Thanks. And thanks for the camping trip, it was awesome."

"Call me, we'll talk about the rental, okay?" Hope waved as she hopped into the truck cab.

Joel took Vicki's things upstairs, making a rude gesture at the asshole across the hall. He hoped even harder it would work out for Vicki to share a place with Hope. He lowered her stuff to the floor before turning to take her in.

It was as if she'd closed off a part of herself. All the warmth and happiness he'd seen over the past day while they'd been camping was locked up tight, and he missed it. He stood without quite knowing what to do. "You going to be okay?"

"Of course." Vicki paced to the window and peeked out

through the slats. She pivoted toward him and forced a smile. "I'm always okay. Thanks for the camping trip. I had fun."

He nodded. "She's not your responsibility."

"I know. I told you that." Vicki shrugged. "Just a bit of a kick in the teeth after the different emotions of the past days. It's nothing I can't work through."

Joel moved in closer. "You want me to stay? We can talk about it."

Vicki met him in the middle of the room and slipped her arms around his waist, tilting her head back to give a glimmer of a real smile. "Oh, you. I'll be fine. You're wonderful, and I had a blast. We can talk later this week, okay? I suppose the horse lessons need to continue."

Joel bent over to give her a sweet kiss.

There wasn't much more to say. "Lessons continue for sure. You're not getting out of them."

She stared across the barn, her shoulders firmly planted against the wall. "Well, I'm good this far."

Joel laughed. "Staying over here isn't going to get you on the horse, not unless you have *loooong* legs."

"Nothing wrong with my leg length," she insisted. Vicki took a deep breath. After her little screaming debacle the last time she met with Sable, she didn't want to embarrass herself again. Still, taking the next steps seemed damn impossible.

"Why don't we stay here for a bit until you're comfortable?"

Hmm, she was learning to recognize that tone in his voice. The slight rasp suggesting sex and pleasure. She lifted her head, wrapped her arms around his neck and accepted his kiss.

And when he lifted her, she folded her legs around him and held on tight.

Suddenly the wall was not just holding her up but him as well as he rocked against her, teasing her body, dragging a response from her as their lips meshed. Wicked *wicked* tongue and snapping bites were followed by soothing caresses.

Getting comfortable? Yeah, she'd pretty much forgotten that there was a horse in the building.

Someone cleared their throat.

Joel dragged his lips off hers, leaning their foreheads together. "You know, there's not *usually* a revolving door on this barn."

Vicki laughed. "So you've said. I don't believe you. Now let me down."

Maybe she should have felt embarrassed to be caught fooling around with him, *again*, but what the hell.

This time Jaxi stood waiting. Her coat was buttoned at the top, the bottom flaring around her distended belly. "So, now that you're finished for a bit... Or, do you want me to come back later?"

"Shut up, Jaxi," Joel stated calmly, no vinegar in the words.

Jaxi grinned.

Vicki stepped forward, tucking herself in front of Joel. "What's up? Do you need help with something?"

Jaxi lifted her hand and displayed a pair of boots. "If you're interested, I have an extra pair. I think they might fit you— you're a six?"

Vicki nodded. Finding boots had become a nightmare. "How did you know?"

Joel snorted. "Jaxi knows everything. Didn't you get the memo?"

"Smartass." Jaxi held them forward. "Mary at the thrift shop mentioned it to me when I was in finding stuff for the girls. If the boots fit, take them."

Vicki was torn. "But..."

Joel accepted the boots from Jaxi then pressed them against Vicki's hands. "You need them to be safe when you ride. Don't turn them down."

"He's right." Jaxi nodded. "I'm surprised Joel didn't ask sooner. It's not safe to ride in your runners."

She gave Joel such a dirty look Vicki felt guilty. "We haven't been out riding yet. But thank you, I really appreciate it."

Jaxi nodded, eyeing the two of them. "Well, I guess I'll head back and rescue the girls from being spoiled rotten by Gramma."

Vicki was watching her face, so she saw the moment happen. Jaxi's eyes widened and her hand snapped to her belly, a gush of air exploding from her lips.

Joel stepped forward, reaching for his sister-in-law's arm. "Jaxi, you okay?"

"Fuck." Jaxi glanced down.

Vicki spotted the wetness darkening her maternity pants. "Oh shit."

"I should have known today of all days, this would happen." Jaxi blew out a slow breath. "Joel, go get Blake."

Joel hauled out his phone, but Jaxi shook her head. "He drove to the southwest fields this morning."

"Shit, no reception." He kissed Jaxi on the forehead. "I'll find him. You hang in there."

"Hanging." She grimaced and shifted her bulky stomach. "Send him straight to the hospital."

Joel was nearly at the barn door. "Vicki, take care of her."

Oh God. He was gone, and she was alone in the barn with a horse and a pregnant woman who didn't like her much.

Jaxi squeezed out another groan. "Okay, honey, it's all you and me now. You got a cell phone?"

Vicki nodded, stepping forward to offer an arm. "Call the ambulance?"

"Yes, but first, help me get to the bales over there."

Jaxi gestured toward the middle of the barn, and Vicki's throat closed. Her breathing sped up.

"Across from Sable's...?" She fought her fear, forced herself to wrap an arm around Jaxi and move slowly toward their target. She ignored everything but the piled-up bales. "You planned on having the baby today?"

"Been having what I thought were Braxton Hicks all night. Guess I was wrong. I might have done this before, but nothing feels the same." Jaxi sat gingerly. "If you can call the ambulance and maybe grab a couple blankets from the tack room—*oooh*, that one hurt."

Jaxi grimaced, rubbing her hands slowly over her belly. Vicki wanted to help her, but couldn't seem to focus on more than one task at a time.

First: Call ambulance.

Vicki pulled out her phone as Jaxi leaned back on the bale behind her, eyes closed, face tight with pain.

She couldn't get the in-labour woman to make the call. Vicki punched in 911 as she kept an eye on Sable. The hairy beast stared at them, her head hanging out the front of the stall. Vicki swallowed past the bitter taste in her mouth and hurried to the back of the barn, sliding along the wall as far away from the horse as was humanly possible.

The very efficient person on the other end got their location, and then wanted Vicki to stay on the line.

Hell, no. "I'll call you back."

Hanging up on emergency services might not be kosher, but she could not keep talking. Only the fact she'd made it into the tack room had stopped another panic attack from setting in, and no one wanted to be on the phone with a shrieking maniac.

The slightly cooler air was calming, reassuring. Vicki dragged in deep breaths and willed her heart rate to slow. Like Joel had mentioned before, the scent of leather became a balm, returning her to the fun times and the caring he'd given her while they'd practiced with the saddle.

If she could have stayed hidden in that room forever, she would have. But Jaxi still sat alone in the barn, and there was no way Vicki could abandon her.

She screwed up her courage, nabbed the requested armload of blankets and hurried from the room.

Ignoring Sable was the only way to survive. Vicki stormed past her and laid a blanket on the open bale beside Jaxi. "I called the ambulance and thought of something else. What's your mother-in-law's number? She'll have to direct the driver, and we should warn her so she's not scared to death by an emergency vehicle arriving in the yard unannounced."

Jaxi eased herself to vertical. "Damn, I'd forgotten that. Good idea."

"Wait," Vicki ordered. "Sorry, but you've got straw on your ass."

She brushed it off before helping Jaxi back down onto the thick padding of the quilt she'd found.

"Trust me, I've had straw worse places." Jaxi gave her the number, and a whirlwind of activity ensued. Vicki reassured Mrs. Coleman, arranged for the little girls to stay with her, then reconnected with emergency. She followed their directions, which mostly meant supporting Jaxi who didn't seem to need much reassuring anymore.

"This baby has got to be a Coleman male." In the slight calm post-contraction, Jaxi released the grip she was using to squeeze the bones in Vicki's hand to pudding. "Stubborn, bad timing...he's coming out the chute like I expect he'll go on."

Vicki wasn't sure what to do, laugh or be overwhelmed by everything happening. "Boy or girl, healthy is all that matters."

Only please, not until the ambulance gets here.

She thought that last part, proud she managed to not say it.

When the paramedics came rushing in the door, the sense of relief was nearly enough to take her to her knees. "I'll call Joel. He might be in range again."

"Tell Blake he'd better hurry. This kid is not taking his sweet time." Jaxi smiled weakly around an emergency attendant. "Thanks for holding my hand."

"No problem."

The blur of motion continued, but it moved away from her. Others took her place in reassuring Jaxi, the paramedics helping her to the ambulance.

Vicki was left alone in the barn, and the sudden quiet

echoed.

She took a deep breath, calming her heart before pulling out her phone. Nothing but Joel's voice mail. He must be in that dead-air zone they'd mentioned.

"Joel? Jaxi's headed for the hospital. Hope you find Blake in time." She wasn't sure what came next. "Um, call me when you get the news. Fingers crossed things go well."

She hung up feeling incredibly—awkward?

Left out?

It wasn't as if she and Jaxi were such bosom buddies that she should have jumped in the ambulance with her. Yet the sensation of being an outsider had never been clearer than at that moment.

For all the lovely gestures of borrowed boots, and passionate kisses, the Colemans had something she didn't. That she got to experience a little of it on the sly—she wasn't sure if her temporary involvement was a good thing or a bad thing.

Hope's comment earlier in the week about *real family* stabbed like a blade. Seeing what family meant, but not truly being a part of it, made Vicki's heart hurt more than when she'd never experienced the joy.

She plopped back down on the bale with the blankets and stared across at Sable's stall. Just her and the horse left, and even the horse fit in better than she did.

She picked up the blankets and returned them to the tack room, shaking off the bits of straw carefully to avoid thinking things through.

Alone. Like usual. Like always.

This time it burned.

Chapter Nineteen

Vicki wasn't returning his calls. Jesse was avoiding him. Altogether the last couple days had been one bucket load of crap after the other.

Although there was something to celebrate. Not only was the Six Pack clan rejoicing in the arrival of the newest Coleman, there was a new reason to tease Blake.

The baby was another girl.

Blake had been astonished. Jaxi just smiled and held the swaddled bundle to Joel when he dropped in for a visit.

He sat next to Jaxi, the soft flannel quilt wrapped around the baby barely leaving room to see her face. "So, Blake. You like pink or something?"

"Of course I love pink. I adore it. It's totally my favourite colour. I'm going to paint the barns pink next time around." Blake laughed along with the others, laid his hand on Jaxi's shoulder and leaned in for a kiss. Then he stood and shook a finger in her face. "Whatever happened to following in my grampa and daddy's footsteps? Having six boys, all that."

Jaxi shrugged. "Hey, you're the one who has to hand over the boy genes. I can't do much if you don't provide the building blocks."

Joel stroked his finger over the baby girl's cheek, amazed at how perfect and tiny she was, little lips pulsing. Nose wiggling. "I don't know why you'd want a boy when she's so beautiful."

Blake growled. "Wait. I'm going to have three girls in their teens at the same time."

"You won't ever put your shotgun away. Just clean it every time the boys come to call. Worked on us with Stacey Walker."

Yeah, that part of the past few days had been incredible.

The rest of it? Sucked.

"You going to keep moping over there or get your ass in gear?" Travis popped past him, a bundle of energy. He cracked a stick against Joel's legs. "More action, less daydreaming."

"What the hell is your issue today? You've been a jerk all afternoon."

"I'm giving back what you're giving me." Travis dragged his hand through his hair. "Okay, that wasn't fair. Yes, I'm pissed off, only not at you, but you're not helping matters."

Joel shoved his gloves in his pocket. "Go ahead and give me hell. What did I do this time?"

"You're moping," Travis repeated. "You in shit with your girl?"

"Not sure. She's not talking to me."

"Oh, great. Yeah, that's a super way to solve problems, I got one of those as well."

Joel eyed his brother. "You and Ashley have a fight?"

Travis paused. "Actually, it's Cassidy who's being a jerk."

That was unexpected. Joel thought back over the past weeks, and couldn't remember seeing Travis's buddy since the summer. "I thought he'd moved out of town. At least, I haven't seen him around in forever."

"Exactly." Travis grabbed a sack from the wheelbarrow and placed it into position while they talked. "He gave me hell a while ago, and I thought he was joking, but the ass took off for real."

"Sad. Stupid, too, like you said. Not talking about troubles doesn't make things better." Joel passed him another sack. "Vicki's probably just busy."

"Not a good reason to let her stew." Travis glanced over. "How are things going with her? I mean other than she's not talking to you."

Joel had thought they were going great. "Hell if I know."

"She ever tell you about..." Travis shook his head. "Never mind."

"What?" Joel jerked to a stop. "You can't make that kind of comment then cut off. Spill."

"Just wondered if you ever talked about what happened in high school. With Eric Tell."

The mysterious Eric question. "Nope. Although her sister mentioned something the other day in passing about Vicki stealing someone's boyfriend, which I think is total bullshit."

Travis brushed his hands clean as he led Joel from the barn. "I'm not going to tell you."

"Asshole." Joel shoved Travis's shoulder. "Why'd you bring it up, then?"

"Because if she had told you, I was going to tell you something else, but if you notice, I don't share other people's secrets. So get your act together and ask her."

Joel still felt like poking Travis, but it was true. Travis was the tightest mouth son-of-a-bitch around. "Since what you're doing is not helpful, bringing up topics then not explaining what's going on, any real suggestions for how to get Vicki to give me a call?"

"Set a date and tell her you're taking her. Show up. You know where to find her, right?"

Easier now than before. "She's just moved into Hope's apartment."

"Bring her out for the night with me and Ashley, then. We can relax and get your girl to forget whatever stupid thing you did."

"Hey, who said I did something wrong?"

Travis grinned. "You're a guy. Means you had to do something wrong. Accept it, and life gets easier."

Vicki couldn't hide any longer. She'd started this façade for one main reason, learning to deal with the stupid horses. It wasn't Joel's fault the other things she'd asked him to help with were making her crazy. She still had to deal with her fears. Calling things off would be insanity.

But she wasn't going to let herself fall into thinking anything was real. No sir, that wound had been cut open and flayed the other day. This was about what she could get. What she *needed* to learn in the next while.

Warm fuzzy feelings didn't belong.

Sexual pleasure was fine. Competence with horses, fine. Even moving in with Hope made sense. It wasn't hurting anyone, and not only did it help Hope, it was a good deal for Vicki since her portion of the rent was lower than she'd been paying. Hope wasn't likely to be around very much at all.

So when Joel called with the news they were going out with Travis and Ashley, Vicki didn't argue.

"No horses, right?"

Joel helped her into the truck, squeezing her fingers. "You've been avoiding me to get out of the lessons, haven't you?"

Vicki jumped at the excuse. "You're right, I've been afraid to go back. I have to keep trying, though."

"I have some good ideas for over the next couple of months that I think will help."

Not real. Not real. Vicki focused as hard as possible on the prospect of becoming comfortable with the beasts and ignored the caring implied in his tone of voice.

Joel grimaced. "I got asked a couple times if we'd broken up, so I guess the gossip chain is still hot on our radar. Which, you know, it's not a bad thing to have them wondering."

Vicki stared, kind of shocked. "Why would it be good for people to think we'd broken up?"

He grinned. "Because that means they thought we were really together in the first place, get it? And now when they see us doing things over the next while, another set of gossips will hopefully get bored and just move on."

"What are we doing tonight?" He had her tucked beside him, warmth bleeding over her so addictively.

"Going exploring, then having a campfire. Just hanging out."

197

They met Travis and Ashley in the Coleman yard. Vicki smiled at Ashley. The other woman had on faded jeans and bright red cowboy boots, her thick winter coat a total contrast to the tight things she'd worn on the dance floor. "Nice jacket."

Ashley ran her hands over the puffed-out pockets. "Down. It's so comfy. Warm and yet soft. Feel."

The other woman grabbed Vicki's hand and duplicated her move of a moment ago. Vicki wasn't sure what caught her attention more, the velvety texture of the fabric, or the fact Ashley had basically pressed Vicki's hands to her boobs.

Travis's gaze darkened as he peeled his gaze off his girlfriend. "If we're ready to go, one truck or two?"

"One." Joel pulled Vicki back to his side. "Mine. Come on, pile in."

She'd had a good time with Matt and Hope two weeks earlier. This was fun of a whole different kind. Joel headed for the river, but at the last moment he took a side trail, turning away from the water and over hilly terrain.

Wheels skittering, engine roaring, they raced down a back lane and directly into the trees.

Vicki held Joel's thigh with one hand, the other pressed against the dashboard to stop from rocking too hard.

In the back, Ashley hooted with delight. "Woohoo, glad you've got good shocks, or I'd be out the window by now."

Travis laughed. "Do up your seatbelt, idiot."

The radio roared. Everyone sang along. Wild passion, high-beat energy raced through Vicki. A night to take whatever came her way. This wasn't about anything except having a good time.

"Stop," Travis ordered.

Joel slammed on the brakes and skidded to a halt, the massive trees overhead closing in like a cathedral. "What you see?"

"You're not going to believe it." Travis was out the door and climbing the limbs of a nearby tree.

Joel rolled down his window, laughing the entire time. "What the hell are you doing?"

Vicki unbuckled so she could lean across Joel's lap and watch as well. Joel took advantage of her position to pull her closer and tuck his face against her neck. "Hmm, you smell good."

"Let me go." She squirmed, but he kept her pinned in place, adjusting her hand so it rested over his groin. He hardened under her touch. Well, that was a nice development. "Or, maybe don't let me go."

Ashley leaned out the back window. "You need a hand? I thought guys peed on trees, not in them."

Vicki snorted.

Travis climbed down one-handed, something shiny clutched in his other. "For that, you get last sip."

Joel swore lightly. "You're kidding me. Is that what I think it is?"

Travis brandished the Mason jar like it was a fine bottle of wine. "Coleman Moonshine, circa 1900."

The golden-tinged liquid rolled in the three-quarter-full glass jar. Vicki stared in amazement. "You found a bottle of moonshine in a tree?"

Travis gestured Ashley out of the way and crawled back in the truck. "You've never heard of the Coleman Moonshine wars?"

Joel snorted. "You make it sound big and impressive."

"It's local history. They should teach this in school," Travis insisted.

They broke out from the edge of the trees and Joel pulled to a stop. "Let's get the fire going then you can spin your tale."

The landscape had changed, and the place was perfect for a bonfire. In front of them was a small hill, the sandy soil eroded away to make a safe spot to build the fire. As the flames grew higher, the light reflected off the golden white of the hill and made all of them glow with a magical gleam.

Joel had the tailgate down, cooler with drinks and snacks pulled to the side. Thick picnic blankets spread on the ground, Vicki climbed into Joel's lap.

"Ready for my story, Travis," she teased.

Ashley had him wrapped around her, his legs extending on either side of hers as the two of them sat on their own blanket beside the flames.

"Great-grampa Stan and Great-grampa Peter were the two brothers who established the Coleman land. That's why we have the two houses on our property. Stan lived in the one our folks use, and Peter built where Blake and Jaxi live. But before they settled down?" Travis whistled. "The stories my dad passed down said the two of them were quite the troublemakers."

"And this is surprising...why? Sounds as if the family genes breed true to this day."

"Smart-ass." Travis kissed Ashley soundly before continuing. "One of the things they did that we don't was brew their own liquor. Which was fine when they were making hootch to stretch out their money. But they had a bad habit of getting drunk, having a fight then hiding the night's production."

Joel stroked Vicki's legs, starting a lovely anticipatory tingle. "Since their still was far back on the property to keep it hidden, the jars got tucked in all sorts of places, and over the years we've slowly found them. Some broken, some intact."

"Most of them are on Moonshine land, which is why it got that name."

Ashley reached for the jar. "Can you still drink it?"

Travis took it from her. "Ah, ah, ah...careful there, sweetheart. That's way stronger than you can handle."

Ashley's response was to laugh out loud and wrap her arms around his neck, kissing him wildly.

Travis somehow kept hold of the jar without dropping it.

Behind her, Joel was laughing as well. "You want to try a sip?"

Vicki gaped at him. "You're not serious. Isn't it like drinking lighter fluid or something?"

Joel shrugged. "Not sure, never drank lighter fluid. I had some moonshine from a jar Daniel found once. It wasn't particularly smooth going down, but it sure warmed me the hell up in a hurry."

She straightened up. Why not? "Sure, I'd love to try some."

Ashley had wrestled the jar from Travis, straddling his thighs as she worked the top. "Stronger than I can handle. Sheesh, I handle you just fine, don't I?"

He waited as she struggled to get the top open, the smirk on his face growing by the second. When she realized he was silently mocking her, she pressed the unopened jar against his chest. "Here. Make yourself useful."

"Don't move." Travis reached around her, twisting the lid. The metal circle around the outside slipped off, leaving the sealed glass top behind. Travis worked the edge and the *pop* was audible across where Vicki sat.

"Ready?" Ashley glanced over her shoulder.

"Let me try it first," Travis warned.

He sniffed the amber liquid, blinking hard. "I hope I have teeth left after this."

Travis raised the jar to his lips and took a small sip, swallowing quickly and gasping out a choked breath.

"That good?" Joel asked.

He hadn't stopped stroking her. Vicki wished it wasn't dead-on winter so he'd be touching bare skin instead of petting her over her clothing. Inspiration hit, and she tugged up her jacket and shirt, pressing his hand to her belly.

She'd forgotten his fingers would be cold.

Her gasp of surprise made Ashley laugh. "You haven't even had a sip, and you're squealing?"

Something about the other woman's attitude made Vicki go for broke and answer a lot more boldly than usual. "Joel's got cold hands."

"Nice." Ashley winked. "That can be a lot of fun. Ice cubes, things like that."

Travis nudged Ashley. "Stop making the girl blush. You want some?" She reached for the jar, but he held it out of reach. "You didn't answer me."

Ashley leaned away, her hands demurely linked behind her. "Yes, please."

It was such a rapid change in her demeanor Vicki blinked in surprise.

Travis nodded, then put the jar back to his mouth and took another sip. Ashley rocked forward and pressed their lips together.

Something wild raced down Vicki's spine. Ashley swallowed, Travis hummed in approval then they both moved on to kissing, flashes of tongue turning Vicki's spectator status into something hotter than she'd imagined.

"You like that?" Joel took advantage of where she'd placed his hand, sliding his fingers farther up to trace along the underside of her bra. He made a disgruntled noise as he attempted to budge the material and got blocked by the underwire.

Vicki laughed. "Yes, I like *that* very much, and I'd love to try it. But first, give me a minute."

She reached behind her and unsnapped her bra. A wildness in the air tonight made her lose her inhibitions. Without even a drop of liquor in her, she was tightly wound and on edge, as if something momentous was waiting to happen.

She leaned away from Joel and slipped her hand up her sleeve, pulling her bra strap past her elbow, out the sleeve and over her hand. One more wiggle and she had hold of the opposite strap.

Normally she would have completely removed her bra out a sleeve, but this time she didn't think swinging the material like a double-barreled slingshot was a good thing, no matter how cocky she felt. Instead she straightened and gave Joel a wink. "There, you can slip it off now."

Joel tugged experimentally, his eyes widening as he pulled the cups from her body and out the gap at her waistline.

"That's a nice trick." He lifted the fabric and shocked her by stroking it over his cheek. "It's still warm from your body."

Oh jeez. "Put that down."

Too late. Travis stood next to them, Ashley watching from her spot on the blanket with bright eyes.

Travis didn't say anything. Just grinned, his gaze trickling over Vicki. He held out the jar and waited until Joel took it from him.

Vicki ignored the flash of heat storming her face. Flushing her chest, making her now-uncontained breasts ache. Joel copied Travis's earlier actions. Filled his mouth with liquid then turned, cupping the back of her neck and pulling her forward until their lips met.

Kissing him was like stepping into an inferno. Flames scorched her throat while his tongue slammed in and he stole her breath. Nothing could have prepared her for the burn or the bliss, because his tongue cooled the pain and stoked the fire at the same time.

The head rush was wild to experience, but it was touching Joel, kissing him, that was the real highlight of the moment.

When they broke apart, her head was spinning slightly and she wasn't sure what had caused it. "Oh yeah, that packs a punch."

Joel nuzzled her neck. "My kisses or the hootch?"

"Definitely the hootch," Vicki teased.

Travis retrieved the jar. "I'm cutting us off." He tweaked Ashley's chin as she muttered a complaint. "I know, such a bore, aren't I? There's nobody going blind while I'm in charge. Switch to the liquor we brought with us."

She nodded, clambering to her feet and racing to the truck where she leaned in the open window and turned up the music. The song about a redneck yacht club wasn't very seasonally appropriate, but it made Vicki smile.

Travis distributed beers, and singing along with the radio resumed. Small talk, easy company. Laughter rose as their conversation veered into stories about Joel and Travis as they grew up and played fast ones on their older brothers.

Vicki sipped her beer slowly, not sure how she would react after the moonshine. The erotic background created by the flickering of the fire and Joel's constant caresses drove a rising need in her core.

Travis and Ashley were more obvious about the petting they were doing. The other woman's coat gaped open to show she had only a shimmering camisole under the thick covering. Travis kissed her often, catching hold of her head and interrupting the conversation whenever he wanted. His hands controlling her.

Vicki swallowed, her heart beating faster than it should. Joel nuzzled her neck, and she would have given anything to be back in her apartment. Or in the tent, or anywhere private for that matter.

Ashley hopped up on the tailgate, swaying her upper body to the music. "Come on, Vicki, let's dance."

She found her footing, hips moving in time with the heavy beat in the song. Vicki watched for a moment, unsure what to do.

Joel stroked her again, his thumb slipping over her nipple and making the hair at the back of her neck stand upright. "Your decision. You don't have to do anything you don't want to."

All her deliberations from earlier in the week, after the incident in the barn, rushed back in. About how she was leaving in the spring and this entire relationship was a sham. She had to protect her heart, not set herself up for more pain.

This was time for casual fun. Nothing permanent about this situation. Why not dance? There were only the two guys. It wasn't as if she were stripping in front of an entire club.

She pushed off the blanket and bounced up, swaying in surprise for a moment as her balance went out of kilter.

Joel caught her with one hand. "Whoa, you okay there, darling?"

She lifted her chin. "I'm more than okay."

Vicki leaned over and kissed him, letting her hands explore his groin as their lips meshed. Yeah, he was already excited. Good thing, because she sure didn't want the sexual buzz of the evening to be hers to experience all alone.

She slipped his grasp and backed away with a wink. "I need some dance time to warm me up."

"I'll warm you up," he growled, but she was out of reach, hoisting herself onto the tailgate with Ashley's help.

"Nice." The other woman swayed, spinning her hips toward the guys and glancing over her shoulder at Travis. "Let's see how long they last before we find ourselves being hauled off for a little ravishing."

Ashley had leaned in close, the words whispering out, her sweet cinnamon breath brushing Vicki's cheek.

"This is a game?"

Ashley ran her hand down Vicki's forearm and slipped their hands together so she could squeeze her fingers tight for a second. "Honey, life's always a game of some type. The rules are win, and have fun while winning. Simple. Right?"

The pulse in the music echoed through Vicki's body. "Yeah, I guess so."

The blonde at her side stepped away and got into the dance, staring down at Travis with a challenge as she swung her hips and slid her hands up her torso.

All that was caught in a second's glance before Vicki turned to see what Joel was doing.

Oh my. He'd eased himself back in his chair, long legs stretched in front of him. The erect state of his cock was easy to see as it pushed the fabric of his jeans. He had a thick sweater on, so there was no way to enjoy the intimate sexiness of his torso, although, *sweet mercy*, the man was built, that much was obvious even through his layers.

Joel lifted his hands and linked his fingers behind his head, his gaze drifting over her.

She was suddenly at a loss as to what to do. "Umm, Ashley? I don't...?"

The other woman swayed to her side, wrapping an arm around her waist even as she kept time with the music. "What's happening, you need a dance lesson? You were doing fine the other day. Just loosen up. Feel the music."

Ashley stepped behind her and put her hands on Vicki's hips. Vicki was simultaneously more tense and more relaxed. With Ashley's help she'd found the beat again, the two of them pressed together and swinging their hips.

But the heat in Joel's eyes when Vicki glanced his way stirred something inside and made her body ache in places that had no right to be turned on. Not when she was basically in another woman's arms. Even though it was Joel Vicki focused on, his eyes locked on where Ashley's hands clutched her.

It should have felt like cheating. Heck, if she'd been dancing this close with another guy in front of her date, she'd have considered it over the line.

This time, seeing Joel adjust in his chair, easing his hips to the side, she didn't think she was in trouble. Not yet. And that pissed her off. A lot.

They were supposed to be boyfriend and girlfriend, but a little girl-on-girl action was okay with him?

Maybe the moonshine had been a lot more potent than she'd imagined because all of a sudden all she could think of was taking this to the next level. She'd gotten her first kiss from Joel, her first of just about everything.

But there were some firsts he couldn't give her, right?

Only a good time, nothing permanent.

She leaned harder on Ashley, reaching a hand around to catch hold of the other woman.

A long, low moan escaped as Ashley returned the favour, sneaking her hand off Vicki's hip and onto her belly. "That's it, I thought you'd like this. Come on, honey, shake your hips. Yeah, now raise your hands and drape them around my neck."

Vicki obeyed so mindlessly she wasn't sure what had come over her. Joel stared, every muscle gone rigid.

"You're driving him crazy," Ashley whispered in her ear, right before what had to be lips pressed to her neck.

Vicki shivered, her body arched as she let her head fall back on Ashley's shoulder. "I think I'm a little insane. What the hell are we doing?"

"Winning the game, honey. Trust me, your guy needs a kick in the butt right now. If I'm not wrong he's about ten seconds from storming over here and hauling you away like you're his prize possession."

Was that what Vicki wanted? To be claimed?

God, *yes*, but it was the wrong answer. She wanted so desperately to belong, and the longing had to be fought with everything in her. She twisted in Ashley's arms, her breathing unsteady as she stared at the other woman, their bodies still touching.

One way to make this clear. It seemed so logical. She'd take charge of her own sexual education from here on. Starting with—

Starting with...

Ashley's eyes were wickedly dark as her pupils and irises blended together into one mesmerizing mass. What Vicki was considering *was* insane, maybe even stupid. This experience had never been on her agenda, but somehow she found herself craving it as she leaned forward and kissed Ashley.

Warm mouth, soft lips. The contact was...thrilling. Not as overwhelming as Joel's kiss, there was no comparison, but the sweetness was delicious. And when Ashley slipped her tongue along Vicki's lips, she opened without a complaint, the kisser now becoming the kissee.

So many sensations overwhelmed her senses. Ashley's body pressed closer, all curves and gentle slopes. Vicki snuck her fingers up and along the smooth skin of Ashley's neck as their tongues brushed. Ashley rubbed their hips together, and Vicki moaned, desire rising fast.

She'd barely had time to register that Ashley tasted faintly like watermelons when big hands wrapped around her waist and she was jerked from the kiss. The other woman winked saucily, licking her lips.

That's all she saw before the view changed and Vicki realized she was in deep shit.

Chapter Twenty

Joel didn't say a word. He'd watched the dance progress and wondered what the hell the girls were up to until he couldn't hold back any longer.

Not only was he achingly hard, he was fucking pissed off. Vicki didn't seem to get the idea of this whole deal between them, and like *hell* was she going to fool around with anyone, guy or girl, while they were a couple.

Possessiveness had never been an issue for him before, but right now he wanted to stamp her with his brand and make it abundantly clear the only person doing any touching, kissing or otherwise, would be *him*.

Out of the corner of his eye he spotted Travis approaching Ashley, but he had more important things to do than pay attention to his brother. He lifted Vicki into the air and spun her, a little squeal escaping her lips.

Her lashes fluttered for a moment before she glanced away.

"Hell no, you don't get to pretend you didn't do that on purpose. Look at me."

Vicki lifted her gaze until her eyes were just visible through her lashes, her chin still tucked down.

Going to play that game, was she? Fine, he could give her what she needed as well as teach her a lesson even if she continued the shy schoolgirl ploy. "Wrap your legs around my waist," he ordered.

Vicki moved quickly, her hands on his shoulders clutching tighter as he jogged to the right of the fire where the rock face showed through the hillside. He pressed her back to the smooth surface, and her eyes popped wide as he ground his erection over her clit.

"Joel, I—"

He swallowed her excuses. As he ravished her mouth, the faint taste of another person made him want to mark Vicki five ways to Sunday. He tugged her coat aside at the waistline and snuck his hand upward. Naked breast filled his palm and he let his growl of satisfaction escape.

He wasn't done kissing her, but needed more. He dragged their mouths apart, hoisted her higher in the air. Vicki caught hold of his head, balancing herself as he shoved up her shirt and in one move took her nipple into his mouth.

"Oh *God*, Joel." Vicki fisted her fingers, pulling his hair. She wasn't hauling him off her, but keeping him close.

He sucked hard, laving his tongue over her nipple until she whimpered. Slow wasn't happening, not tonight. Joel broke off, lowered her feet to the dirt and reached for her zipper. "Off. Get them off."

Vicki had her lower lip between her teeth. "Strip?"

He squeezed her ass. "Right here, right fucking now."

She lowered her zipper, glancing over his shoulder.

"Don't look at anyone but me." Joel yanked one side of her jeans down, panties going with it. The heat off her body made something inside crack. "I'm the only one you need to worry about, got it? Stop thinking about the others and focus on us. On *me*. I'm the one who's going to fuck you until you can't walk."

That wide-eyed-doe look did something to him. For a split second he worried he'd gone too far before he noticed her breathing had kicked up a notch, and she was clutching his sweater to keep him close, not push him away.

Everything else vanished but the driving need to be inside her.

He whipped a condom out of his pocket and pressed it to her palm. Vicki swallowed, crowded as she was between his body and the rocky outcrop. Joel slammed down his zipper and hauled out his cock, the erect length hard and more than ready.

Condom wrapper abandoned to the ground, he rolled the

latex on before focusing his attention on his now-silent girlfriend.

She had one leg still in her jeans, the other bare. He was fully dressed but for his cock.

"You ready for me?" Joel smoothed his fingers along her sex, slipping through the folds and finding what he'd hoped. "You're good and turned on, aren't you?"

"God, *yes.*"

She leaned her head back on the rock and thrust her hips toward him, as if she couldn't get enough. He pressed his finger into her core and she sucked in air.

Joel growled. "You like this a lot. The idea of being fucked right out in the open."

He sure the hell did. He spread her on a second digit, then a third while she panted lightly, her fingers digging into his shoulders even through the layers he wore.

He slipped his fingers from her heat, hoisted her in the air, and lined them up, his cock nudging her sex. He settled her shoulders against the rock wall.

Their eyes met and he drove deep.

The cry of pleasure from her lips only made it easier to continue, pumping into her frantically, thrusting like a mad man. The fabric from her empty jean leg dangled toward the ground, flapping as they moved. Vicki had her eyes closed, sheer ecstasy on her face.

Everything leading up to this moment meant Joel teetered on a thread. His climax built like pressure behind a dam, balls tightening, electric shocks sliding along his spine. He had less than a dozen strokes left before he'd lose it.

A slight adjustment allowed him to squeeze his hand between their bodies all the way down to her clit. She gasped when he touched her, eyes flying open to stare, breathless, as he pinched the sensitive nub.

Another thrust.

Another.

Vicki squeezed her legs tighter around him, pulling in time

with his thrusts and driving his cock deeper. It felt so damn good he forgot everything except the need to make her come before he did. Had to be soon because, dammit, he wasn't going to last.

Another stroke, harder to her clit.

Another thrust, deeper this time as he angled his hips. Vicki moaned sweetly, a long, low noise edging higher. Joel worked her harder, and her body quivered under him, nearly there...nearly there...

She jerked hard enough he almost lost his balance. He did lose his control. Climax spilling out, balls emptying so hard his legs went rubbery.

Vicki gasped as he thrust a couple more times, her passage so tight around him he couldn't bear to leave.

Until they both stopped shaking, Joel leaned into her, supporting them with the meager energy left in his lower limbs. Cold air swirled around them, and he stroked her naked leg where it rested over his hip, warming her with his palm.

"Hmm, that feels nice." Vicki whispered the words, her breathing nearly back to normal. "Joel?"

He leaned his shoulders away just enough to see her face. "Yeah?"

She stroked his cheek and smiled contentedly. "I liked that. Totally hot."

So had he, but he hadn't forgotten why he'd been insane. Frantic sex had eased his anger, and the way she burrowed in against his neck, he didn't think she was pissed off at all he'd been a demanding asshole this time around.

Which was good, because he'd enjoyed the sex a lot. But this wasn't the end, it was the beginning.

He wasn't about to start the next step now, with his cock still embedded in her body, but once they were back to civilization, they were going to have a long-postponed conversation. About her disappearance the days before, the fuck-it-all attitude she'd had tonight. Hell, even dig a little deeper into a few other areas that up to now they'd avoided in the good old time they'd been having while hanging out.

Screw going slow. It was past time for some secrets to be shared.

Vicki accepted the cup of hot chocolate from Joel, staring around her in amazement.

He hadn't taken her home after they'd driven back to the ranch house and dropped off Ashley and Travis. Well, not true. He'd taken her home and told her to pack a bag, then he'd hustled her out the door and into his truck. Driving into the mountains for an hour in the deepening black was a little like moving into a fantasy world.

The heat under her fingers was the only solid, non-confusing part, so she focused on it. A few sips at a time to center herself before she had to break the silence.

The tiny cabin had a small counter on one wall, the door to a bathroom on another, and the rest of the room was pretty much taken up with bed. This little corner she'd claimed was right in front of the wood-burning fireplace Joel had gotten going only moments after ushering her in the door.

The entire evening had bordered on the fantastic, and she was still reeling.

"How did you set this up so quickly?" She stroked the carpet under her fingers, luxuriating in the softness.

"Friend of the family. We have a standing invitation. I checked the website, and it wasn't booked for the next couple nights, so it's ours."

Vicki shifted position as Joel lowered himself to the floor, his blue eyes catching hold of hers and not letting go.

She wasn't sure why they were there, but that expression he wore scared her a little. "It's pretty, but I don't understand why we took off so fast."

Joel leaned back on the foot of the bed, stretching his legs in front of him. "We need to talk, and there was a definite lack of places we could be uninterrupted. My place was out. Hope could stop in at any time at your new place."

"Forget the barn, since everyone we know finds us there eventually, right?"

He smiled at her joke. "Yeah..."

He wanted to talk. Vicki held herself very still. She didn't think he'd haul her all the way out to a cabin to tell her he'd had enough of their little game. He'd been really pissed off when she'd...it seemed unreal now...kissed Ashley, but his anger had vanished after they'd had the incredible sex.

Vicki waited. No way was she going to open up the conversation without knowing what he was looking for. She still trusted him. There was no way she would have come with him for the night if she didn't.

Although she quickly shoved a few reinforcement bricks into the wall she had to maintain around her heart.

He didn't keep her on tenterhooks for long. Reached over and plucked the cup from her hand and put it to the side. When he kept hold of her fingers and caressed them, she wanted to snatch her hands back because his touch was so tender she was going to come apart.

Joel cleared his throat. "I'm a stupid shit."

She couldn't help it. Vicki burst out laughing. "That's not what I expected you to say."

"It's true, though." His thumb stroked the back of her hand as he carried on. "I understand more why, for the past few years, Blake and Daniel have told me I'm too young to grasp what's going on. Why Matt shakes his head and pokes at me that some day when I *grow up* things will make more sense. I'm a shit because all the time we've been together I've been far more focused on me. Like some typical kid whose world is a ten-foot space, and they're the center of the fucking universe."

Whoa. She sure hadn't expected him to start ragging on himself. "We're young. Aren't we supposed to be a little selfish?"

Joel shook his head. "No excuses. I bet you haven't had a real chance to be young for a lot longer than is right."

She lowered her gaze, unable to meet his anymore. She

shrugged. "It's just the way it is."

Joel lifted her chin, his fingers gentle on her skin. "Over the past couple months, I've learned things about you, and your life, and while I'm growing up, I've still been sliding. So I want you to know. The rest of the time we're together, I'm going to do it right."

She wasn't sure what he thought he'd been doing wrong. "I'm lost..."

"We got a three-part deal, right? You getting happy around horses, changing our reputations, and learning about sex."

"We're doing all those things." Vicki edged closer, poking him on the chest. "It's not your fault I jammed out of the horse thing. We'll move ahead, there's still time. And the sex, holy hell, you've been awesome in teaching me about that. And you said it yourself, people are seeing us as a couple, that's good, right?"

Joel nodded. "It is, but it's not enough. You wanted to know what it's like to have a boyfriend, and I wanted a girlfriend, and hell if I didn't fuck that part up."

Nope. "This is going in one ear and out the other. What have you mucked up so bad, because I can't see it."

Joel made a face. "That's because you don't know any better, but I do. So here's my commitment. I'm going to take care of you like I should be, and hopefully that means you'll notice a difference, deal?"

Vicki hesitated. The only thing she saw coming from him giving her *more* was more trouble. She'd get even further attached to the Coleman clan, and yet not truly belong.

"It's not real, though, Joel. We're just doing this until the spring."

"There's a good example of what I mean. Who says this isn't real? We're friends, and friends help each other." He paused, regrouped. "We *are* friends, right?"

Oh hell. Vicki stopped completely and thought it through. There was only one possible answer. "Of course we are."

Joel eased back and nodded. "Good. Then there's

something I need to know, as one friend to another. What happened with Eric Tell?"

Vicki wondered if running to the bathroom and hiding was an option.

Joel raised a brow. "I can tell you the version I got if that helps, and you fill in the blanks. Rumour says you two slept together during his senior year, which I know is total bullshit. You hate his guts, that much is obvious, but the rest I don't get."

He had her hand again, stroking it as if attempting to settle her. The entire evening blurred together until she realized she had two options.

She either went forward from this moment and trusted Joel completely, or she didn't. Not sharing with him meant all her secrets stayed hidden, but it also meant all the barriers she'd put up stayed up. For once in her life she longed to be completely honest with someone. To be able to trust them and let them in.

Joel had been nothing but wonderful, and she ached so hard to let go of her walls, it was impossible to resist.

Maybe she'd regret this. Maybe she was asking for more pain like she'd felt the previous week, but she had to know if it was possible to have a real friend.

Vicki took a deep breath, hoping this wasn't going to change her world in ways she'd come to regret.

"Before I tell you about Eric, you tell me something. Tell me about my family, and don't try to be polite and save my tender feelings. Because the two things are connected."

He looked rather uncomfortable for a moment. "Again, I know less details and more rumours. Your mom..." she glared until he finished his sentence, "...she's got a new *friend* every now and again. Older men who take care of her for a while before she switches."

"She's been doing it her entire life as far as I know, which is why me, Lynn and Sarah have three different fathers."

Joel shook his head. "Damn."

"Go on."

He nodded. "Sarah...takes after your ma."

Vicki let out a guffaw. "Now, that's a nice way to put it."

"Lynn. I never heard much about Lynn. She moved to Edmonton right after high school, right?"

She nodded. "And me?"

Joel sighed. "You dropped out of school the same summer Lynn left, moved out on your own."

"And slept with half the town."

Denial came instantly. "Actually, once you left school, you fell off the radar. I mean, the Hansol name got used a lot, but not yours specifically."

What she figured. "It's so awesome that this town has been giving me hell for years completely based on two members of the family."

"Eric—what happened?" he prodded again.

God, it hurt to share even now. "Eric did sleep with a Hansol girl, only it was Lynn."

Joel paused, stiff with shock.

"I overheard the senior guys talking about having one of those stupid bets. How many girls they could sleep with before graduation. You know, the contests that aren't supposed to happen, but do."

Anger was rising on Joel's face. "Go on."

"I was in the Home-Ec room and heard them in the hall boasting about conquests, reducing sex to sheer numbers. I was disgusted at the time, but when I got home I discovered it was worse than I'd imagined because Lynn was all excited to tell me about her new boyfriend. Seems Eric Tell realized my sweet sister was about as good a target as he could find."

Oh Lord, here was the moment. She lifted her eyes to Joel's. "Lynn's got Asperger's. She's not bad, but it means there are certain things she just doesn't get. She's borderline on the spectrum, so my mom was never forced to get her real help during school. It was too much bother to fill in paperwork and such. Any teachers who made a comment were poo-pooed, and since Lynn got passing marks, they had no choice but to move her forward year after year. It's the social side she doesn't get."

"Like knowing how to act with others?"

"Exactly." Vicki wrapped her arms around her legs. "A routine helps, which is why I used to haul her into Home-Ec every lunch break for some quiet time. Having a boyfriend was just a cool thing. Everyone else in high school talked about wanting a boyfriend. When Eric told her that's what he was, she was thrilled. When I found out what he'd done, I went a little crazy. Raced down to the football field and stormed into the changing room."

"Oh hell, that would have been incredible to see."

"Yeah, well once the shouting and running for towels was over, I marched up and got in his face. Told him he was an asshole, and that I didn't appreciate being used for some kind of bet. That if he'd wanted to sleep with me once and be done, he should have been man enough to just tell me."

A frown creased Joel's forehead. "Wait, you said he slept with *you*?"

She nodded. "Lynn didn't need the reputation of being another of the loose Hansol girls, and she didn't need any other assholes in the school realizing how her mind works. She's fanatical about her friends, Joel. Will do anything for them, anything they ask at all, even if it's not in her best interest. She didn't *understand*, and like all the years before, I did what I had to do to protect her."

"And he just agreed with you? Didn't mention Lynn at all?"

"The rest of the guys started hooting and cheering him, you know like he was some great hero or something. Yeah, he wasn't going to argue at that moment. Just took their adoration and trampled me underfoot."

"So you lost your reputation to save hers."

"Yeah." Fear hovered, and she fought it down. She had to trust him. "This is why you can't tell anyone the truth. I know Lynn is safely away, but I don't ever want this discussed in front of her. I don't want him connected with her in any way."

217

He was nodding but still staring into the fire. "Something doesn't make sense. Eric knew you'd lied, and being the kind of ass that he is, why didn't he try holding this over your head? He knows it was Lynn…"

Vicki paused. "Well, first he kept quiet because he was in the hospital with a concussion and a broken arm."

It was clear Joel wasn't too choked up about Eric getting hurt. "That part is true? Damn, you really did beat him up."

She wished she had. It would have been more satisfying than the truth. "He was standing on a wet floor, clutching a towel around his waist. When I went to kick him in the nuts he slipped and did it to himself. Of course, rumours twisted fast enough into me attacking him out of the blue."

Anger flared in Joel's eyes. "Needs to have his balls removed."

"I've had many a pleasant daydream about that." She swallowed. "The other reason he's never said anything is I have two birth certificates."

Confusion was written all over him.

Vicki dove back into her explanation. "With all the places my mom lived before hauling us to Rocky, she was constantly losing things. I was born somewhere in rural Saskatchewan, but when she got here and had to register me for school, she applied for a new copy. Only what she got wasn't a copy, it's a different version. Maybe she messed with my age to get me into some free childcare program, or someone in the system might have made a typo, I don't know for sure. But I found both copies, so I have two."

"How does that keep Eric from telling about Lynn?"

Vicki slowed. "All the guys heard him acknowledge he slept with me. Once I had that, I had him trapped. I showed him my birth certificate, the second one that I keep hidden. It says I'm three years younger than he expected, which would have meant he slept with a minor. It doesn't matter if me being that much younger is believable or not, it's a legal document and would be enough to get him a record, if not jail time, even now."

She had him floored. Joel blinked hard and shook his head. "Whoa. Okay, remind me never to piss you off."

"It wasn't about me. The deal I offered was he leaves Lynn alone. No comments, no *nothing* about her, and I keep my mouth shut. He goes after her in any way, I go after him." Vicki stared into the fire, clutching her legs as she waded through to the end. "For years he's pushed the limits. I take the cracks about myself, and Sarah and Mom. Hell, they made their bed, they can lie in it. But Lynn is off limits."

"He's a bastard through and through for even starting this war between you. Was Lynn okay?" He radiated fury, and something about his anger helped defuse hers. Like she finally had someone to share the load with. He rested a hand on her arm and she caught his fingers.

"She is now. I contacted social services and got them to listen. Lynn got accepted into a group home, and she's safe. No chance of Sarah's leftovers strolling down the hall and making a move on us."

His fingers tightened around hers to the point of pain as he reacted to that one. "No. Fucking. Way."

"Why do you think I moved out when I did? Lynn was gone, so I left as well. I was sick and tired of waking up with strange men hovering, wondering if they dared take a try." Vicki twisted her back to the sidewall so she could look at him. This sharing was killing her, but now that she'd started she couldn't seem to stop. "I had to drop out of school. Moving out meant getting a place of my own, and paying rent became a priority. A job and going to school don't mix very easily. Not when you're sixteen and earning minimum wage."

"Plus getting set upon by small-town bigots and even your own family." Joel took a deep breath, and damn if he didn't wipe his eyes.

God, she really was going to lose it now.

He took her to bed and cuddled her. His tenderness was what she needed. Nothing more to explain, nothing to admit or confess. Just the honest truth out there.

She lay nestled against him with her head resting on his

chest for the longest time. Joel ran his fingers through her hair as she relaxed off the adrenaline high.

He spoke softly as he continued to care for her. "I'm so sorry you've been alone and dealing with this. You are incredible. I hope you know that. No matter what uncaring words people have tossed your way over the years, the truth is you were real family to Lynn, and she's lucky to have you."

She nodded. "Thanks."

A couple more minutes passed and he laughed. "Okay, this might sound stupid, but how old are you?"

"I'm pretty sure the older birth certificate is right, Joel. The other one is only good as a threat over Eric. At thirteen I could have consensual sex with a fifteen year old, but he was eighteen. It's enough."

Joel shook his head. "I'll say it again, you're amazing."

She didn't feel amazing, she felt exhausted. "Sharing that took a lot out of me. I've never told anyone before."

"I'm glad you told me." Joel rolled her to vertical and kissed her cheek briefly. "Come on, let's crash for the night. We can do more talking in the morning."

Vicki fought the yawn that wanted to overwhelm her. "And other things?"

"Maybe..." Joel tapped her on the butt toward the bathroom. "Hey, when is your birthday for real?"

"April fourteenth. You can give me a pony ride," she joked.

Joel grinned. Vicki turned away, her load lighter than she'd carried for a long, long time.

Chapter Twenty-One

Things had changed a lot.

It was about two weeks since Joel had promised to truly be there for her, and she'd felt a difference. Not only the situations around her, but inside. She was still worried about getting too attached, but planting a label on their relationship of being *good friends* made it easier. Some people had been good friends for years and years, right?

Joel had taken to doing a ton of little things that made her squirm at times, but she couldn't deny the pleasure his attention brought. He stopped in with a coffee and doughnuts, and visited during her break time. He texted her off and on through the day. Short but sweet notes.

He made her a playlist of his favourite songs and asked her what she liked to listen to.

Good *friends*. She clung to it with both hands and tried to ignore all the warning signs she felt anything more than friendship.

Walking into the barn without a qualm proved another area where she'd made progress, and this one she had no reservations about whatsoever. May might be far off, but in terms of moving forward, she had come a long way.

She spotted Joel working with a pitchfork and hurried to his side.

The very real smile he gave her made her warm. Not sexually, but deep inside where she'd never had someone to count on before.

"Hey, darling. You're a little early." Joel opened his arms, and she scooted against him, breathing in the scent of working male. Musky but not too overpowering. He kissed her quickly then pointed in front of him. "I need to finish dealing with this before we can do anything."

"No problem. I unloaded an emergency shipment over lunch, so Mr. Orson let me go early. I can help with chores, if you'd like." Vicki bounced on her toes, so full of energy she was ready to burst.

Joel looked her over. "You're damn chipper today."

"I had a good breakfast," she deadpanned.

He grinned. "Told you that made a difference. No, you don't have to help. I'm nearly done. Hang out or, if you're feeling brave, go explore the barn. There's a surprise I plan to show you."

Surprises were good. "You got the entire herd tucked out of sight with noise makers, waiting to leap out at me, right?"

"Damn, you figured it out." Joel returned to his task. "Nope, only full-grown horse in here is Sable."

Vicki watched him work for a bit, the slow motions he used mesmerizing. It wasn't him being lazy, but the kind of conservation of energy she'd witnessed all the Colemans employ while they toiled.

She glanced at her boots and deliberately walked away with steady steps, even-paced. A lot different than the mad sprint she usually used to get places.

It might be a little silly, but after walking the length of the entrance a few times, she figured she had it down. A country song playing in her head, she wandered around the corner, still working on this cowboy ramble, or whatever it was she'd discovered. It was fun to walk like this, and it took a moment to realize she'd strolled into the row where Sable's stall was.

She paused, waiting for Sable to do the usual and stick her nose out.

Nothing.

Vicki listened harder, but the only sounds were from the front corner where Joel worked.

Wait. There. A rustle gave the horse away. Sable wasn't going to freak her out today. In fact...

Vicki felt as bold as she'd ever been. Sable was behind the gate, she couldn't get out. Maybe going and leaning on the wall opposite her stall would be good practice.

She took a couple steps and stopped. Oops, that wasn't the cowboy ramble, that was the Vicki *my ass is on fire* two-step. She deliberately slowed and, focusing on the bales opposite Sable's stall, sauntered forward.

Vicki kept her back to the front of the stall, her heart fluttering nervously. Except for when she'd been forced past the day Jaxi went into labour, this was the closest she'd voluntarily gotten to a horse in forever.

She pivoted and stared across the distance, only to discover Sable had no interest in her whatsoever. Nope, after all that worry, the damn horse was busy nudging something on the ground.

Oh. My. God.

Vicki's tongue went numb, and she couldn't have talked if she wanted to. There was a tiny horse on the straw-strewn floor, a little black spot on its forehead.

Sable had her baby. A quick glance ensured this wasn't a recent development, unless horses had their babies with a lot less fuss than humans. The place looked too spotless clean for the baby to have just been born.

Vicki took one step closer. Then another, expecting Sable to leap at the gate to protect her newborn.

Sable did look up, but she only made this horse sound that was very content and not scary at all. Either that or it was the noise they made to lure in unsuspecting humans. But Sable didn't seem into her.

Which, Vicki couldn't blame her. "You got your baby, didn't you? Wow. She's pretty. Or he. I'm not being rude, just, it's not that easy to tell."

Vicki paused. She was three feet away from the stall, and she was talking to a horse. It was a bloody miracle and fucking weird at the same time. She shifted uncomfortably, not ready to go any farther, but kind of amazed she was where she was.

Silence warned her Joel was done. She turned toward where she expected him because getting scared by his approach and screaming would undo the positive vibes stealing over her.

His grin when he spotted her was a huge reward. "Well, look at you. You found the surprise."

She nodded, moving in slow motion as if she'd been stuck in a deep freeze for a while. "I'm not freaking out."

Joel joined her, his smooth stride eating up the space between them. "You're not, and that's super."

He wrapped her in his arms and squeezed her tight in a hug, and Vicki sighed with happiness.

When he let her go, it was to grab her hand. "You want to be properly introduced?"

"Go inside there?" With Sable? *Ummm.*

"No." Joel tucked her under his arm. "We'll give Sable a break and keep the visiting to a distance. But if you peek through, you can whisper a hello to Comet."

"You've named him...her...already?" Vicki leaned against Joel's side as she looked the baby over.

"Dad did. Something to do with bloodlines. His sire was Shooting Star."

"Cool." Yeah, this wasn't bad. Vicki smiled up at Joel. "This is a nice surprise."

"Nice seeing you so close to the stall without me having to entice you there."

"Oh." Vicki smiled wider. "Enticement? You mean I went and blew a chance to win a prize?"

Joel wiggled his brows, and Vicki laughed, lowering her voice because, you know, there was a baby right there in front of them.

Sable made that strange sound again, and Joel let Vicki loose. "Just a minute, Sable's feeling neglected."

He reached in and stroked the horse's nose, patting her on the side and cooing over her as if she were the baby. Sable shook her head as she leaned into Joel's touch.

Yeah, Vicki understood that sentiment. The man had magic hands, and if she were the one being petted right now, she'd be pressing closer and looking for more attention as well.

Vicki slipped her fingers into Joel's free hand and squeezed tight.

Joel gave Sable one last brush, then led Vicki away. "I'm so proud of you."

"I'm proud of me too," Vicki confessed.

She did a check as Joel guided her. Heart rate seemed normal. She hadn't screamed. She adjusted her step to go a touch faster to keep up with Joel's longer stride, but she still attempted to imitate the Coleman cowboy walk.

Joel stopped them at the barn door. "Hmm, don't know what it is, but put a pretty girl in cowboy boots and it makes her even prettier."

"You sweet talker, you."

"Come on, ready for your reward?"

That expression he wore was the naughty one. The one warning of physical pleasure and bliss. "Well, Joel Coleman, it looks as if you intend to seduce me or something nefarious."

"Nothing nefarious, I'm going to give you another lesson, and we're both going to have a hell of a good time."

Joel glanced around Traders, a pleased sensation trickling over him. The family was out in full force, and this time there had been no hesitation in welcoming Vicki.

Watching her bloom under the attention made him smile.

She deserved so much more than she'd gotten over the years, and if for the next little while he could help her, it was worth it.

"I'm playing pool for a bit, you okay?"

She glanced up from where she was planted between Lisa and Hope and nodded. "No problem."

"We've got her." Hope winked, and Joel was more grateful

for his family than ever.

Except for one individual with a fucking bad attitude. Jesse had gotten worse instead of better over the past few weeks, and Joel was thoroughly sick of it. It was stupid shit, like not making enough coffee for two, or parking his damn truck across the roadway at an angle that meant Joel had to park on the road and walk.

Inconsiderate, childish things to let Joel know Jesse was pissed, but hell if his twin would tell him why.

"Need a partner?" He offered the olive branch regardless of what he'd prefer to say.

Jesse glanced over his shoulder. "You have time to play? You might need to run out of here, you know, if Vicki needs something."

Matt thumped Jesse on the shoulder. "Shut up and quit being an ass. You want to play another round or not?"

Travis motioned to Joel. "Partner with me. We'll kick their butts."

The game proceeded with a little more vigour than usual. Suddenly it seemed vital to beat Jesse at whatever this was about, which wasn't a damn pool game, but some other fight.

Travis chuckled, leaning down to whisper softly, "You scowl any harder and you're going to break your face."

Damn. "Maybe I'll break Jesse's face. He's being a jerk."

Across the table Jesse crowed at having made his shot, loud enough to draw attention from the rest of the room, patrons frowning.

"We all get that label at some time or another," Travis pointed out. "Maybe it's his turn?"

"Never the right time for this stupidity." Joel straightened and hissed at his brother. "Jesse, stop the clowning around and play the damn game."

"Oh, I'm sorry, am I not doing things the way you want me to? Gee, so sad." Jesse lined up to sink another shot, and Joel's temper flared.

Matt circled the table and rested his hand on Joel's

shoulder. "Easy there, big guy. Jesse's being a brat, but if you keep looking at him like that, people will expect murder."

Joel nodded and dragged in a steadying breath. He wasn't sure why Jesse was pushing all his buttons.

It didn't get any better as the evening went on, especially when Jesse sauntered over to where the girls were visiting and plopped down on the arm of Vicki's chair.

Joel bristled and laid his pool cue on the table so he wasn't tempted to skewer Jesse with it.

The cousins laughed at something Jesse said, but poor Vicki was leaning as far to the side of her chair as possible, trying to escape the arm Jesse had laid across the backrest.

Her gaze darted into the rest of the room, then fell, her expression tightening. Joel followed her line of vision and spotted a couple groups of girls whispering madly behind their hands as they gestured toward the Coleman table.

Fuck it all. This was exactly what they were supposed to avoid. What he'd promised Vicki they would not have to deal with. One poorly timed move by Jesse, and the past two months of Vicki and him being a couple was in jeopardy.

Joel grabbed Jesse by the back of the shirt and jerked him off the chair. He intended to make it less of a yank, but the anger burning inside from his brother's fucked-up behavior didn't help his reaction.

Jesse ended up sprawled on the floor, scrambling to his feet with his fists at the ready.

"What the hell was that for?"

Joel gestured toward the door. "Outside. And keep this quiet and polite, or you'll regret it."

"Fuck you." In spite of his words, Jesse grabbed his hat and waved curtly to the crew before striding out of the pub, Joel hard on his heels.

Outside it was brisk. The snow hadn't arrived yet, but the wintery temperatures were enough to cool Joel off. He relaxed his fists and gave Jesse the benefit of a doubt as they stepped into the parking lot and away from any listening ears.

Vivian Arend

They stopped beside Jesse's truck.

"I'm sorry for jerking you off the chair. I was worried..." To hell with it. He met Jesse's eyes and admitted the truth. "I was worried people would see you leaning in on Vicki and think she's fooling around with you as well."

Jesse rolled his eyes. "I haven't touched the woman, and I'm not going to. Who gives a shit what people think?"

"She does."

"She's a goddamn *Hansol*. People already assume she's fucking most of the single guys in town, and if she's anything like the rest of her family, half the married ones as well."

Joel fought to keep his temper. "She's not her family. We had this conversation before, you remember? So when she cares about what people are saying, I'd appreciate if you gave a damn and helped us out here. It's not that hard of an idea, giving someone a break. Helping them a little."

Jesse stared for a moment, pacing toward the back of his truck. His eyes narrowed. "Is that why you're dating her? As a favour?"

Joel wasn't going to admit any such thing, not when the situation had changed. "I like her, she likes me. Period. But it doesn't help that you're being so..."

Jesse raised a brow. "So, what?"

"You're a bastard these days." Joel shook his head when Jesse pulled more faces. "Don't act like you're so damn surprised. The past couple months you've been hard to work with, and—"

"How the hell would you know?" Jesse demanded. "Calling me a bastard. Hello, pot meet kettle. You've gone around the bend since you started seeing Vicki, and I don't like the changes."

Joel jerked to a stop. "I've changed?"

"Yes. God damn." Jesse slammed a foot into his tire and stomped away, cussing. He twirled back, anger painting his features. "But let's get this straight off the start. It's not like I'm pissed that you're fooling around without me."

228

"That's what it seems like."

"Fuck it. Doing the same girl was a kink, that's all." Jesse folded his arms. "And I can't believe I'm saying this, because it's so fucking emo I should be all of twelve, but it's the time we spent together I miss, okay? It's like, you don't want to fool around with the same girl, fine. That means you also don't want to hang out with me? Or go to parties? It's as if you're fucking avoiding me."

Joel stared at his brother in shock. "Of course I'm not avoiding you, idiot."

Jesse lifted a hand and showed fingers as he spoke. "Friday nights at Traders, if you show, you're sitting with her, or dancing with her, or watching her, or you're not here. Chores, you've been switching out and working with Travis or Matt most of the time. What's the issue, do I smell?"

It was Joel's turn to want to roll his eyes, but he kept in control and listened to the continuing tirade.

"I asked you to come out to the party in Red Deer, you didn't feel like it. You didn't want to head to Calgary for the concert. You said no to the dance in Sundre."

"Vicki couldn't go that night." Joel swore. "Do you not get this? I'm not on some kind of anti-Jesse campaign, just I'm doing things with her—"

"And Travis and Matt, and fuck, even Daniel and Blake more than me."

Joel stilled. Really listened. *Hell.* "You feel left out, don't you?"

"Oh, screw that."

"No, that's what you said, you miss spending time with me."

Jesse dragged his hand through his hair. "No. Yes. Hell, I don't know anymore."

Joel shook his head. This was something he'd never anticipated, and yet suddenly it made sense. "Jesse, I'm sorry. I didn't mean to leave you out. It's just that Vicki..."

Damn. He was stuck. He couldn't tell Jesse about her fears

regarding their reputation without sharing things with his twin he had no right to share.

"Yeah, that's the problem, isn't it? Vicki."

"Stop pouting like a two year old," Joel snapped. "I'm trying to figure out what I can say to fix this, but you're making it damn tough when you're being a spoiled ass."

All the good things about the family that Joel had been so proud to show off to Vicki, the opposite emotion seemed to be staring him down right now.

Jesse was jealous. That was the only possible answer, and there was no solution for it. The fact was whichever of them had gotten involved with someone first, the other was going to be left out.

The days of living in each other's pockets were over.

"Jesse, I'll work on being around more, but I can't guarantee I'll hang out with you as much as I used to. It's not that I don't enjoy your company, but I like time with the others too."

He wasn't doing this well. Jesse stiffened even more, his usually happy smile fading away. "So that's it, then. You're going to give up on family for a girl."

This was ridiculous. It was obvious Jesse wasn't listening and didn't want to hear, so Joel wasn't going to try to explain anymore. "I'm not giving up on family, Jesse, but I don't want to stay a kid. And growing up means changing. No matter how much you dislike that, it's true."

Jesse nodded, lips set together. "I'll see you around then."

He yanked open his truck door and jumped in. Joel stepped out of the way to avoid being sprayed with gravel as Jesse gunned it out of the parking lot and fishtailed onto the highway without stopping.

Stupid, immature asshole. Regret filled Joel, though, that there was a chasm between the two of them. But bar dropping Vicki completely and going back to being at Jesse's beck and call, he didn't see a solution.

Even come the spring when Vicki was gone, he didn't want

to return to being Jesse's stooge. He liked doing stuff with his brother, but he didn't want to have to rescue him, or bail him out, or follow meekly behind for the rest of his life.

It was time to grow up. This was just the start. What would it be like down the road when he fell in love?

The thought made this weird sensation twist inside, both imagining Vicki being gone, and finding someone new. He was enjoying his time with her very much, and as he rejoined her inside, scooping her up and placing her in his lap to the great amusement of his cousins, Joel found a little respite from his tension.

Vicki cupped his face gently. "You okay?"

He should have been the one asking her, and here she was, caring for him. It was humbling. "Jesse's sorry. He didn't mean to do anything to hurt you."

Joel didn't feel at all guilty for putting words into his brother's mouth. It wasn't strictly a lie. Jesse hadn't thought through his actions, like everything else he was doing without thinking lately.

Vicki smiled and accepted his kiss, wrapping her arms around his neck as she melted against his body.

"Get a room," Travis shouted.

Joel pulled back so he could rest his forehead against hers. "Sounds like a great idea to me. What do you say we do that a little later?"

Vicki blushed, and Joel grinned, turning to the table and pouring a beer, ready to spend a few more hours with family.

At least the part that was acting like family right now.

Chapter Twenty-Two

Chaos reigned in the living room of his parents' house. The nephews hadn't unwrapped their presents, they'd torn the paper to shreds, egged on by Jesse. The scent of Christmas dinner lingered in the air. Joel had to loosen his belt a notch to deal with the slight bit of overindulgence he'd partaken in.

But the biggest present he had was seeing his family together and happy. Or as happy as they got these days.

Travis leaned back in one of the La-Z-Boys, the two smallest of the nephews swarming over him as they attempted to get him to join them for a game. Blake and Jaxi's toddlers were alternately crawling through the wrapping paper and having the brightly coloured bits of paper pulled from their mouths, or they were dancing in that weird toddler way to the music he'd put on just for them. Christmas tunes with sort of a Chipmunk twist, adding a strange flavour to the setting.

Everywhere he looked people shuffled around the room or were seated at the massive family table. The after-dinner drinks had come out, bottles stacked to one side. Blake and their dad had cleared a space to play crib and were hard at it.

Vicki wandered through the chaos all wide-eyed, which made Joel smile.

He was glad she was having fun. That had become his number one goal over the past weeks. Jesse, on the other hand, had remained a standoffish stick-in-the-mud, going out of his way to avoid Joel during the most basic of chores.

The contrast burned, but there didn't seem to be anything he could do to make things better.

Blake laughed, laying his hand down in defeat as he got skunked for the third time. "You have the best luck at cards, Dad."

Mike Coleman raised his glass, the ice cubes clinking together. "You're too easily distracted. Once you've got six kids, then we'll get closer in skill level. *Ouch.*"

He rubbed the back of his head where Jaxi had elbowed him as she walked past.

Jaxi turned, her arms full of dirty dishes she was taking to the kitchen. "When your son figures out a way to carry and deliver the next three children, you can talk to us about having six kids, got it?"

She disappeared past the swinging door, and Blake and Mike exchanged glances. Mike cleared his throat. "So. You're stopping at three?"

Blake shrugged. "Give her a few more months to forget childbirth, and she might change her mind. Right now she's still at the *wake up in the middle of the night and punch me* stage. Like it's all my fault she was pregnant."

Mike laughed, but both of them got really busy when Jaxi reentered the room.

Blake rose to his feet. "Chores. Who else is joining me on this blustery winter day? Jesse? You're up, aren't you?"

Joel stepped forward. "I'll come out—and Vicki, I want to show her something."

If he'd expected his twin to say thank you for taking over the cold task, he'd have waited a damn long time. Jesse didn't so much as acknowledge his offer, just went back to pouring a drink before he plopped down beside Travis, the TV remote in his hand.

Joel ignored him, although he did notice their dad watching with disapproval.

Vicki nodded. "Give me a minute to change?"

"Meet me in the west barn when you're ready." Joel grabbed his coat before joining Blake on the journey across the yard.

The snow had arrived in style a week before Christmas Eve, lying in thick drifts everywhere. They'd used the tractors to push the roadways clear. There were narrower trails between the barns, paths stomped down by the nephews' enthusiastic feet when they visited Gramma and Grampa and headed to the barns for some all important fort-building and kitten-chasing.

Blake pulled on gloves, glancing over as they headed forward. "So, you and Vicki, things going okay?"

Joel nodded. "Yeah, she's a great girl."

"She is." Blake cleared his throat. "I'm sorry I was an ass back when she first started hanging around."

"No problem. You're not *still* an ass, that's the important part."

Blake snorted. "Yeah, one at a time in any family, isn't that the rule?"

"God, I hope so." He couldn't imagine if Travis was being a shit right now as well as Jesse. His twin was bad enough.

Blake asked him something, and he had to get him to repeat it, distracted by Jesse's continued childish behavior.

"Are you serious about her?"

"Who?"

Blake cranked open the barn door and the heat of animal bodies and the sounds of the flock made him raise his voice. "Who the hell do you think I mean? The tooth fairy?"

Shit. "Vicki? She's a friend."

"Yeah, a close friend." Blake passed over a coverall. "You're being careful about sex?"

Good grief. "A lot more careful than my big brother who, if I recall correctly, had his wife pregnant before they got married."

Blake had the grace to look a little embarrassed. "Yeah, well, slightly different situation."

Joel paused in pulling up his coverall. "What the hell does that mean?"

"Don't get your britches in a twist. I was a lot older than you when Jaxi and I got together. If this thing between you and Vicki is serious, that's your business. Just, don't rush. In the big scheme of things you both have a lot of time."

Joel gave his big brother a smack on the arm. "Good to

know your heart is in the right place."

"Hey, I love the kids, and I love being married, but when I was your age, I wasn't ready for it. I want the best for you, and for Vicki, whatever that means."

Joel nodded. He'd been thinking about it a lot lately himself. "Thanks. I appreciate it, and you're right. We're young, and we're not rushing, so relax."

They divvied up chores, Blake taking off for the other barn to deal with the horses.

Joel snuck in a few tasks before the door opened and Vicki entered.

"Joel?"

He waved. "Over here."

She hung onto the door, looking around cautiously.

He straightened up. Damn. He'd forgotten. "Don't worry. This barn is full of sheep. And lambs, right now. Not a horse in sight."

"Thank you." Vicki paced forward. "Is it stupid that they are not the same thing? Sheep don't freak me out."

"Good, because you're going to be getting a big dose of them for the next while."

Vicki narrowed her eyes. "You making me do your chores again, Joel Coleman?"

"Of course. I'm no dummy." He picked her up and spun her in a circle, her laughter streaming out louder than the bleating and rustling of the sheep.

"Put me down, you big oaf." She banged on his shoulder with her fist.

First he kissed her lustily, taking pleasure in her eager response. Yeah, they'd had no lack of enjoyment in the bedroom. And on the kitchen counter, and in the shower... The list was getting rather extensive now that she had a private place with the apartment and a sturdier bed for them to play on.

He lowered her slowly, rubbing them together as he did so.

"Hmm, nice. Is that my Christmas present?" Vicki blinked innocently. "Or do I get more?"

Oh yeah. Now he didn't want to do the rest of his chores. "You have more than one present, if it comes to that."

Her eyes sparkled. "Sounds good to me. So, boss. What's the lesson for today?"

It was the most brilliant of plans. "You get to wrestle sheep."

Vicki stared in disbelief. "Really? Like, why?"

He grinned. "You're not afraid of them, right?"

She thought it through, hard. "I don't think so. I mean, I don't usually have tons to do with them, but they're just another stinky animal of the smaller and more shaggy variety."

"I'm not even going to argue with you on the smelly part."

That didn't sound good. Vicki squared her shoulders and thought positive thoughts. "So far you've been an awesome teacher, Joel. I trust you. Do your worst."

He took a moment to strip off the coverall he wore over his regular jeans and shirt before he grabbed her by the hand and led her deeper in to the barn. "My worst is going to make you happy."

"Usually does." She nudged him, pleased to see that sexy grin of his break out.

The past months had been incredible. He'd meant every word he'd said in the cabin about being there for her, and for the first time in her life she felt as if she had a best friend.

With bonus screaming hot sex. Life was about as good as it had ever been, and she owed it all to Joel.

She'd gotten a Christmas card from Lynn, and a phone call. Her sister was doing well, and still excited about the adventures every day brought. Vicki agreed. This was wonderful, finally moving forward.

Her future looked a whole lot brighter.

It was impossible to resist. She threw her arms around him

and kissed him this time, trying to put a little more of how grateful she was into her touch.

He hummed but broke them apart, stroking her cheek as he smiled down. "As much as I hate to interrupt you, we need to keep moving."

Moving forward. All the time. She totally agreed.

He led her to a pen that was four times the size of one of the horse stalls and held at least a dozen sheep.

She climbed up on the gate and peered in. "Lots of the furry buggers in there, aren't there?"

"Yup."

Joel stood beside her and rubbed her back.

Vicki waited, but he didn't seem to be going ahead with the explaining bit. "So. This wrestling business..."

"Not really wrestling." Joel pointed into the pen. "More like dancing with them, in a way."

She followed the line of his finger and cursed. "Joel Coleman, is that my Christmas present in there?"

He nodded.

Damn. "You get the weirdest ideas. This is going to help me with my horse phobia, how?"

"Animals are animals, darling. Doesn't matter if they're horse or sheep, once they get used to having you around, they're going to get up close and personal. I figure it's easier to practice with the short smelly variety than the tall ones."

Good point. "Exactly what does 'get personal' mean?"

"They'll bump you." He hip-checked her lightly, and she laughed.

"God, you're insane."

"Yeah, I've been told that before." Joel rested his folded arms on the top of the gate. "You going to rescue your present before they unwrap it for you?"

"Good thing they aren't goats. Those guys eat everything, right?"

"You don't even want to know."

Vicki eyed the gate, but opening it didn't seem like a good idea. With her luck, half the beasties would get out before she'd get the thing closed. Instead, she climbed up and swung a leg over the top.

Joel grinned, taking the time to stroke her thigh. "Nice work jeans, by the way."

The jeans in question had a hole in one knee from the last time he'd had her in the barn, and there was a worn patch on her ass she swore was from when he'd dragged her down the hallway and into her bedroom.

Vicki ignored him and crawled down the other side. The sooner she got her present, the sooner she could get to the part of the day when she gave *him* a present.

When she landed on her feet, a few of the sheep jolted and ran to the far side of the pen, but the rest were all too interested in the box in the middle of the space to pay much attention to her.

"They won't bite, right?"

"Only if you bite first."

"Jackass. So reassuring. A simple *no* would have worked."

He chuckled but didn't say anything else.

Vicki took a deep breath and stepped forward. One sheep moved aside, another. This was going to be way too easy. "Looks as if your little plan isn't going to work. They're parting like the Red Sea."

Well, until that moment. She reached for the package right when one of the fuzzy beasts sidestepped and knocked her hand away.

She reached forward again, and this time one of them bumped her shins hard enough to rock her on her feet.

"Fuck."

Joel laughed. "Watch it," he warned.

Vicki spread her stance and braced herself to stay vertical. "Stupid things."

"Hey, right now they have your present, and you don't. Who's the stupid one?"

She whipped back to face him. "You did not just compare my intelligence to a sheep, did you?"

He ducked behind the gate. "They're actually very clever animals."

Vicki laughed. "Oh man, are you in trouble."

But first, she had this puzzle to solve. She glared down, slightly pissed off they were blocking her this easily. "Shoo. Go on, get out of here."

"That's it. Now don't be afraid to give them a little guidance."

"A kick in the ribs?"

"Sheep don't fly very well. Just use your knees."

And like that, it made sense. Vicki waded forward, applying pressure to the stupider beasts that refused to budge. It wasn't as if she was hurting them, but it was enough to get the more stubborn ones out of her way.

"Open it while you're in there," Joel ordered.

God. "Bossy, bossy."

It wasn't a big deal anymore. Now that she had the method of dealing with the sheep figured out, she had to work to keep her balance, but it wasn't impossible by any means. She knelt to get at the packing tape, and ended up with a sheep staring her eye to eye.

She raised an elbow and used it to force him back while she stripped off the tape and popped the top open.

Inside a pretty pair of new cowboy boots gleamed at her.

"Oh, Joel."

She rescued them from the box, nabbed the box with her other hand, and holding both high in the air, waded through the sea of walking cotton balls.

"You're a pro." Joel reached over the gate and grabbed her burdens.

That was right about the time one of the sheep got *real* up close and personal and took out the back of her knees. Vicki grasped the wood slats frantically, catching herself from falling.

Joel dropped everything to trap her hands in place. "Whoa, don't blow it now."

She hauled herself up, climbing to the top and staring him down. "Interesting choice of words..."

He frowned, offering her a hand as she made her way over and rejoined him. "What mischief you got planned?"

Enough. She peeked around cautiously, but it seemed to be only them and sheep. "How long before your brother comes looking for you?"

"Never. He'll just head into the house after he's done. Why?"

She tugged him into the next empty stall. "Because I want to give you your Christmas present."

Joel laughed as she planted a hand on his chest and backed him toward the wall. His pupils dilated as she dropped to her knees, hands reaching for his waist.

"Oh, darling."

"See, I'm nice." Vicki loosened his belt and popped the buttons on his fly. "I'm not making you wrestle anything."

"You're gonna be wrestling something in a minute..."

They both smiled. Joel leaned back on the solid wood and opened his legs wider around her.

Of all the sexual lessons she'd learned, this was one of the most sheer, out-and-out fun. Pulling his cock forward and feeling the heavy weight in her palm. Sliding her fingers up and down his girth and watching his face tighten with pleasure.

It was power in its purest form, to take a strong man like Joel to his knees in bliss.

She leaned forward, still looking up at him from under her lashes. She applied one small lick to the end of his cock as if he were an ice-cream cone, and was rewarded with a shudder.

So. Much. Fun. Teasing him with her tongue, rubbing the sensitive spot right under the head she'd learned drove him mad. Wrapping her lips around the tip for a second to get him good and wet then sucking hard as she popped off.

"*God*, Vicki."

He thickened in her grasp. She waited for him to make the next move. It was becoming a bit of a game, because he didn't seem to know every time she gave him a blowjob, he eventually caved and did the same thing.

And she loved it.

Vicki pumped her fist faster. Squeezing harder than she'd thought safe, but he'd taught her how he liked it. Worked her mouth over him until he was nice and wet, and she could take more of his length. She hadn't managed to do any of that deep-throat stuff yet, but he didn't seem unhappy with her attempts.

Joel threaded his fingers through her hair, and she hummed, earning a harder thrust.

"Sweet mercy, woman. When you do that, I feel it all the way to the back of my brain."

With a mouthful of cock she wasn't about to ask which brain, but the quip still made her smile.

He caught hold of her then so it was no longer her moving over him, but him in control. Vicki opened wide and brought her tongue into play as best she could, sucking when he dragged his hips back.

So gentle, even as he fucked her mouth. Saliva slicked his length, escaping to moisten her cheeks. The taste of his seed snuck onto her tongue as his breathing sped up.

"So damn good." Joel stroked a hair back from her face and tucked it behind her ear. "I ain't lasting long. You want to swallow? Decide fast."

This time she did. Instead of pulling back to watch him finish himself—spraying into his own hand or over her chest like he'd done in the past—she held him tighter.

"Ease off," he ordered.

Guided by his hands she leaned away enough his cock rested on her lower lip. She went to town with her tongue as he stroked himself rapidly. And when he gasped, the first shots of come exploding from his cock, she surrounded him again and swallowed him down as far as she could go.

"*Fuck.*"

It was all over but for the shaking. Joel lost control and let her take care of him.

"You killed me." Joel cupped her head, his cock continuing to jerk in her mouth as she played with his softening shaft. "Goddamn killed me dead."

She was still trapped, nose to his groin, the scent of sex in the air around them. Joel stroked his fingers free, released her and pulled her up to lean on him as he sprawled against the wall.

"Let me remember how to walk. I think you sucked my brains out my dick that time."

Vicki laughed. "Merry Christmas, Joel."

He smiled down at her. "Merry Christmas to you too."

Chapter Twenty-Three

Vicki opened the oven and pulled out another cookie sheet of finger food, transferring the hot tray to the counter top and stepping away to allow Tamara Coleman to load the wonton wrappers onto serving bowls.

"It's people like you who give the Coleman family a rep for incredible parties." Karen Coleman lifted the lid on a Crock-Pot and breathed in deeply, letting loose a moan of pleasure. "God, do we have to share? How about we stay here and eat all night instead of going into the living room with the greedy lot of them?"

There was already enough of a crowd in the tiny kitchen, Vicki wasn't sure what Karen meant. "Tamara's apartment is nice, but it's not made for occupancy of...well, how many are there in the clan?"

Tamara pushed her glasses up her nose. "Don't bother trying to count. It's not the actual blood relatives, it's the number of friends, lovers and other mischief-makers they bring with them that adds up." She turned to her sister. "Still don't see why you didn't accept Dad's offer to hold the party at the Whiskey Creek Ranch. We could have all fit much easier."

Karen scooped the last spoonful from the pot and stuck a bunch of forks into the bowl. She sighed. "Right. You know very well if we'd had it there, we'd never get out of the kitchen. At least here we can leave if we want to."

The loud beat of the New Year's party music reverberated through the apartment, spilling through the door as Matt entered to grab more soda from the fridge, and another cousin, Steve, shouted after him to bring out the rum.

Tamara ducked out of the way, passing the plates she'd filled to Steve before turning to nod at her sister.

"True. I'd forgotten that part. Not living under his roof makes it much easier." She grimaced at Vicki. "Sorry. Dad's old-fashioned. The fact I'm a woman living in the evil city, let alone that I have my nursing degree makes him all kinds of crazy."

Vicki nodded, wrapping her brain around another form of family. With no dad in the picture, ever, she hadn't considered the ramifications of having a dominant male figure in her life. "Wow. I...didn't think that still happened."

Karen leaned back on the counter. "Dad means well, in his stifling, misogynistic, cave-man way."

Tamara pulled the meatballs from her sister's hands and tilted her head toward the living room. "You're the one putting up with it on a daily basis. You've got more masochist tendencies than Travis."

Vicki laughed at that description of Travis. Yeah, right. He was one hundred percent, grade-A bossy male, but it wasn't her place to discuss what she'd noticed in Ashley and Travis's relationship.

She washed her hands and got ready to head back into the party to find Joel when Karen tugged her sleeve. "Hey, if you don't mind. Can I talk to you for a minute?"

"Sure."

Drat. Here was one of those incredibly awkward moments. Doing things with the Colemans meant running into Joel's cousin at times, and over the past month the questioning glances cast at her and Joel had grown more intense. Vicki didn't know if the little tidbit regarding her horse issues had gotten loose or what.

Her response had been to avoid Karen as much as possible, which tonight, obviously, wasn't going to work.

Karen brought her into the quiet hallway leading toward Tamara's bedroom. "Feel free to tell me to mind my own business at any time, okay?"

Vicki loosened her teeth off her bottom lip where she'd been chewing it. "Did I do something wrong?"

"No, of course not. Well, when I offered you the position

with the trail rides, I didn't know you and Joel were seeing each other. Trust me, I am all for us women deciding what's best for our lives in terms of work situations. I still want you to be involved, but at the same time, I don't want you to feel you have to stick to a commitment we only made verbally in the fall."

The fluttering in her stomach ensured Vicki wasn't going to eat any more of her own treats tonight. Would her and Joel's friendship mean the end of her ticket out of Rocky? "You still want me involved. Like the position is still open?"

Karen nodded slowly. "I don't want to be the cause of trouble between you and Joel, though. I mean, he's kind of stuck here in Rocky, with his ranching and all, and if you're gone... Long-distance relationships are not easy."

Wow. Here was a situation she'd never thought of. "Well, thanks, but I think we'll be okay."

Her reassurances didn't seem to make it any better. Now Karen was out-and-out frowning. She cleared her throat. "Again, you can tell me to go to hell, but I have to say it. I hope you're not leading him on."

Oh jeez, this was going from bad to worse. "No, really, things are okay between me and Joel. He knows my plans for the spring, and he's good with it. Really."

Karen's disapproval was sharp enough to cut. "He's one of the gentle ones in the clan. Don't break his heart, okay?"

Vicki smiled. "I don't think there's any worry of that."

"You don't?" Karen tipped her head in the direction of the party. "I've seen the way he looks at you, and, girl, he is completely gone."

Karen was obviously a romantic. Or Joel was doing a better job of acting than they thought. "I'll keep that in mind."

She got away without any more of an inquisition, taking a deep breath before heading into the jam-packed living space.

Joel spotted her immediately, leaving the group he'd been chatting with. He crossed the room with his long-legged stroll that ate up the distance between them like it was nothing.

He tucked her under his arm, the smile on his face

warming her with its familiar heat. "You finish getting ready all those goodies you insisted on bringing?"

She nodded. "It was only right to bring something, and you know I like cooking. I'm glad I could contribute."

"They're glad you could contribute," he joked. "I would have brought a couple bags of chips and some dip."

"You would not."

He smiled as he reached for a glass. "You want anything with it?"

She'd given up that lie. Alcohol wasn't necessary for her to have a good time. "Just the Coke, thanks."

He settled them in a clear space on a love seat, and she leaned into his side. The place was more crowded than anything she'd attended, and yet a lot more comfortable than she'd dreamed possible.

Of course, considering the majority of people in the room were Colemans or their friends had something to do with that. Over the past month, most of the town folk had stopped making snide comments to her face. Didn't mean they had changed their opinion, but at least they weren't airing those particular thoughts as often or as loudly as before.

A musical laugh rang out from the front door and she stiffened in her seat.

It couldn't be.

She leaned forward to peer through the crowd, but too many bulky bodies stood between her and her target.

Joel played his fingers over her shoulder. "What's up?"

"I thought I just heard... No, it's impossible."

He lifted a brow. "What?"

She heard the laugh again and jumped to her feet. Damn being short. If she could have crawled on the furniture to get a better view, she would have.

Joel stood as well, trying to follow her gaze. "You're not being very party-like right now. It's tough to win at Eye Spy when I don't know what I'm looking for. Oh *fuck...*"

"Yeah." He'd pretty much summed it up. Sarah was at the front door, and she had her arm draped over Jesse's elbow, her body pressed intimately close.

Fuck. *Fuck.*

Vicki's first response was to hide.

The second was a familiar flash of anger. Brazen bitch. Her sister didn't do anything without an agenda. "You don't mind if I go see what the hell is going on, do you?"

Joel was at her side as they worked their way across the room. "Don't think this is yours to fight alone."

"I don't want to fight, I want to cause massive pain and then never have to see her again in my life."

"Sounds good to me. The causing-massive-pain part, only I get dibs on Jesse."

Joel stepped in front of her, effectively blocking her from getting close enough to Sarah to rip her ears off. His bulk also blocked Jesse from moving any farther into the room. "This is unexpected."

"Just dropping in on a family event. We won't stay long. Other things to do." Jesse grinned, his smirk less attractive than she'd remembered. It was as if his eyes had grown colder. "Of course, you both know Sarah."

Joel pointed back the way they'd come in. "Outside, Jesse. Let's talk without an audience."

Music still blasted, but little pockets of discussion were rising in corners.

"Sarah said she needed a washroom. Why don't you go ahead, sweetheart? We'll be done chatting by the time you get back." Joel was forced to step aside as Jesse slapped Sarah on the bottom and directed her farther into the apartment.

Vicki was torn. Did she go after her sister or stay with Joel?

Sarah vanished fast enough the decision was made for her. Vicki slipped out the door just in time to grab hold of Joel's arm and stop him from slamming his fist into his twin's face. "Whoa. That bit I said earlier about causing massive pain? Let's rethink that, okay?"

Because as mad as she was, she hated that she'd come between the two brothers.

Joel checked himself at Vicki's touch.

The pause allowed Jesse to back out of range and turn to sneer at Vicki. "You are a hell of a lot less fun than I thought you'd be. Other than being a pain in the ass, you're simply...needy, aren't you?"

Asshole. Joel glared daggers at his brother. "Leave Vicki out of this and explain what the hell you're doing showing up with Sarah."

"Hey, having a good time, you know. Nothing wrong with giving someone a chance."

Sarcasm dripped from his words.

The door at the entrance to the apartment slammed open, and Travis sauntered in. "Hell, it's a Six Pack party in the hallway. Who's in shit now?"

"Mind your own fucking business," Jesse snapped.

"Ahh, that answers my question." Travis stepped between the twins, pausing for a moment as he faced Jesse. "You're too dumb to realize this, but the guilty party always speaks first. And you know what's really odd? It usually seems to be you flapping your jaw far quicker than Joel."

"Stay out of it, Travis. I can deal with him." Joel tugged Vicki to his side, wishing he could insist she go back into the party, but it was as much her fight as his.

"There's nothing to deal with, jerk. I'm here, I brought a date, that's it." Jesse sniffed at Travis. "Speaking of dates, where's Ashley?"

Travis stiffened. "Fuck off, Jesse."

"Ha. Then I did hear right, she dumped you. Damn, you can't seem to keep a girl happy. Maybe you need to do like me and Joel." Jesse pointed at Vicki. "I mean, you're taken, and I nabbed Sarah for the night, but there's one more Hansol whore still available—"

Joel couldn't fathom the words had really been said.

Disbelief made him hesitate just long enough that by the time he went to smack some sense into his ass of a brother, Vicki had beaten him to it. She leapt from beside him and slammed her fist into Jesse's smirking face.

It took a moment of scuffling before Travis had Jesse in a headlock and Joel had his wildcat of a woman pulled free.

"Let me go. I'm going to kill the fucker." Vicki swung even when she must have known it was futile. Joel had her around the waist, holding her struggling body tight to his as he attempted to calm her.

"Let us have the fun, we've been waiting for longer." Travis jerked Jesse off his feet, biceps bulging as he kept his brother trapped in position. "Don't think about fighting back. You're in deep shit."

Fury whipped through Joel that Jesse would take whatever was pissing him off and make this battle into hurting Vicki. Wading in and using his fists to beat some sense into his brother would have been fun, but clearly wasn't going to work. "You have a problem with me, you talk to me, but you leave Vicki and Lynn out of this."

Travis released Jesse from his grasp, tossing him down the hallway. "I second that. I don't care if you want to poke at me or meet me outside the barn so I can rearrange your face. In my books, Vicki deserves more respect than you do."

"Now why would you defend her as well?" Jesse scrambled to his feet, wiping blood from his nose. He turned to face Joel. "Sharing with Travis this time? I guess you still haven't figured out how to fuck a woman on your own."

Silence descended on the hallway so hard Joel heard his blood pound past his eardrums. He couldn't let go and beat Jesse like he deserved or Vicki would be loose, and murder really would be done.

Travis held up a hand, speaking quietly to Vicki. "Ignore him. He's being an ass, and he's not worth it. Joel's got a damn fine woman in you, but I don't want you the way Jesse implied. I consider you a sister, and that's all I've ever said in public, and that's all that will be said. So if you want me to pound

Jesse on your behalf, you go ahead and let me know."

"No one has to beat him up." She relaxed, and when she tapped his arm, Joel set her on her feet. She nestled against his chest, glaring across at Jesse. "Your words, your actions, tonight and earlier. All of it makes me realize what I should have already known. Just because people are related doesn't mean someone will be like their family. I'm nothing like my sister, and, Jesse, you're nothing at all like your brothers."

"Just words, sweetheart. They're not going to make me cry into my pillow tonight."

"They should," she snapped. "I'm proud I'm not like Sarah, but you should be damn ashamed you're not more like Joel or Travis or Matt. I'd trust them with my life. I wouldn't trust you with dirt."

"Why, sweetie, what a sad way to talk about your sister." Sarah slipped out of the apartment door and stepped into the mess.

Jesse's face had flushed bright red at Vicki's accusation. Travis stood warily to the right, Joel protecting Vicki on the left.

Only Sarah moved, Vicki still as a statue as her sister paced closer.

Sarah tilted her head. "You're not like me? Maybe you should rethink that. You seemed to have weaseled your way into a protective family who are taking good care of you. Mama would be proud."

"Fuck you." The words came out soft and low, but lifeless, as if Vicki had no more fight left.

Joel saw it coming this time. When Sarah lifted her hand he caught her wrist before she could take a swing at Vicki. "You're not welcome here. I think you should go. You and Jesse, both."

"It's a Coleman family party. You've got no right to kick me out." Jesse blustered a bit as Sarah retreated to his side. Joel noticed he didn't take her hand or draw her close, more like turned aside as if she weren't even there.

Sarah noticed as well, her gaze darting between Jesse and

the others. Her eyes narrowed for a second before she hauled back and used the slap Joel had stopped earlier.

"What the hell was that for?" Jesse pressed a hand to his cheek where Sarah had laid into him.

She sniffed. "Fuck you for using me to pick a fight with your family."

Sarah swung on her heel and vanished out the apartment doors. Tension rose higher even as Joel stroked the back of Vicki's neck, willing her to relax.

"Gee, even the whores think you're a jerk," Vicki muttered.

Travis snorted.

Jesse glared in her direction, and his continued rotten attitude was the final straw. Joel stepped forward. "Had enough of you tonight. No, you're not welcome at the Coleman party. Not until you damn well remember what it means to be family."

"I agree." Travis gestured down the hall. "You only showed your face to take a piss on everyone anyway. Go home, Jesse. Go home until you grow up."

Jesse didn't say a word, just left.

Joel died a little inside at the loss, at the confusion and anger they'd tossed about like matchsticks. It hurt like hell to see his brother wrench farther apart from them all.

But he put his attention on the good he did have, turning Vicki toward him and kissing her cheek tenderly. "You're an incredible woman. Don't you forget that."

"I'm so sorry. I shouldn't have—"

"Stop." Joel cupped her face in his hands and put everything he could into his words. "Jesse made his choice, and it's not your fault. He was wrong. Period. I'm sick of him and his shitty attitude, and I'm sorry he hurt you."

She nodded, only she was blinking away tears. "I'm sorry he hurt you as well. Damn weird parties you people throw."

"This is not a typical Coleman..." Travis paused.

Joel swore, remembering another toxic New Year's party only a couple years earlier.

"Well, maybe it is." Travis straightened his jacket and gestured toward the door. "Come on, I need a drink."

Vicki caught his arm. "Ashley?"

Travis shook his head in an exaggerated manner. "You'd really make me discuss this *before* I toss back a couple strong ones? Evil woman."

Joel spoke up. "I thought things were going well."

"I thought you were good together," Vicki added.

Travis shrugged. "Yeah, but for one little argument she won't give an inch on. It's okay, or it will be down the road. She needs time to cool off."

"I hope it's soon." Vicki patted his arm, then linked her fingers into Joel's as she moved back against his side. "Thank you for defending me."

Travis nodded. "I meant it. You're alright. And I owed you."

She frowned, and suddenly Joel wasn't sure where this was going anymore.

Travis stared off into space for a minute before hauling his gaze back to meet hers. "In high school. I knew the guys were setting up that damn bet. I've kicked my own ass a million times I didn't tell them it was stupid or that I didn't do something to stop it. I'm sorry for the pain it caused you."

"Whoa." Vicki shook her head. "You...knew?"

Oh hell. How much did Travis know? Joel let her squeeze his fingers bloodless.

Travis took a deep breath. "It wasn't right what Eric did, taking advantage of you. I'm sorry."

Breath whooshed out of her like air from a released balloon as Joel scrambled to put the facts into place.

Travis was missing the fine details.

Vicki nodded slowly. "Thank you for telling me."

He lifted his dark eyes and allowed a smile to break free. "I wasn't very good at standing up for what I thought was right back then. I'm trying harder these days."

Vicki smiled and reached on her tiptoes to press a kiss to

Travis's cheek. "I meant what I said earlier. I trust you, and the rest of the Colemans. You're good people, Travis. And Joel's a wonderful friend. I'm thankful to have you guys in my life."

Travis cleared his throat. "Can we go drink now?"

Ring out the old, bring in the new. It was a mix of sadness and hope they were staring down as they reentered the apartment and walked into the noisy crowd.

Travis disappeared after winking at Vicki. Joel found a place for them in the thick of an animated exchange between Tamara and the three youngest Colemans: Rafe, Lisa and Lee.

Joel forced Jesse out of his mind. He had to, or it would drive him mad. He'd already gone through a dozen different ways they might have avoided the situation, and yet none were real solutions.

Jesse had chosen his path.

Joel concentrated instead on the woman in his arms, on trying to find ways to get her to relax and enjoy the evening. Slowly Vicki opened up again, her sadness fading and laughter coming quicker as they shared jokes and meaningless conversation with people who had no agenda other than to enjoy themselves. Joel breathed easier as the hours passed, but he couldn't help wondering.

In light of everything that was changing, what was the coming year going to hold?

Chapter Twenty-Four

"I don't suppose we could put this off for a few more weeks?" Vicki was certain she wasn't ready for this. Would never be ready.

And yet the confidence on his face said something different.

Joel shrugged. "Your choice, but eventually you need to get up on a horse, and I see no reason to postpone it any longer. You've only got a couple more months before you have to give your final yes or no to the job."

"I can't even wait that long. It's not fair to Karen if I bail at the last minute, and she has to scramble for a new cook." Vicki fought with herself. He was right, and with all the practice she'd had building up to this moment, there was no reason not to try.

February had come damn fast, though, in the big scheme of things.

By now, she'd waded through enough sheep they really were nothing but walking bundles of fluff. She'd saddled and unsaddled the sawhorse so often she could buckle straps with her eyes shut.

Even spending time around Trigger had been built into her training. Since New Year's, Joel had introduced one fresh challenge after another. He'd coaxed her from watching him walk the beast in a circle, to having her join them, to finally "helping" hold the lead rope.

Trigger seemed to think the entire exercise rather boring except that at the end of each lesson Joel always pressed a couple bits of carrot or apple slices into Vicki's hand. The first day she'd been certain she'd end up with missing fingers, but now it was more a case of convincing the stupid oaf there were no extra treats in her pockets, because Trigger didn't hesitate in sticking his nose where he had no right.

Today Joel upped the ante again. This was no longer leading the creature. He wanted her to get on its back and actually ride.

"Is it safe?" His snort of amusement pissed her off, and she smacked her fist into his chest. "Don't *do* that."

His arms went around her, settling and calming. "It's okay. It's more than okay. I'll stick close beside you, and Trigger isn't going to do anything to harm you."

God. "You owe me a big-time reward for this."

"Oral sex. Until you can't stand."

Vicki laughed even as she quickly glanced around the barn. "Damn it, Joel, stop."

"The oral sex? No way, you're too delicious. And the sounds you make when you're coming?" He gave a low growl.

"Stop talking about it out loud," she whispered.

If past history was any indication, somewhere in the barn, or outside and only moments away from springing around the corner, was bound to be a Coleman.

They had the stupidest luck when it came to being caught fooling around. The last time it had been Matt who'd backed out of the tack room with his eyes averted, huge grin on his face. Vicki's cheeks flushed at the memory—being bent over the sawhorse and taken from behind had been fun, but she could do without everyone in the family knowing.

Although the fact they were fucking like bunnies was probably a given by this point.

Joel gave her his hand. "Come on, darling. You have big-girl boots, you can do this."

She nodded and gripped his fingers tighter. Together they walked into the stall where Trigger was chomping the wisp of hay he'd pulled from in front of him. The yellow strawlike bit disappeared an inch at a time.

Vicki concentrated on keeping her breathing even. She had come a long way to be able to get this close to the beast without running in fear.

"You're doing wonderfully." Joel rubbed Trigger on the

forehead. "Hello, dude. You ready to help take care of someone special for me?"

"Take care of." Vicki shivered, but kept it under control. "Always sounds as if you're going to drag me into the yard and bury me."

"Nah. You're too good at helping with my chores. No way do I want you gone."

"Jerk."

They smiled at each other, and suddenly, things were going to be okay.

They led the horse into the round pen. The motions of saddling him went smoothly, although Vicki stayed back as much as possible. Joel smiled, a knowing grin on his face as he tugged her forward and squeezed her tight. When he guided her to Trigger's left side and stretched her hand upward to the pommel of the saddle, there was nothing but confidence in his actions. "Just like we've done a million times on Goliath."

Her wooden horse for the win.

Vicki let herself go into auto-mode. Foot in stirrup. Hands on the saddle. With all the practice Joel had made her do, the next motions followed instinctively. She pushed up, lifted her leg over Trigger's rump and, to her great surprise, ended solidly in position.

She was on a horse. "Fuck."

Joel laughed, still holding onto Trigger's halter. "You like it?"

"I'm...no, let's not go that far." She wasn't throwing up, screaming or peeing her pants in terror. She'd take this as a great improvement. "Don't you dare let go."

"Wouldn't dream of it." He smiled, and she beat down the impulse to tell him exactly what she felt. That expression of pride on his face did something to her. It wasn't just that he had continued to fulfill their bargain. It was more.

The *more than* she'd grown to feel wasn't hers to share. It was driving her crazy, but no way would she make sharing her new emotions a part of this deal. They'd set the boundaries. She wouldn't cross them.

But would she ever love to be able to say what she'd learned. What was inside screaming to break out. How much she really cared about him. How much being with him had changed her and given her hope.

How much she loved him.

God, she was a stupid twit.

Joel patted Trigger firmly. "You two ready for the next thing?"

The juxtaposition of her thoughts and his comment made her want to cry. Yes, she was ready, for what was never to be...

"Okay." The word came out a little creaky, but he probably blamed the hesitation on her fears, not on the lump of regret building in her throat.

Joel led Trigger forward slowly, and Vicki worked on releasing the death grip she'd taken on the pommel. Focused on using her thighs to grasp tighter. Her thoughts still raced far faster than Joel paced with the horse.

She was going to get her wish and get the hell out of Rocky. Escape the place that held so many terrible memories and had trapped her. Yet escape meant leaving behind all the good things she'd experienced in the past while.

Sadness coated the pleasure and left her cold inside.

She didn't think it was all one-sided, either. He liked her as well. Everything about the man said he had some feelings for her—his gentleness and patience. It might have been a verbal deal between them in the start, but it must be more now.

Things had changed. She was sure of it.

Only if she told Joel how she felt, and he admitted this was more than a casual romp between friends? Then what the hell would they do?

She'd run into her mother in the grocery store the other day, and the meeting had left Vicki's nerves on edge and brittle as Debbie let the accusations fly, cutting remarks that Vicki should be old enough to allow to roll off her back, but couldn't.

Her sister's behavior wasn't any better. Sarah had been

caught fooling around with another married man who should have known to keep his zipper up. But the ensuing rush of gossip meant the Hansol name got a fresh whipping through town, and the judgmental glances increased again. The snide remarks. The women who curled themselves protectively around their guys when she and Joel walked into Traders.

As if she'd want their men while holding on to Joel? Stupid bitches.

Still, the actions hurt. Another layer of pain to deal with. Which meant she was back to her dilemma. She could stay in town and continue to be dumped on, and maybe, if she were reading things correctly, she'd get to be with Joel. Or she could make a fresh start somewhere else without her heart.

Fucking great choices.

"You're so comfortable up there you're wool-gathering," Joel teased.

Vicki dragged herself back to reality, shocked to find he was right. "Trigger is kind of like Goliath on steroids. He's not as scary, because you're holding him. Don't stop holding him or anything," she hastened to add. "This is enough for now."

Joel patted her leg. "You are doing great. Loosen up, though. If you sit like that for any length of time, you'll be so sore at the end of the ride you'll be walking funny."

"Loosen up?" Vicki stared at her hands, at the saddle under her fingers. She had a hold on the leather, but she wasn't white-knuckling it anymore. "I think this is about as loose as you're going to get."

He kept Trigger moving forward, but shifted closer. He slid his hand up her thigh. "No, I think you can do better."

No bloody way. "Joel Coleman, if you're going to start something sexual, you can fuck right off."

His eyes widened. "Okay, you're still a little stressed."

"You think?"

Joel laughed. "I'm not headed for any intimate parts, darling. Trust me."

That was the problem. She did trust him, and yet was it

enough? "Don't push me too hard. I'm going to break."

He soothed her, and Trigger at the same time for all she knew, the sound stroking her, but it was too late. Tension had flooded in. Her heart rate had increased, and she really didn't want to be there anymore.

Like some miracle worker he read her mind. "Come here."

He opened his arms and she leaned over, clutched his neck and allowed him to pull her from the horse. He cradled her with one hand, pausing only to loop Trigger's lead rope over a hook before carrying her out of the round pen.

Foolish regret washed over her in a wave. "Damn it, I was doing so well."

"You are amazing. You got up on the back of a horse. All by yourself. That calls for a celebration."

"More moonshine shots?"

He snorted. "Not likely. I think I mentioned something else."

Vicki stared into his face as he carried her to the side of the barn. His eyes sparkled with mischief, his muscles tense under her fingers. "What are you planning...? Oh, you're not serious."

She caught hold tighter as he eased her between his body and the ladder fixed vertically to the wall. "The lesson isn't finished."

"Oh God, you're insane." The idiot went straight up the ladder and into the hayloft, carrying her body weight as well as his own as if she were a feather.

The lighting was thinner up here, no bright fluorescent bulbs overhead. Joel nuzzled her neck as he brought her to where the bales were stacked unevenly, a little bench all ready for him. He sat with her still in his arms, her knees ending up straddling him. "Stand up."

"You just left Trigger loose in the arena. Saddled and bridled."

He undid her jeans and tugged them off her hips. "You're not listening to me."

"You abandoned your horse." Oh Lord, what was he up to?

259

She caught his shoulders for balance as he pulled the fabric off one foot, then the other.

"Trigger will hang out until we're done. It's like saddle training them when they're younger."

Her fingers moved of their own accord and slipped through his soft hair. "Joel?"

He ran his hands over her naked hips, gaze lingering for a moment on her pussy before he met her eyes. "I want you."

God. If only. Vicki batted down the emotions and slapped her brain until it was focused on nothing but the physical side of that comment. "I'm yours."

If she'd expected him to go slow, she'd have lost the bet. He jerked her forward and covered her with his mouth, tongue dipping between her folds. His fingers gripped her ass cheeks as he squeezed and played, that damn talented tongue lapping her entire length before stopping to torment her clit.

She dug her hands into his hair and held on tight.

Enthusiasm he had in spades, no doubt about that, eating greedily, driving her crazy. One hand snuck around her hip, caressing her skin until a finger pressed into her, and she groaned out his name.

"You like this, hmm?" He pumped slowly, stroking the most sensitive spots inside, and her legs quivered. Another flurry of his tongue over her clit, and the first orgasm hit, her sheath clutching at the two digits he now spread her on. "Oh, darling, yeah. That's the way. Cream on my fingers. Mmm, you taste good."

She wanted him to shut up and get his tongue back on her, but the words were driving her as much as his touch. "Don't stop."

Begging. Begging for more, more than he could even know.

He licked and nibbled until she was ready to scream, the constant thrust into her sex flinging her closer to the edge so rapidly she couldn't breathe. When he pulled his fingers free, she muttered unhappily.

"You just wait, I'm going to fill you up pretty good with

something else." He fumbled at his groin, and she peered down to see he had already rolled on a condom, his thick cock rising from his open pants.

"Hell, yeah." Vicki dropped into his lap and speared herself on his erection, her head falling back in ecstasy as he stretched her wide. "Oh *God*, Joel."

He caught her hips in his hands and rocked her up and down, the wide head of his shaft creating the perfect internal caress. "That's it. Move over me. Use your thighs. Fuck, that's good."

Vicki leaned in and took his lips, the taste of what he'd been doing a moment earlier lingering on his tongue as he helped her fuck herself on his cock. All the way up until he'd nearly break free, then a hard plunge down, her body undulating over him.

He hummed against her lips. "Only thing that would make this better would you being butt-naked, those tits swinging every time you ride."

Vicki closed her eyes and gripped his shoulders tighter. "Some other time."

"Nice and smooth, right, feel these muscles?" He stroked her ass, her lower back, returning to massage her butt as he helped carry her weight. "Feel how relaxed you are? That's the way to ride. Everything moving and easy."

A stream of laughter bubbled up. "Joel Coleman, is this a riding lesson?"

He nuzzled her neck and brought their bodies closer, dragging a hand between them to tease her clit as he fucked deeper into her body. "Ride your cowboy, darling. Make it good."

Pleasure broke and she couldn't do more than gasp, words eluding her as her body caught hold of his cock and tore his orgasm free as well. Joel squeezed his eyes shut, and she stared into his face as he came, all control gone in that moment, nothing but the physical delight they'd shared.

The face of the man she'd fallen in love with.

A loud slam broke from the right, sunshine flooding over

them as the hayloft doors swung wide to the cold bright day.

"Shit." Joel jerked her jeans around her, attempting to cover her naked ass as Jesse stared at them from beside the open doors.

He took in their position, not giving them any privacy. His expression made it clear he was pissed.

"You mind?" Joel called.

"I'm doing my bloody work. Shouldn't have to give a warning call before I walk into the damn barn. Just..." Jesse grabbed a bale and tossed it through the opening, "...fuck each other blind for all I care, but do it in the goddamn trailer. I'm moving out. You can have it to yourself and stop providing free shows for everyone in the family. Unless that's part of what turns you on."

He didn't give them a minute alone. Vicki waited until his back was briefly turned so she could clamber off and race around the corner, hiding behind the bales as she scrambled to straighten her underwear and jeans. It was like some weird nightmare she couldn't wake from.

"You're moving out?" Joel repeated.

"Steve and Trevor have room for me in their place."

"You don't have to do that."

"I think I do," Jesse snapped. "I don't want to talk about it. The decision is made."

Vicki died a little more inside. She might not like Jesse very much, but this was her fault as well, coming between the brothers. Another part of why staying in Rocky wasn't a good thing.

Joel stepped into view and looked her over. "You okay?"

"Embarrassed," she whispered. It wasn't how she wanted this session to end. And it certainly wasn't how she wanted Joel and Jesse to end, either.

Joel held out a hand, wrapping his fingers around hers and tugging her to his body. He kissed the top of her head. "Don't be. Honestly."

"Yeah, don't be embarrassed," Jesse cut in. "It's not as if

I've never seen ass—"

"Fuck off, Jesse," Joel ordered.

The slam of another bale smacking into the bed of the pickup truck below rang like a warning klaxon in the silence that followed. Jesse glanced over one final time, then deliberately turned his back and returned to dropping bales.

Joel led her to the ladder and went down first. Vicki glanced over her shoulder to see Jesse staring after her, anger in his eyes, frustration and...a touch of sadness?

She swallowed hard and faced the wall. It wasn't her place to make him happy. In fact, she couldn't understand how the two brothers had turned out to be so different from each other. Guilt poked her even as she admitted she wanted nothing further to do with Jesse.

If she weren't in the picture, would they be able to patch things up?

Falling in love wasn't supposed to hurt this hard.

Chapter Twenty-Five

Twenty-one candles crowded the surface of the cake. Vicki stared, not so much in shock at the number of them, but at the entire celebration raging around her.

The Colemans had insisted on hosting her a birthday party.

"You need help?" Robbie leaned harder against her leg. He'd basically jumped her the moment she and Joel had walked into the big ranch house. Joel raised a brow, but said nothing when Robbie determinedly separated their linked fingers so he could take control and tug Vicki off.

And now, after the meal was over, she still had a cling-on by her side.

"I can help, if you'd like. I'm a good candle blower-outer."

Beth laid a hand on her son's shoulder. "Let Vicki have some of the fun, okay?"

"I don't mind." Vicki smiled at the little guy. She stopped herself before sharing she'd never blown out candles before, deciding last second her lack of experience wasn't worth bringing up. She was getting the chance now, no matter that the occasion was bittersweet.

She'd done it, Joel and her. She still didn't love the beasties, but she was comfortable enough around horses to survive the summer.

She left in just over two weeks.

Little fingers poked her arm. "You making a wish or somethin'?"

Vicki nodded. "I am. You ready to help me?"

Beth caught Robbie as he shoved himself too far forward. "Whoa there, mister, you don't need to be kissing the cake to do your job."

Laughter curled around the clan, and in spite of not having made a wish, Vicki leaned forward and blew.

Besides, there was only one wish in her heart these days.

The enthusiastic helper at her side probably took out most of the skinny candles, but she did see a couple flames waver and extinguish after she aimed their direction. All except one, which flickered then roared back to full potency.

She drew a breath to try again then paused, surprised by the chorus of whistles and catcalls that broke out. Lots of grinning faces greeted her, Joel being jabbed in the ribs good-naturedly by Blake.

What the heck?

One quick tug and she had Robbie's full attention. "Why are they laughing?"

He pointed his finger at the still-burning candle. "You missed one. That means you got a boyfriend."

Her gaze shot to meet Joel's, and he smiled, sweet and sexy at the same time. Her heart broke a tiny bit further even as she soaked in the experience.

"Well," she said to the group at large. "I guess I do."

Cake and ice cream consumed, the crowd sauntered outside to take in the fresh spring air.

"Thankfully the winter was short." Hope leaned her elbows on the railing and watched the nephews kick a soccer ball around the yard. Nearby, Blake and Jaxi's nearly two-year-old twins were pretending to be horses, whinnying and pawing the ground with their feet. "Damn, those kids are cute. There should be a law against it."

"Makes you want some of your own?" Vicki wasn't ready for kids, no matter how cute they were.

Hope shrugged. "I think I'm immune for a few years. There's still a lot of things Matt and I want to do before we start a family, especially with the shop finally making some money instead of sucking my savings dry."

"Kids are fun, but yeah, not something to rush into." Jaxi stroked the soft curls of the baby held against her chest in a cotton hammock contraption.

Vicki glanced over her shoulder at the truck pulling into the yard. "More company?"

"Karen."

Once again guilt hit. Joel knew her time was limited, but they hadn't shared that with the rest of the family yet. He had told her to wait. He'd obviously been in on the plans for the birthday party and probably didn't want to blow the surprise with announcements she would shortly disappear.

A group split apart to greet Karen. The woman expertly backed the horse trailer into position at the gate one paddock over from where the kids played. She jumped from the truck cab and waved, pulling on a pair of gloves as she walked to the trailer door.

Hope wandered off toward the guys while Jaxi shifted position as well, moving closer to where her girls continued to laugh and play, ignoring the grown-up action.

Vicki caught herself smiling at their antics as she turned back to focus on Joel. "New horses?"

Joel lingered at her side, his hand resting on her lower back as he propped himself against the railing. "One. Dad bought a stud at auction last week, and Karen offered to pick him up when she grabbed the couple the Whiskey Creek clan purchased."

Vicki leaned into his touch, watching as the trailer was opened. Movement showed through the open windows as the horse shuffled position. The sound of his discontent in being enclosed escaped, stomping hooves and other more vocal complaints.

It was incredible to think she could be here, experiencing this. Because of the things Joel had done, the things he'd taught her. The way all of the family had taken her in.

Except one.

She looked around the yard, not wanting to bring up the sore spot, but curious if Jesse had cut and run for the day or if he would show up at some point to make his obvious displeasure clear.

"He's gone."

Vicki glanced up.

Joel's arm was around Vicki but his focus remained on the action by the horse trailer. "If you're looking for my sad-assed twin, he left a message he had something really important to do this weekend, and he'll be back when he gets back."

Guilt. Strong and powerful. "I'm so sorry—"

"Stop it." She had all his attention now. Joel cupped her cheeks and kissed her hard before capturing her gaze, the blue in his eyes reflecting the spring sky. "Remember? We've had this conversation. His actions are his responsibility. You've done nothing wrong, so ignore him. His loss, anyway, he missed some awesome cake and ice cream."

She forced a smile because he was right. This was—

A terrible metallic screech sounded, jerking their attention to the trailer. Karen's truck rolled forward, shuddering to a stop a few feet from where it had begun. The ramp Karen was guiding the horse down bounced unsteadily, and she threw out her hands to catch her balance.

The horse spooked, lurching upright on the lead rope she held and lifting her feet off the ground.

"Shit." Joel took off at a dead run, little puffs of dust rising from under his boots.

Blake and Mike moved into position to help when a loud gun-like blast rang out, and the horse freaked further. He lowered his head and stormed forward, pivoting as soon as he'd cleared the roof of the trailer. Karen clung to the rope, but she was holding a wild beast.

With a space open between the ramp and the gate, the animal was set on escape. He spun, and this time Karen flew free, arms spread, legs wide. She landed with a sickening crash half-on, half-off the ramp, her cry of pain sharp and bitter.

The horse made a break for the main road, which put him on a direct path past where Vicki stood against the railing. The lead rope hung loose from the horse's halter. His tail was up, nostrils flaring. He tossed his head and snorted out his fears.

Robbie darted from under the fence in hot pursuit of his rolling ball, and Vicki's stomach fell.

The world flipped into slow motion, it really did. There was no time to think, only do. She was the closest person by far, with the men gathered by the trailer and Jaxi burdened with the baby. Out of the corner of her eye she saw one of the guys sprinting toward them, but she knew he'd never make it in time. Instinct kicked in, born of all those lessons Joel had made her repeat again and again.

There was a sickening taste of fear at the back of her throat, her limbs gone numb. In spite of her rising nausea, she rushed forward. There was nothing else she could do.

The fact a far more experienced horsewoman had just been thrown didn't change the urgency. All she saw were dangerous front hooves slamming into the ground, and Robbie in the way.

He finally heard the shouting. He lifted his head as he twisted, face gone white as the horse bore down on him.

Vicki dashed between the horse and the boy, waved her arms and shouted. With macabre fascination she watched the beast rush toward her, waiting for the pain of impact to arrive, fully expecting to be trampled.

Only he jerked to a stop and sniffed hard. Her heart might have stopped as well. She had gone stone cold, and everything around them faded away until it was just her and the horse in a tiny corner of the world.

Terror of a different sort rocked her, images of the beast lifting his forequarters then slamming down on Robbie. To stop him from rearing she clutched the lead rope, snatching at his mane with the other. "Easy now. Whoa."

Her feet were firmly on the ground, anchoring the horse in position. Her ploy seemed to have worked, at least until he lifted his head. With her hands gripping the lead rope and his mane, she rose into the air. Dangling from his head she might have been a fly for all the attention he paid her.

He took off without lunging, though. Moving down the lane

at a slower speed, Robbie left behind.

The demon-possessed horse had calmed, but still seemed intent on fleeing from the ranch with Vicki stuck like a burr to his neck. She hung on for dear life while being jolted as he trotted out the main gate. She couldn't get her fingers to release.

"Come on, it's okay. Easy. *Easy.*"

Like she'd learned to imitate the Coleman cowboy stroll, she did her best to copy how Joel always talked around the animals. Smooth and calm. A total lie from what she felt inside, but she got the words out. Somehow? They sounded as if she was taking a stroll in the park.

"Easy, boy."

Then a miracle happened. The hell horse slowed to a walk.

Hope rose. Her heart still pounded enough to make the blood roar in her ears, but the beast was settling. His head dropped low enough her feet touched the ground.

"That's it. Good boy."

She glanced back toward the ranch. She thought she'd heard another horse, and sure enough, there was Joel, riding bareback, a coil of rope in his hand. He approached slowly, but the wild beastie in front of her twitched.

"He's scared of you," she warned.

"Easy, boy. Easy." Joel glanced at Vicki. "Hold him steady. You're doing great."

He slipped off Trigger and paced forward cautiously. He *shh*ed the horse a few times as he got closer, wrapping his hand over hers on the rope. "You can let go now."

No. No, she didn't think she could. Her fingers were locked in that position for the rest of her life. Vicki nodded, though, and slowly stepped away, the smooth fibers pulling from her crooked fingers as she increased the distance between them.

Joel's attention remained fixed on the runaway as he spoke soft and slow. "Lead Trigger back to the barn," he ordered.

After the hundreds of times she'd crawled on his back, after dealing with the panicked new beast, it didn't seem nearly as scary anymore to grasp hold of the sedate Trigger's mane and tug him toward the barn. "Come on, big guy."

Her stomach tightened as they moved, but now it had nothing to do with the horse at her side. Whatever had caused her phobia in the first place had been replaced with confidence she knew what to do.

No, the agony twisting her had less to do with the stinky beast and everything to do with having to say goodbye in a few days. Goodbye to Robbie, who she spotted ahead, wrapped in his dad's arms. Dirt streaked his face from his little hands rubbing his teary eyes.

She'd be leaving the Colemans, most of whom had opened their homes and their hearts.

And leaving...

God, she couldn't even think it without choking up.

Mike Coleman met her near the corral. He surrounded her with an arm and pressed his lips to her forehead. "You done good. You done real good."

Blake gave her a hug of his own before taking Trigger and guiding him back inside the railings.

Vicki swallowed hard and set her resolve. It had been the most incredible experience of her life, being with the Colemans. They'd shown her how family was supposed to act. Well, Jesse's actions proved even in the best of families, nothing was perfect. But she'd only been invited in for a short while, and as much as she wanted this to be real—it wasn't.

Somewhere down the road, in a better location, after a fresh start, she hoped she'd find this again, and when she did? She'd do everything in her power to make it last forever.

She took in the slowly settling chaos. Karen was laid out on the ramp, her face tight with pain, one leg bent at an awkward angle. Hope, Matt and Travis were all there, supporting her. Marion, Beth and Jaxi had most of the children rounded up and were guiding them inside. Robbie remained in Daniel's arms, the two of them talking seriously as Daniel carried him toward the barn.

Joel soothed the wary beast back into the yard even as an ambulance siren drew nearer.

It was like trying to memorize a sunset, every moment precious yet vanishing quickly. Watching him made all kinds of memories pop to mind, bringing both joy and tears of frustration.

He led the horse past her, and Mike took over, Blake at his side to ensure the animal went where he belonged this time.

Joel folded her against his body and kissed the top of her head. "Darling, that was the most incredible thing I've ever seen. I'm so proud of you."

"I'll start shaking once I go home. Oh my God, Joel, what did I do?"

"What had to be done." He kissed her again then walked her toward the barn, his arm still draped around her shoulders. "What you were trained to do."

She didn't believe it when he brought her into the corral, to Trigger's side and offered a leg up. "You want me to ride him bareback? Now?"

She glanced around at the turmoil-filled yard.

Joel nodded. "Trust me. Mount up."

Heart and mind still a whirl, she followed his orders and found herself on Trigger's broad back, fingers twisted in the stiff hair of his mane. A moment later Joel joined her, settling his hand around her waist and snuggling their torsos tight as he nudged Trigger forward. "First rule of horses. Get right back in the saddle."

Swaying together as Trigger circled the yard, Vicki found it hard to argue with Joel, if only for the fact she got to be nestled in his arms once more.

And when Daniel appeared, leading Robbie on another horse, Vicki had to smile.

Joel rested his chin over her shoulder, their cheeks touching. "Be proud of yourself. This proves nothing's going to stop you from doing your job this summer. You did it. Your dreams are coming true."

If that was so, why did she feel as if her hopes and dreams were slipping from her fingers?

The ache between his shoulders wasn't caused by any chores he remembered doing. Joel rubbed his neck with one hand briefly then gave up and poured his glass full to the brim.

"You drowning your sorrows or getting ready to fight?" His cousin Gabe spun the chair opposite him and sat in it backward.

"Both. Neither." Joel gestured to the pitcher. "Help yourself. I asked Jesse to join me, but hell if I know if he's going to show."

"Your brother still playing that game?" Gabe shook his head. "Asshole."

Joel laughed, the sound tainted with bitterness. "Yeah, have to agree with you there."

Gabe glanced around the pub. "Slow night. Not a lot of the clan out."

"Busy or broken. Calves are still dropping at our place and the Moonshine spread. I'm off until tomorrow noon, and Blake swore I get to pull for the next twenty-four hours straight. Whiskey Creek clan is going crazy trying to deal with Karen being laid up with that busted leg."

Gabe eyed him far too knowingly. "And Vicki?"

"She and Hope are packing. Nothing but clothes left, and they said they didn't want any guys around."

His cousin sipped his beer then stared up at the ceiling. "I heard she's leaving."

Fuck. Joel couldn't speak for a moment. It wasn't that he didn't know this was coming, but every time the reality hit, it hurt a hell of a lot more. "Yeah. She's cooking for Karen's crew for the summer."

"She'll be back in the fall?"

Joel swallowed hard. "Don't know. Probably not."

There was nothing to bring her back, and a lot to keep her away. Once she'd found a chance outside of Rocky, he couldn't ever see her wanting to return.

"You okay with that?"

Joel glared at his cousin. "You interfering again? I thought your wife was curing you of your need to be everyone's savior."

Gabe grinned. "Once an Angel, always an Angel..."

Joel tossed a napkin in his face.

His cousin sobered. "I thought you two were good together. I'd hate to see you making some kind of mistake because you're too afraid to go after what you want."

A string of curses rose inside, but he held them back. He and Gabe were close in temperament. If he'd spent years saving Jesse, Gabe had done the same for most of the rest of the Coleman clan. Guardian angel was right.

He met Gabe's eyes steadily and confessed the truth. "It's not a case of being afraid, asshole. It was an act. Us being together. Couple reasons for it, but it was only meant to last until now. And if you ever share that with anyone I will call you a liar, and then I'll bury you."

"It was an act?" Gabe wiped his mouth for a moment, and Joel wasn't sure if the man was trying to figure out what to say or hiding a smile. Definitely a smile. Gabe leaned forward. "Well, if you want to know a secret, me and Allison? Started out pretty much that way as well."

Joel thought for a minute. Nope. Couldn't see any connection between his cousin's marriage, and his and Vicki's little ploy. "Bullshit."

"Not bull, but never mind that for a minute. You happy she's going?" Gabe glanced at the nearly empty beer pitcher.

Joel sighed. "No. But it's what she's always wanted. Rocky is full of hurtful memories and stupid people who keep on tormenting her. How the hell can I ask her to give up on her dreams because I like having her around?"

"Oh, well, you can't." Gabe sat back and lifted his glass. "That would be totally stupid."

The instinct to fight was rising. "Fuck off, Gabe, and tell me what you're playing at."

Gabe glanced down the length of the room at his wife who was perched on the arm of a chair chatting with her sister. Allison caught him looking and smiled back, the expression shining out like a rainbow. Gabe didn't take his eyes off her as he spoke. "Liking someone is for when you're in high school. Loving someone is what makes people change their lives for another person."

Joel froze.

Gabe turned back. "Makes a huge difference, you know. You want to be like Jesse and sleep your way through all of southern Alberta for another couple years? Or are you grown up enough to know what you want is what you've already got? Worth fighting for."

Joel ignored the question of Vicki for a minute, because what he wanted didn't seem possible. "Jesse hates my guts right now."

"So?"

Shit. "Didn't expect that response."

His cousin shrugged. "You need his approval to live your life?"

"Hell, no. Just seems as if he could not want to follow me and still get along. Instead he's cut himself off from the entire family. I've lost my brother."

"You haven't lost him, he's chosen to run off and be an ass." Gabe paused. "You can't blame yourself for others' actions. You can't fix them unless they want to be fixed, and even then they have to do the changing, not you. It's a tough lesson, Joel, but it's real."

Joel pondered that for a minute. He'd been trying his best to be forgiving. He hadn't given up on connecting with his brother even while he was damn pissed for the way Jesse had treated Vicki. Some day he hoped they'd be able to mend that situation. But he wasn't going to change to make Jesse happy, which kind of meant, right now, Jesse wasn't going to be happy.

As sad as that truth was, it seemed to be the only choice.

But Vicki?

"I don't want her to go," he confessed.

Gabe stared over the table. "Then don't. I mean, don't let her go without telling her."

"Asking her to stay somewhere she hates is damn selfish. I don't want her to give up her dream."

"What if you're part of her dream? Why would you deny her, and yourself, everything you could have?"

Joel played with his empty glass. "There's no easy solution."

Gabe cleared his throat. "Not when you try to find the answers all by yourself, idiot."

His raised brow was the final punctuation mark Joel needed to light the fucking fire under his ass. Good grief, Gabe was right. And Joel was wrong, in so much of what he'd focused on over the past two months.

He threw money on the table as he shoved his chair back. "You mind if I run out on you?"

Gabe shook his head. "Nothing to mind. Go get her, tiger."

Joel pushed through the doors of Traders, his brain whirling with possibilities.

He and Vicki had started this with three goals. The first had been met beyond their expectations. The second, well, he'd learned small-town gossip refused to let up completely, but it was time to finish up the third with a bit of flair. Maybe he wouldn't have to lose the best thing that had ever happened to him.

Only if he wanted to do it right in the short time he had remaining, it was going to take a little planning...

Chapter Twenty-Six

Joel's cryptic voice mail had said nothing more than he wanted to meet her by the river at nine.

Vicki fought her sadness. Her life was packed into a shockingly small pile of boxes and the two panniers of clothing for her bike.

It seemed the final days of living in her hometown should be faced with more fanfare. Things still weren't perfect, and her family continued to haunt her. The past memories burned, and the current snide comments and the accusations she didn't deserve had slowed but not vanished.

Add in the icy-cold reception she'd gotten from Jesse Coleman the few times she'd been unlucky and met him while on her own, God, it was enough to make her crazy.

Even running into Eric Tell and having him pass by without attempting to rile her up wasn't as sweet with the bitter taste of Jesse and Joel's ruined relationship flavouring everything.

Getting out of Rocky was the only way to save herself and Joel more pain. It was as if she were cutting out her heart and leaving the best of her behind, though.

She'd debated this over and over. Saying something about how she felt would be horrid, and like hell would she give any indication she was dying inside. Two more days until she turned her bike north and left forever.

The tears she wiped from her eyes were the only weakness she'd allow.

She taped the lid of the final box. Wrote a note to Hope who had offered to store the boxes in the shed at her and Matt's place. Hope hadn't said anything in condemnation when Vicki had told her she was leaving, only her eyes had looked volumes. As if the woman knew this wasn't what Vicki really wanted, no matter how much the words from her mouth insisted it was.

If Joel had been her first real best friend, Hope had become her first girlfriend. They hadn't spent many nights together in the apartment before Hope and Matt got married, but enough that Vicki was going to miss her. And she felt like crap for not having shared more about her plans in the first place.

Another reality of having people you considered family? She'd hurt others without intending to.

She pulled the apartment door shut after her. Hope and Matt would grab the boxes later that night. Now, all she had were Saturday and Sunday in Rocky before her life changed for good. Joel had asked her to spend them with him.

One final weekend in his arms. It wasn't just the sex they would share, it was him. Being with him, having him near. There was no way she could refuse the invitation even though she should have. She would have to hide her emotions the entire forty-eight hours.

She took the steep stairs down from the second-story apartment and made her way to her bike.

A bouquet of wildflowers was strapped to the handlebars.

Vicki stood without moving for a full minute before she threw the panniers into position and reached for the card poking from the foliage.

I've never given you flowers and that's something a boyfriend should do. Hope you like them. See you at the river? I have one more surprise.

It wasn't safe riding with tears in her eyes, but she had no choice.

His truck was pulled to the right of the tree where they'd first met so long ago. She parked to the side, not worrying this time about hiding her wheels.

The entire lanky length of him stepped out from behind the vehicle, and she soaked in the sight.

He waited until she'd removed her helmet before coming

over and picking her up. Bodies meshed close as she gave in and let herself enjoy being in his arms. Once more savouring his strength as he held them together, their mouths connected, tongues and lips battling hungrily.

Vicki wrapped her legs around him, the strong muscles of his torso so familiar now, so wonderful to touch. She pulled back and sighed. "Hey, you."

He stared into her eyes, and for a moment she forgot how to breathe. "Thanks for coming."

They stood there, not talking. Not kissing or anything, yet unable to turn away from each other. She forced out a whisper. "This is crazy. You should put me down."

Joel nodded and lowered her. "Sorry. I'm a little distracted."

"Me too."

Joel tilted her chin with a stroke of his fingers. "Hey. No long faces. You did it. You did the most important thing you set out to do."

Yeah, she had. She'd also done what she'd never intended. She'd fallen in love.

"Thanks to you." Vicki accepted the hand he held out. "So, you going to have a busy summer?"

Joel cleared his throat. "Before I answer that, I have to apologize."

Vicki thought back, but couldn't see why. "Umm, for what?"

He pointed toward her bike. "There were a couple things I missed. Like the flowers, and something else. And if we're going to finish this, I have to make sure it's done right."

He talked so easily about things being over. Vicki pasted on a smile and forced herself to copy his nonchalance. She followed him around the tree. "Goofball. What else did you forget?"

He turned her to face the tree, tugging her body back to lean on him.

There was an enormous heart carved into the wide trunk, with *Joel + Vicki* filling the center of the space. The raw wood looked fresh, the marks recent.

She sucked for air, but none seemed to be available to fill her lungs. Joel stroked his hand down her side as he knelt behind her, creating a place for her to sit on his strong thigh. He turned her face toward him, cupping her cheek. "It's supposed to be self-explanatory, but to make sure you don't miss the message, I'll say it as well. I love you."

"Oh my God." Vicki blinked back tears. "You do?"

"Like crazy. Completely, totally, head over heels." He smiled, the sweet sexy version that made her knees shake and her body ache. "If you keep staring at me with those wide eyes of yours, not saying anything, I'm going to think I freaked you out forever."

"You love me?"

Joel grinned. "Vicki, darling? You going to—?"

Maybe she was supposed to do something else, but there was no other response. She flung her arms around his neck and kissed him until she needed to let go or pass out from the stars spinning in her head.

When she leaned away, his grin had grown wider. "You got anything to say?"

"We're insane. How can this be? What's going to happen? I leave in two days, and oh my *God*, you love me?"

Joel held her face tenderly. "One step at a time. I'm not going to let you go *anywhere* until you say it. You do love me, don't you? I didn't imagine you feel the same as me?"

"You didn't dream it up. I'm...how did you say it? Crazy about you. Totally and completely, head over heels." She shook her head. "But this wasn't supposed to happen. I'm moving away. I can't cancel on Karen now. Not with the other last-minute changes she's had to deal with."

"I don't want you to cancel. I think you should go work for the summer." Joel rearranged her so she was curled up in his lap, his broad back leaning on the tree beside where he'd posted for everyone to see how he felt.

"You want me to leave you?"

"Oh hell, no. Part of me wants you to stay right here, close. Now that I've told you how I feel, I want to spend the next days and months and years saying it until it sinks in for real. Only..." He wiped a tear from the corner of her eye. "Only...we're young. We've got so much time ahead of us, and so many things to look forward to. Maybe, if you and I think about it together, we can figure out what's right for both of us, now and down the road."

Vicki's heart pounded. "But you love me?"

He laughed out loud. "And you love me. That's the starting point. Yes."

"Fuck, yeah." It was incredible, and yet there was so much rushing her brain right now. "I'm going to hate being away from you for the entire summer."

Joel nodded. "I'll miss you too, but you're right. Karen needs you to keep your commitment. So I'll come visit you on your days off."

She sat in shock. "You'll drive seven hours to visit me?"

"Hell, I'd drive farther than that. You're worth it. And when the job is over, you can move back here, move in with me."

A sliver of icy cold snuck into her happiness.

Jesse.

She stroked Joel's cheek. "I know I've said this before, but I need to say it again. I'm sorry I came between you and your brother."

Joel's gaze traced her face. "And I'll say it again as well—it wasn't your fault. He and I had come to a crossroads. A place in our lives where things had to change, and if it hadn't been you, it would have been something else. I still care about the jerk, but I don't like what he's become. I don't think we should close the door on him if he wants to make things right. But he's picked his path, and if I want him to respect our decisions, I have to respect his. As wrong and stupid and as bullheaded as he's being."

He was right, but the guilt remained. Doubts rushed in as she wondered how they'd deal with everything. "This is a dream..."

He pulled her closer, their torsos tight together until his warmth poured over her. "No, it's one hundred percent real. And it's still your choice, but hell if I could let you walk out of my life without telling you how I feel."

Vicki followed the outline of the heart with a fingertip. "This is more than just *telling* me."

"Okay, fine, I'm claiming you." He smiled, stroking her arms as if he couldn't get enough of touching her. "You can go away for a while, but you'd better enjoy your freedom because it's the last time you get to be without me for the rest of your life."

Everything was still a blur. "I keep thinking I'm going to wake up back at the empty apartment, and the past hour will have been nothing but my wishful imagination."

"It's real." He tweaked her nose. "Darling, we've got so much to talk about, but we need to start with this. I want to be with you, but I'm tied up tight to the ranch for the next five years. I owe my parents that long at least to pay them back for college and everything else they've given me. Please tell me you can handle living in Rocky for a short while?"

Her stomach rolled, not from the idea of returning to the Coleman spread, but from him suggesting he would leave. "You don't want to ranch?"

"I want to be with you." His gaze drifted over the fields. She twisted to take it in, the land spreading toward the horizon in colours of golden brown and fading green, all topped by the cloudless blue sky. His fingers, firm yet gentle, turned her face to him, sincerity shining in his eyes as he spoke. "I love the land, Vicki, but I love you more. If Rocky is too full of bad memories and hurtful family for you to be happy here, we'll move. It'll be tough, but we'll find a way to make a living somewhere else if that's what we decide is best."

That announcement was what broke through her final lingering disbelief. It was one thing for him to say *I love you*, but for him to be willing to sacrifice everything?

God.

Vicki swallowed around the lump in her throat. "I would

never, ever want you to give up your home for me. Ranching is part of who you are, and part of why I love you."

His grin flashed out. "It's still a possibility, if we need it. Because this is about you and me now. Making a family together. And Lynn. I want to get to meet her again. Want her to be able to visit us wherever we settle."

Vicki was going to break into a million pieces of happiness and start sparkling like a fucking rainbow or something. "You're incredible, Joel Coleman. I love you so damn much."

"Finally she says it like she means it. Now I can give you this..." He tugged her hand up and slipped something hard on her finger. "We can buy a different ring down the road, but since you're leaving in a few days I hope you'll wear it as a promise. And in terms of getting married—"

"Married?" Her heart was doing back flips.

Joel paused. "Did I freak you out? I guess I'm more old-fashioned than I realized. We can live together for as long as you want, but I mean this forever, Vicki. Not a whim, not something we're doing because we're trying to achieve a goal. Well, other than the goal of being in love."

Vicki shook herself out of shock, lifted her hand and stared at what he'd put on her. "Your school ring. Wow, I never figured I'd get one."

Joel raised his brows. "That's another thing on the *talk about* list. You could finish your high school through correspondence, maybe even head to college for some classes if you'd like. I hear the local college has a decent cooking program."

This was all happening too fast. "You serious?"

"If it's important to you, we'll find a way to make it happen." He snuck a kiss, and she held on tight, loving the joy shining in his eyes. "We'll have to stick to the basics for a while to be able to afford things, but together, we can do anything we put our minds to. You know that. Look at how well we dealt with the stinky, scary beasts."

She tapped him with her fist, more in play than in earnest.

"You stop that. They're not so scary anymore."

"But still stinky?"

"Hell, yeah." She settled in tight, working her way under his arms so she could believe this was forever. That he never was going to let her go. "I love you, Joel. I really, really do. Thank you for everything you've done to make me a part of your family, and a part of your life."

He squeezed her tight. "Think you kinda did a bit of it yourself, but you're welcome."

She rested, his heart beating steadily under her ear. The rhythm reminded her of the horse's footfalls when Joel led Trigger in easy circles in the arena.

Having that kind of comparison come to mind was pretty amazing.

Something else came to mind. They might have a long time in front of them, but right now, the moments they had before she left were passing far too quickly. "You know, I love the flowers and the carving, but I think you owe me a few other lessons as well... Stuff you missed during our teaching sessions."

Joel hummed lightly as he stroked her hair, the spring breeze playing over them as they admired the countryside rolled out below them. "What you figure we're still missing?"

"Well, we ain't never had sex in the back of your truck, for one—"

"Hell, yeah." Suddenly, she wasn't sitting comfortably. Nope, she was in mid-air, her gut landing on his shoulder as Joel shot to his feet.

"Joel," Vicki gasped as he jogged around the corner toward his truck. She laughed as he jerked down the tailgate then lowered her to the bed. "You goof."

"Time's a wasting." He reached behind her into the truck carry box and yanked out a thick horse blanket. "Strip, darling."

She did, he did, clothes flying everywhere with the enthusiasm of youth and the ticking of a deadline. He had her calling his name faster than she'd imagined possible, his hands and tongue and cock driving her past the point of no return.

He hung over her, both of them breathing hard, bodies still connected. "That's a fine lesson. *What to do with a naked woman in the back of your pickup.*"

Vicki lifted her hand and wiggled her finger in his face. "I'm not naked. Not anymore. Always going to have something on."

He nuzzled her neck, and she sighed, the sound turning into a moan as he latched on below her ear and started all over.

She'd never have to be alone, ever again. Not really. Not when she carried his love inside wherever she went.

"I love you, Joel Coleman." She whispered the words and the spring air drifted them skyward with the promise of new life and new growth. So many things to look forward to in the future.

But right now? They had each other. They had the moment, and a handful of condoms.

Hell, yeah, life was good.

About the Author

Vivian Arend in one word: *Adventurous*. In a sentence: *Willing to try just about anything once*. That wide-eyed attitude has taken her around North America, through parts of Europe, and into Central and South America, often with no running water.

Her optimistic outlook also meant that when challenged to write a book, she gave it a shot, and discovered creating worlds to play in was nearly as addictive as traveling the real one. Now a *New York Times* and *USA TODAY* bestselling author of both contemporary and paranormal stories, Vivian continues to explore, write and otherwise keep herself well entertained.

Website: www.vivianarend.com
Blog: www.vivianarend.com/blog
Twitter: www.twitter.com/VivianArend
Facebook: www.facebook.com/VivianArend

Sometimes even Angels must learn to fly...

Rocky Mountain Angel
© *2012 Vivian Arend*
Six Pack Ranch, Book 4

Allison Parker needs a convincing excuse to come home to Rocky Mountain House. A hopelessly romantic reason that won't let her mother suspect the truth—that Allison has discovered Mom is keeping a terrible secret from the family.

Gabe Coleman is struggling with two of the roughest parts of ranching: dealing with his bull-headed mule of a father, and making enough to pay the bills. When his old friend Allison offers to help him develop his ideas for organic ranching—in trade for pretending to be her fiancé—it sounds like the perfect set-up.

Yet the deception leads them in an unexpected direction, where their shared daily hells are erased by nights of heavenly distraction. It's not supposed to be real, but once the gates are opened, there's no denying they've found in each other a little bit of Paradise.

To break free of the past and face the future, though, will take more than temporary pleasures. It'll take putting their hearts on the line.

Warning: Tortured hero with a guardian-angel complex, grief-stricken heroine willing to sacrifice everything for family. Break out the tissues, this trip to the ranch is a heartbreaker on the way to the HEA.

Available now in ebook and print from Samhain Publishing.

It's all about the story...

Romance

HORROR

www.samhainpublishing.com